PEST

A small town is gripped by an ancient
sickness in this chilling thriller

ANNA WILLETT

THE
BOOK
FOLKS

Published by

The Book Folks

London, 2020

© Anna Willett

ISBN 978-1-913516-66-6

www.thebookfolks.com

pest – 1. A fatal epidemic disease. Now *rare*. 2. A troublesome, annoying, or destructive person, animal, or thing.

Chapter One

Wind, urgent and powerful, slapped the pane like a wet hand. Startled by the suddenness of the sound, Maggie sat forward on the sofa. The book she'd been reading tumbled from her grasp and hit the floor. Living alone, she'd become sensitive to sound and movement, especially at night. Noting the rising storm beating at the windows, she grabbed the thriller up from the rug and dumped it on the coffee table beside the empty wine glass.

While the mournful howling unnerved her, the wind was little more than an annoyance. She yawned and scratched her head. The temptation to curl up on the sofa and go back to sleep was enticing, but not worth a sore neck in the morning. Grabbing the glass, she padded into the kitchen on burning soles. *Shouldn't being your own boss mean easy living?* She chuckled at the thought. Owning a business was hard work and long hours.

By the time she reached the sink and dumped the glass, the clamouring storm had intensified. Nights like this made her question the wisdom of living on the outskirts of a small town. She missed the sound of traffic and sirens. Somehow, being alone was easier when surrounded by noise. A sudden *thud*, like the sound of something falling against the path along the side of the house, startled her. She waited, listening for more. The *thud* was followed by a metallic *clink* as if a can were rolling along the concrete walkway.

"Damn." It had to be the wheelie-bin blowing over.

The last thing she wanted was to go out in the storm, but if the bin blew over, there'd be rubbish all over the back lawn by morning. Muttering another curse, Maggie flicked on the outside light. The instant she opened the back door, a gust hit her, tearing at her clothes.

The bin *had* blown over, tumbling across the lawn and spilling its contents onto the stone path that ran around the back of the house. Darting down the stairs, she wrestled the bin back into a standing position. Struggling to keep her body shielded from the relentless gale, she crouched and began gathering a mess of empty milk cartons, cans, and damp food wrappings. Her hair whipped around her face, sticking to her mouth. The back of her pyjamas flew up, exposing her bare flesh to the relentless gale.

Maggie stood on feet numb with cold and wheeled the bin around the rear of the house, wedging it on the far side of the back steps. With any luck, the building would block the storm's reach. She ducked her head down against the icy gust and ran around to the foot of the stairs. Desperate to get inside and away from the freezing wind, Maggie clambered up the steps. Before hauling the door open, she snatched a glance over her shoulder.

The lights didn't quite reach the shed, but a full moon lent enough silvery glow for her to make out the shapes of bushes and trees. In the seconds it took for her to identify the familiar outlines, something shifted. Maggie gasped and stepped back. *What was that?* Her hair whipped across her eyes. Momentarily blinded, she scrambled for the door. She fumbled with the knob, heart galloping in her chest. Behind her, the storm shrieked like an injured child, and not wanting to turn back and risk another look, she managed to wrench the back door open and stumble inside.

It was nothing. Nothing. Just a bit of rubbish caught on the wind. Maggie slid the bolt in place and turned the latch. Stepping away from the door, she tried to sort through what she'd seen darting between the trees. *Nothing. I didn't see anything.* But she had. Something jerked out from behind the tree, moving with stealth and purpose. But it was dark. With the wind blowing so hard, *everything* was moving. It was impossible to say what she'd seen. *Probably nothing.*

The display on the microwave told her it was 10.15. *Too late to call anyone?* The list of people she knew well enough to reach out to this late was woefully short. There was Tess, but she had a young baby. The only other person she could think of was Doug, the old guy who helped her fix up the house when she first moved to Thorn Tree. He reminded her of her grandfather, solid and kind. She almost reached for her phone, but then reconsidered. Doug's wife, Maureen, was undergoing chemo. Disturbing the elderly couple was out of the question. Maggie ran her fingers through her hair. There was always the police.

She forced herself to slow down and think. What had she really seen? What would she tell the cops? *I saw something move in the dark.* But had she really seen anything? What if the cops arrived and found a plastic bag stuck in the tree? An image flashed in her mind, vivid and painful. Her ex-husband, Richard, cheeks puffed out in anger and spittle flying from his mouth. *You're useless. So used to leeching off your rich grandfather, you can't do anything for yourself.* His constant put-downs rang in her ears.

She thought of the senior officer in charge of the small police station in Thorn Tree. He was well-known in the town; tall, stony-eyed. Maggie had never actually spoken to him. For some reason the idea of looking like a fool – *no*, worse, a helpless woman – in front of the senior sergeant, kept her from reaching for her phone.

"Okay." She swallowed. "I can sort this out." Her voice sounded shaky, unconvincing.

There was a torch in the cupboard under the sink, she grabbed it and clicked the switch. The light flickered. She banged the shaft against her thigh and the globe settled into a blue-white glare. Looking around the kitchen, her gaze landed on the knife block. Maggie slid the largest knife out of the wooden husk and headed for the back door.

The outside lights were still on, washing the small deck and stairs in an arc of yellow. Beyond, the trees shifted and creaked in the wind, the leaves rustling like dead fingers over a dusty floor. Maggie shivered and moved forward. Taking measured steps, she descended the stairs. The torch light bounced off the bushes, tracing a line through the trees. *What if someone's hiding, waiting...* Her mind faltered. Coming outside to confront a possible intruder was insane. She glanced back at the house. The sensible thing would be to go inside, lock the door and call the police. But doing the sensible thing wasn't her style – not anymore.

Holding the knife out in front of her, Maggie stepped across the stone path. She trained the light on the area between the trees just to the right of the shed. Nothing but shimmering branches washed in wintery grey light. Heart jumping, she moved a little closer.

The gale blew harder, pulling at her long auburn hair. The wind carried an odour, dank and earthy, as if something rotten had been exposed to the air. Maggie noticed the knife shaking in her grip as she eased a low branch aside and shone the light between the trees.

"Urgh." The cry broke from her lips accompanied by a cloud of mist that hung in the frigid air. She felt bile hit the back of her throat, not quite making it up over her tongue.

She pressed the side of her hand to her mouth, as she tried to keep herself from screaming. What looked like the remains of a cat lay scattered on a carpet of crushed leaves and broken twigs. The thing had been torn apart, its flesh dappling the low-lying bushes.

Reeling back from the bloody mess, Maggie turned and ran for the house. Her feet hit the stairs with a *thump* heavy enough to shake the deck. Desperate to put a door between her and the dead animal, the knife slid out of her grasp and went spinning over the edge of the platform. She kept moving, pulling the door open and half falling into the kitchen. Not until the latch dropped with a satisfying *clunk*, did she dare slow down.

Maggie had no idea what could have killed the cat, if that's what it was. The pulpy mess could have been a large rabbit or a possum. Not that it mattered, the thing was dead. *Torn to pieces.* It had to be a feral dog, something with teeth and claws large enough to do that sort of damage. She closed her eyes and the image of something lurching between the trees played out in her mind. How close had she come to being attacked by the animal?

Leaving all the downstairs lights on, Maggie went up to her bedroom and crawled under the covers. It had been four years since she'd shared a bed with anyone. Most nights she was able to convince herself that sleeping alone was better, but tonight she wished a pair of arms waited to hold her close while the storm raged against the house.

Chapter Two

The early morning sun revealed the damage left by the storm. A few large branches down, a sheet of tin off the roof of one of the sheds, leaves and branches strewn over the lawn like a woodland carpet complete with a fine wisp of dawn mist. Maggie sipped her coffee, working up the nerve to venture into the trees. By the time she fell asleep last night, she'd almost convinced herself the whole thing had been an overreaction. A dead possum, killed by a fox, the most logical explanation, one that was much more appealing than a savage dog lurking in the bush.

Even so, it took another sip of strong coffee before she had the courage to put her cup down and set foot on the back lawn. The scene was just as she remembered from the previous evening except in the light of day, there was no denying the dead creature was a cat. As if to confirm its death, a sweet, meaty stench hung in the air. Maggie gagged and covered her mouth.

Out of the corner of her eye, she caught movement. Stomach still churning, she almost tumbled backwards as a large crow danced out from behind the bush with a scrap of something dangling from its beak. Something red and fleshy. Maggie turned and ran. The yard was a mess, not to mention the dead cat being slowly eaten by birds. With no time or desire to spend hours clearing the garden, she headed inside to call Doug.

The line was engaged. Maggie supposed he was inundated with calls after the storm. She glanced out of the kitchen window, picturing the cat's body crawling with flies, and shuddered. The phone vibrated in her hand, making her jump and almost drop the mobile.

"Hi, Maggie."

"Oh hi, Tess." Maggie tensed. Her friend wouldn't call at 6.45 on a Saturday morning unless there was a problem.

"Look, I'm sorry." Before Maggie could ask why she was apologising, Tess launched into an explanation. "I know I said I'd pop into the café this morning and go over the new menu with Cilla, but the baby is sick, and I just don't want to cart him around." There was an anxious edge to her friend's usually calm voice.

"No. I mean, yes, of course. What's wrong with Eddie?" Maggie asked as she rubbed a finger between her furrowed eyebrows.

"I'm not sure. He started crying just after eleven last night. At first, I thought the storm was bothering him, but then he felt so hot." She paused, and Maggie heard her take a shaky breath. "I'm calling the doctor next."

"Good idea. Once Dr Cole has a look at him, you'll both feel better."

"Yes. Yes, I know. It's just he's so small and… fragile?" Tess's voice wavered.

"I know, but he's a strong, healthy baby and you're doing exactly the right thing getting him checked out. These things come and go quickly with little ones. I bet he'll be as right as rain by tonight." Maggie bit her bottom lip. She wanted Tess to feel better, but couldn't help remembering the sound the wind made as it shrilled against the windows, reminding her of a child wailing.

"That's what Ollie said, but I–"

A piercing cry fractured the quiet. The noise faded to a gurgling wail. It wasn't like any sound Maggie had ever heard Eddie *or* any other baby make. Her hand flew to her throat and rested just above her heart.

"I have to go."

"Okay. Call me if you need anything."

"Thanks." Tess clicked off and the line went silent. Maggie let out a deep breath and tossed the phone in her bag. Eddie's cry didn't sound right; even over the phone he sounded pained. *Not that I'd know anything about babies*, she thought with a hint of bitterness. Her ex-husband had been far too self-involved to even consider having children. Her inexperience notwithstanding, Eddie's tortured cries and the panicky edge to Tess's voice left Maggie unnerved and anxious. When she opened up shop three years ago and Tess walked into the Hawk's Nest Café, her down-to-earth attitude and casual confidence said more than any resume ever could. They struck up an instant friendship. If Tess was worried, Maggie feared something might really be wrong.

* * *

On the drive into town, she couldn't get Tess's call out of her head. The urgency in Eddie's cry and the fear in her friend's voice kept rolling around in her mind. Forcing her attention back to the road, Maggie noticed a fallen tree branch laying at an angle on the opposite side of the bitumen. She thought of the dead cat and the unanswered call to Doug Loggie. Checking the mirrors and the road ahead, she reached over, attempting to fish the phone out of her handbag. It slipped just beyond her fingertips and into the bag's side pocket. With another quick glance ahead, Maggie ducked across the seat and grabbed the bag. A high-pitched wail startled her into an upright position. The wheel spun in her fingers, the car veering left. Wrestling the vehicle back on course, she snatched a glance in the rear-view mirror just as the siren wailed for the second time.

"Damn. Damn, damn."

She eased on the brake and pulled the car over to the side of the road. Looking behind her, Maggie caught sight of a large-framed cop stepping out of a white police vehicle. Senior Sergeant Harness Gibson walked slowly as if he had all the time in the world, stopping only to examine something at the rear of the car.

"Morning," he said, leaning a large hand on the open window.

"Hi, how are you?" she asked and as soon as the words were out of her mouth, she knew she sounded too casual.

"Have you had any drinks containing alcohol this morning?"

"What? Of course not." Now she'd gone from casual to shrill. "Look, Officer Gibson, I was just reaching over for my bag. I made sure no one was coming. I mean, the road was deserted."

She knew she was babbling, so she closed her mouth, swallowed and waited for him to speak.

"Can I see your license?"

Maggie searched through her bag and found her purse. After what felt like an eternity, she extracted the licence and handed it to Gibson. His face was unreadable, eyes hidden behind dark sunglasses.

"Wait here." He turned and strode off towards his car.

Maggie had seen the cop around town but never up close. She'd even wondered if he was single but didn't have the courage to bring the subject up to Tess. Not really sure what made her hold back, Maggie often hoped he'd come into the café so she might get the chance to speak to him. Now, here she sat with the perfect opportunity, and all she could manage was a shriek and a string of incoherent babble. *Very alluring!*

"Here you go, Ms Hawkbetter." He put his hand on the lowered window and offered her the licence back.

"Oh, thanks."

Her cheeks burned, the blush sudden and uncharacteristic. Hoping he hadn't noticed her discomfort, Maggie reached out and took the licence. Her fingers brushed against his. Quickly shifting her eyes away from his face, her gaze landed on his crotch. She turned her head and tried to shove her licence back in her bag when her elbow hit the horn. The ear-piercing *bleep* made her jump.

"Sorry," she said and forced her face into a weirdly lopsided smile, hoping to cover her embarrassment.

"Keep your eyes on the road, okay?" He smiled and just for a second, dimples appeared in his stubbly cheeks.

"Yes, sorry. I mean yes, thanks."

Maggie put the window up and pulled back onto the road. In the mirror, she saw Gibson standing on the side of the road, hands on hips watching her drive away.

By the time Maggie arrived at the Hawk's Nest, she'd mentally rerun the encounter with Gibson at least ten times. In each new version, she thought of something clever and witty to say when he asked if she'd been drinking. *Not that it matters now*, she told herself with an inward cringe. After the clumsy way she'd acted, he either thought of her as an idiot or not at all.

The lane behind the café was deserted when Maggie pulled in and turned off the car. She took out her phone and sent Doug a message asking him if he could stop by the house the next day and take a look at the backyard. The damage wasn't that severe or urgent. The simple truth was that she considered Doug a friend, and after the incident the night before, she was glad of an excuse to have him around.

Maggie got out of the car and entered the café through the back door. She enjoyed the early morning quiet. It gave her time to prepare for the day's onslaught – at least, it felt like an onslaught when the place was buzzing. Business would slow this week as the summer vacation crowd made their final exodus and although Maggie would be sorry to lose the extra income, she looked forward to the calm, regular trade that the locals provided during autumn and winter.

She turned on the lights and put the float in the till. Setting up was always the same: lights, chairs, float and food prep. It was a comforting routine because no matter what else happened, people always wanted to eat, and Maggie was more than happy to provide the food.

The kitchen was a large square with a small cold room in the far-right corner. Along the back wall sat two sinks and the oversized stove as well as an industrial dishwasher which Maggie regarded with almost tender adoration. She pulled down two large saucepans from the four rows of shelves over the steel bench-tops and placed them next to the stove. Then she yanked open the cold room door and went inside. Surveying the shelves, she checked that they had the necessary supplies for a busy day's service. Noticing they were down to their last four litres of milk, she made a mental note to send Cilla out for more. Grabbing two cartons of eggs, she headed back to the kitchen.

As she filled the pots with water, the back door slammed open with enough force to shake the walls. Maggie jumped, sloshing water over her shoes.

"Jesus! Take it easy." There was a tremor in her voice. "Sorry, Jackson. I'm a bit jumpy after the storm."

Jackson gave her a sheepish look and ducked under the doorframe, careful to avoid hitting his head. He carried a box of vegetables from his father's market garden which he dumped on the workbench. Jackson Palmer had worked for Maggie as a kitchen hand for about a year, choosing the café over toiling on his parents' farm.

"I've got some lettuce, cucumbers, tomatoes, zucchini and beans for you. Dad picked them this morning. He's so pissed about the storm last night; it blew away half his cherry tomatoes. I saw Doug out at Mr Tolman's house.

Looks like a tree limb went through his front window. Doug had a chain around it and was towing it out when I drove past. They must have been on the phone to him at the crack of dawn."

"How much do I owe your dad?" Maggie asked, trying to keep up with Jackson's story.

"He didn't say, but fifty dollars should cover it." He paused. "When's Tess coming in?"

"Eddie's sick," she answered, handing him the money.

"Huh, there must be something going around." He picked up a tomato and tossed it in the air, catching the piece of fruit with ease. "My little sister didn't feel too good when she got up this morning. Said she felt hot and had weird dreams."

"Summer cold?" Maggie offered.

"Yeah, that's what Mum said, but my gran swears it's something else. '*A cruel wind blew in something bad last night,*' she reckons."

Maggie had only been half-listening up to this point but was suddenly interested. "What did she mean by *something bad?*"

"I don't know. Mum told her to stop frightening Asha with her crazy Indian stories." He chuckled and started unloading the vegetables.

Maggie knew it was silly, but she wanted to know what Jackson's grandmother was talking about. She thought of the earthy odour wafting through the trees during the storm and wondered what the old woman meant by *something bad.*

Her mind turned to Eddie and the way he'd howled with pain. He was such a bright little baby. She thought about the silky feel of his soft, downy, blond hair as she'd cradled his head two nights ago. She couldn't help smiling. When Tess had finished feeding him, she gave him to Maggie so she could burp him. It was one of the few times in her thirty-four years that she'd held a baby, cradling him against her shoulder and patting his little back until he gave an almighty belch. Maggie remembered the dreamy look in his dark blue eyes.

She flicked on the gas under the pots, deciding to drop by Tess's after work and say hello to the little fella. She might be able to give Tess a half-hour break and still have time to dash home and change for the party. The thought of seeing the baby lifted her spirits enough to allow her to focus on chopping vegetables and setting up the salads.

* * *

By 4.30 in the afternoon the Hawk's Nest Café was empty. Cilla swept the floors and wiped down the tables while Maggie and Jackson worked in the kitchen. Jackson moved in and out of the cold room, covering trays and putting food away while Maggie stacked the dishwasher.

"Any plans for tonight?" She slammed the washer shut and pressed the button to start the cycle.

"I might go to the pub with some friends. Nothing very exciting." Jackson closed the cold room door. He walked over and stood on the other side of the dishwasher facing Maggie. "Why?"

"I've got to go to Agnes's party tonight and I'm dreading it. I guess I just wanted to torture myself by hearing about how much more fun you'd be having." Maggie laughed, waiting for Jackson to join, but instead he frowned and looked down at the floor.

"You can come with us to the pub if you want, or I can take you to the party so you won't have to go on your own."

Maggie watched him as he studied the floor. His ink-black hair and ever-present tan hinted at his one-quarter Indian heritage. If he were ten years older, she'd probably let him break her heart.

"That's nice of you, but I wouldn't dream of spoiling your plans *or* subjecting you to an evening with Agnes. She'd probably be all aflutter over a young guy like you and I don't think I could stomach it." Maggie couldn't help chuckling as she pictured Agnes flirting with Jackson.

Jackson nodded and swiped at the workbench with a damp cloth. Still smiling, Maggie grabbed her phone, deciding now would be the best time to ring Tess and tell her she'd pop over in half an hour. She dialled her friend's number and waited. When the phone rang out, she tried Tess's mobile. Nothing but static.

"Strange."

"What's that?" Jackson asked.

"Oh, it's nothing. I just can't get hold of Tess and I want to find out how the baby's doing."

"Well, if they were up all night, they've probably turned off their phones and gone to bed."

Maggie turned, surprised by Jackson's common sense. *That's the smartest thing to ever come out of his mouth.* She immediately chastised herself for thinking such a thing. He had a kind heart.

"You're right, Jackson. Thanks."

The boy blushed and looked pleased with himself. Maggie went through to the café and found Cilla refilling the sugar holders. Maggie flipped the sign on the door to *closed* and locked up.

"Why don't you leave that for Monday and get going?"

"Okay, thanks." Cilla gave her a tired smile. "After last night, I'm beat."

Maggie gave the door a shake, then standing on tiptoes, she slid the bolt at the top in place. "Why's that?" she asked, only half-listening.

"Robert was up half the night with his asthma."

Maggie stopped moving and watched the woman stow a tray of sugar packets under the counter.

"Do you think he's coming down with something?" She tried to keep her tone casual while her stomach did an uncomfortable flip.

"I hope not," Cilla said as she reached around to untie her apron. "If he gets any worse, I'll take him to Dr Cole."

Maggie nodded and followed Cilla into the kitchen. She had to stop worrying. Kids got sick, no big mystery. *There are always bugs going around.* But still, three children all feeling unwell at the same time seemed a little out of the ordinary. Maggie picked up her bag and keys and headed for the door. She waited while Jackson and Cilla exited then turned off the lights.

"See you," Cilla called over her shoulder as she trotted down the lane towards her car.

Jackson lingered, watching as Maggie made sure the door was locked.

"Okay, well, have a good night." Maggie turned to leave.

"Um… you too. Don't worry about Tess. If there was a problem, she'd have called you by now."

"You're right. She would have called. I guess I'll just give her and Ollie some space. If Eddie *has* settled down, they won't want a ringing phone waking him." Jackson stared at her and bit his bottom lip. She had the feeling he wanted to say something, so she waited.

"Enjoy the party." He turned and headed for his car, walking with his head down and his hands in his pockets.

She watched him for a second then shook her head and unlocked her car.

Chapter Three

Maggie pulled up in front of Agnes's house behind a row of cars. Trust Agnes to go over the top and have valet parking in a town full of open spaces and quiet streets. As mayor of Thorn Tree, Agnes Wells got an itch for the spotlight at least three times a year. Tonight was her annual summer's end party where she'd pull in the last of the important tourists staying in town as well as city council members and local business owners for one last hurrah. Maggie had learned it was wise to attend these gatherings or risk the consequences. She'd missed a party two years ago only to receive a curt letter from the local council informing her that her bins were blocking the lane and needed to be moved or she'd face a fine. Maggie learned her lesson the hard way and attended every party since. Tonight would be no exception.

Why do these parties always make me nervous, like an awkward teenager? She took her hands off the steering wheel and rubbed them on the front of her pants. She'd considered dropping by Tess's on her way to the party, but at the last minute changed her mind. Jackson was probably right, Tess and Ollie were new parents, probably exhausted. Instead Maggie checked her phone to see if Tess had sent a text. Nothing. Maybe she'd been right to leave them alone.

The valet climbed in the car ahead and drove it around the corner and out of sight. Maggie sighed and checked the clock on the dash: 8.45. It would have been easier to just park one or two streets away and walk over. She pulled down the visor and checked her reflection in the vanity mirror.

It had taken her less than twenty minutes to get ready, doing little more than showering, putting on mascara and combing her hair so it fell around her shoulders. The red silk blouse and black pants were an attempt at casual sophistication, but she'd most likely be woefully underdressed. Not that it mattered what she looked like, it would be the same people she saw almost every day with a few elderly tourists thrown into the mix. It wouldn't make much difference if she had a bucket on her head. With that thought, she almost put her hair in a ponytail but stopped. This wasn't work, even if it felt like it.

She stepped out of her car and handed her keys to the valet. At the side gate, a young woman dressed in a black T-shirt and pants welcomed her. She could hear soft music and conversation wafting from the rear of the house.

"Enjoy the party."

"Thank you." Maggie gave the girl a polite smile. She sounded exotic, most likely a backpacker in town for the fruit-picking season. *Agnes probably paid these kids a pittance to spend all night serving and then cleaning up into the early hours.*

The house screamed money with its modern finishes — crisp with lots of sharp stone edges and huge windows. Maggie rounded the path to the back of the property and as always, she was struck by the impressive entertaining area. Surprisingly, the property showed no evidence of the storm. *Maybe the wind doesn't blow on Agnes's house.*

Floodlights bathed the pool area in a golden glow. Soft fairy lights winked in the trees, giving the garden a magical feel. Tables draped in black cloth and decorated with gold centrepieces were set up on one side of the pool. Waiters wearing identical black outfits circled the crowd offering drinks and finger foods. Maggie noticed that everything was set out just as it had been at the last party, only this time with gold accents instead of purple.

Looking around, she spotted some familiar faces and more than a few new ones. A tall, glamorous woman wearing a form-fitting blue cocktail dress leaned one tanned elbow on the back of her chair, engaged in what looked like a very animated conversation with a grey-haired man in his late fifties. His square-jawed face and horn-rimmed glasses were familiar, but Maggie couldn't quite place him. A quick burst of laughter came from the buffet table where a young woman in a short lace dress whispered something into the ear of one of the waiters. With the valet parking and the dressy crowd, she was suddenly glad she'd at least made the effort with her hair and makeup.

"Maggie, you look lovely. I almost didn't recognise you. I mean, you look so different out of your apron." Agnes smiled and slipped her arm through Maggie's so she could steer her around the party.

Maggie frowned at the backhanded compliment and wondered when, if ever, Agnes had seen her in an apron. It definitely wasn't in the café. In the entire time Maggie had been in Thorn Tree, Agnes had never once set foot in the Hawk's Nest. *Probably because we don't create little works of art in the cappuccino foam.*

Still puzzled over Agnes's apron comment, Maggie allowed herself to be guided around the pool. Agnes's grip on her arm was strong for a small, elderly woman. Even in heels, her perfectly coiffed iron-grey head barely reached Maggie's shoulder.

"Have you met our newest resident? She's a writer." Agnes spoke with astonishment as though she was announcing the existence of aliens.

"A travel writer. Not very exciting, I'm afraid. I'm Prapti, Prapti Gautam," the woman said.

"Prapti, this is Maggie Hawkbetter. She owns the Hawk's Nest Café on Guild Street," Agnes continued.

Prapti turned her head, but the rest of her body remained motionless. There was something snakelike in the way the woman moved. She was striking in a dark statuesque way, yet Maggie's neck tingled with aversion.

"I'm very happy to meet you, Maggie." Prapti spoke through a wide smile.

"Yes. Welcome to Thorn Tree." It was all Maggie could think of to say. She was glad the party was crowded because she had no desire to be alone with the woman.

Prapti's long neck swooped forward. "Hawkbetter, what an unusual name. Is it English?" Prapti asked.

"No." Maggie looked over the woman's shoulder, hoping to catch someone's eye so she'd have an excuse to end the conversation. But everywhere she looked, guests were engaged in conversation.

"My great-grandfather was half Cherokee," Maggie said, forcing herself to focus on answering Prapti's question. "His name was Blue Hawk, but he changed it to Hawkbetter when he married my great-grandmother and they immigrated to Australia."

"Well, what an interesting surprise. A Cherokee businesswoman in this little corner of South Western Australia."

Prapti's smile stretched, but there was an edge to her words, and Maggie found herself bristling.

"I would hardly call myself a Cherokee. I was born in Perth," Maggie snapped.

"I'm sorry; I didn't mean to offend you. I didn't realise you felt defensive about your heritage." Prapti chuckled, a deep guttural sound that set Maggie's teeth on edge. Judging by the wide grin on the woman's face, she was enjoying being offensive.

Agnes joined in the laughter, her bulging eyes darting between Prapti and Maggie. In that moment, it was as if Prapti had reached into Maggie's brain and found the insecure schoolgirl who'd been teased unmercifully for revealing her Native American heritage. Suddenly the surrounding chatter and laughter seemed cruel and mocking. A sheen of sweat broke out on Maggie's forehead. She wanted to say something, put Prapti in her place. But most of all she wanted to prove to herself that she wasn't that self-conscious little girl who couldn't stand up to the bullies. She needed to prove it to herself *and* Richard.

Her mouth opened, but the only retort that came to mind was, *go fuck yourself.* Instead, she smiled.

"Enjoy your time in our town, Prapti."

Maggie thought she caught a flash of disappointment on the woman's face before turning and walking away.

Maggie made her way through a trio of guests and found herself at the buffet table. Her stomach soured at the thought of food, but she forced herself to feign interest in the assortment of tiny portions of jellied salmon and arancini. Her first instinct had been to head for the gate and make her escape, but running from a party in tears was something she would have done when she was still married to Richard. Living alone, opening her own business were all things she'd never thought herself capable of, and she'd be damned if a few snide comments would send her backsliding into an insecure mess, not when she'd worked so long and hard to pull herself into a new life.

"I thought you handled that very well. I would've told her to go fuck herself." The voice was deep and instantly familiar. Maggie turned and looked into the unsmiling face of Harness Gibson. Seeing her surprise, Harness smiled and suddenly they were both laughing.

"Why have I never seen you at one of Agnes's parties?" Maggie asked, still smiling.

"Why don't I get you a glass of wine and tell you all about it? Red or white?" he asked.

"White, thanks."

Five minutes later they were seated on a bench in Agnes's front yard with the sounds of the party a forgotten background noise. Maggie sipped her wine, unsure of what to say now that they were alone.

"Sorry about this morning," Harness began, and then stopped.

"Don't worry about it. I must have looked like a madwoman swerving all over the road." Maggie waved a dismissive hand, but Harness looked serious.

"I was right to pull you over, but when I saw it was you, I acted like an ass. So... sorry."

"Sergeant Gibson, I'm confused. We've never met before this morning, right?" she asked.

"Right, and call me Ness." He gave her a tight smile then looked away. "I've seen you around."

Maggie wondered why he was having such a hard time looking at her. Could he be nervous?

"I was just having a bad morning," he added.

She took a sip of wine, searching for something to say.

"Prapti's an unusual woman," she said, trying to change the subject.

"That's a nice way of saying she's a bitch."

His bluntness took her by surprise. She caught herself looking at him in a new way. He was dressed casually in black jeans and a pale blue open-necked shirt. The base of his neck was lightly tanned with just a hint of light-coloured chest hair visible above the top button. She wondered if he had a girlfriend. Maybe it was the wine on an empty stomach, but before she could stop herself, the words were out.

"Are you seeing anyone?"

He looked surprised but smiled. His hands were resting on his legs. Maggie wondered what the skin on his palms would feel like. She looked away, worried he'd look into her eyes and know what she was thinking. Not really sure what to do next, Maggie decided it might be time to leave before she got herself into trouble.

"Look, Harness, I..."

"Call me Ness."

"Ness." The name felt strange on her tongue, too intimate. "I can't face going back into the party. I think I'll head home. It was nice of you to sit with me, but don't feel like you have to stay any longer."

"I don't feel like going back in either. I live next to the station house. It's only a few streets away. Walk back with me and have a beer?" His tone was casual, relaxed even, but Maggie had the feeling he wanted more than just a drink.

"All right." She answered without hesitation, sending her stomach flipping over as if she were in an elevator.

Maggie had many regrets about her life. Staying married to a verbally abusive narcissist was the main one, but there were others. Not long after separating from Richard, she went out for drinks with some work friends and met a man. It was nothing more than a casual encounter, but when he asked her to go home with him, she was shocked by how tempted she was to do something wild and reckless. In the end, she turned him down, mostly because her moral training told her having sex with someone just for pleasure was wrong. But there was also a small part of her that knew her reluctance was less about morality and more about fear. She'd regretted that decision for the last three years, especially on nights when the wind was howling at her windows. Maggie decided that for good or bad, tonight wouldn't be another wasted opportunity.

* * *

The moon was full and silvery in the cloudless night sky. A slight breeze cooled the air. The temperature was pleasantly warm after the previous evening's storm. As

Maggie and Harness walked, their footsteps echoed along the empty street, giving the town a deserted feel.

"Why is it that you've never been in the Hawk's Nest? There's not that many places to eat in Thorn Tree," she asked, partly to fill the silence, but also because she really was curious.

"I'm usually busy, so I eat at the station house. If I have more time, I go home to eat. One of the perks of living next door to the station." He shrugged. "But now I know the owner, I might have to start dropping in." He turned slightly and gave her a grin, dimples dancing in and out of sight in the blink of an eye.

Maggie laughed and shook her head.

"What?" he asked, still grinning.

"Nothing. I was just thinking about this morning. This morning and tonight. Every time we meet, I seem to be involved in some kind of drama. Are you sure you're ready to risk coming into my café?"

"I think you're worth it." As they walked, his fingers brushed against hers. "That woman really got to you, didn't she?"

"You mean Prapti?"

"Yes. Prapti." Harness stopped and turned so that he was looking down into Maggie's eyes. "What she said, about you being a Cherokee, it hurt you, didn't it?"

"I..." She hesitated. "I'm proud of who I am, but I suppose I am sensitive about it." She stopped, not sure how much of herself she should reveal. She'd only known him for a few hours, but her instincts told her she could trust him.

"I was teased about it when I was at school. I know it's silly to still be so touchy, but I guess it still stings a bit."

"We all have buttons. When they're pressed in just the right way, it hurts." He paused and looked away. "Some hurt more than others."

Maggie wondered if he was talking about her or his own pain. She thought of asking, but reminded herself they'd just met.

"Well, you were right about one thing," she said, and started walking again.

"Yeah? What was that?" His voice was deep, almost husky.

"Prapti *is* a bitch!"

He laughed and took hold of her hand, guiding her across the road. Maggie felt a tingle of excitement in the pit of her stomach. It had been a long time since she'd felt this carefree.

"I don't usually wander off with strange men. This is something new for me." She tried to keep her tone light, but at the same time she wanted to make sure he knew she didn't sleep around. Hell, she wasn't even sure that he wanted to sleep with her. This could just be some pity thing after what happened at the party.

Harness stopped walking and turned to look at her before answering.

"Maggie, I don't make a habit of this either. I'd like to get to know you better. You're funny and interesting." He reached out and touched a strand of her hair, rolling it between his fingers. "And sexy."

Without waiting for her to speak, he slid his hand around her waist, leaned down and kissed her. His lips were soft. A slight rasp of stubble brushed against her cheek. It was a surprisingly sweet kiss but with enough promise to take her breath away. She caught the faint hint of lemon-scented soap. When he pulled back, Maggie felt a bit off balance. It had been a long time since she'd been kissed, but she was sure it had never felt quite that good. She turned her head and looked out onto the darkened street. Her eyes caught a movement in the shadows just over his shoulder.

"Harness," she said, her voice was little more than a whisper. "Someone's out there."

Maggie strained into the darkness as a figure emerged from the trees. Still just a shadow, but obviously human, it moved with an odd shuffling gait. Progressing towards them, feet sliding over the bitumen like sandpaper on gravel, its pace remained unaltered. Maggie's mind jumped back to the shape she'd seen moving in her garden the night before. She grabbed Harness's arm, glad that this time, she wasn't alone.

"Hey, mate, do you need help?" Harness's voice echoed as he stepped off the curb and walked towards the figure. Maggie kept hold of his arm, allowing herself to be pulled along with him.

The shape shuffled into the moonlight. Maggie's hand dropped from Harness's arm. Her heart jack-knifed into her throat as recognition hit her like a fist.

"Oh God, Tess!" Maggie pushed past Harness and rushed to her friend.

Tess wore a dirty, torn nightdress that clung to her blood-smeared legs. Her feet were bare and filthy, covered with cuts and scrapes. She turned to look at Maggie with blank eyes. It was then that Maggie took in the wrapped bundle clutched in her friend's arms. Tess stopped moving and held the baby out.

"Help him?" Her voice came out as little more than a croak. Her body trembled as if about to give out.

Maggie reached for the baby, noting its frightening weightlessness. As Tess released the infant, her legs buckled. Harness swooped forward and, in one fluid movement, caught her under the arms. He picked her up and turned to Maggie.

"Let's get them to the station house."

Maggie moved to follow but the feel of the baby in her arms brought her to a halt. The blue bundle was still, without weight. She sucked in a breath that lodged in her throat like a piece of cold steel. With trembling fingers, she moved the soft blue blanket from around Eddie's face. A groan slipped past her lips as her vision blurred with tears.

25

His little face, once pink and chubby, was now blackened around milky eyes, his mouth frozen in a silent wail. A tiny grey tongue protruded from swollen, blue lips. Maggie staggered towards a lamppost, needing support.

"Oh, Eddie, baby, what's happened to you?" She placed two fingers against his cheek and shuddered.

"Maggie, come on. We need to get them off the street." Harness's voice came from the corner, the streetlight throwing shadows over his eyes and mouth.

She wanted to cry out, tell him something was wrong with the baby, but the words didn't want to come. Saying it out loud would make it real and just for a few more minutes, Maggie wanted to deny the truth. Clutching the baby against her chest, she followed Harness as he led the way to the police station.

Chapter Four

Annabel Chapel leaned forward and pressed her index finger to the windowpane, tracing her name on the icy glass. The window seat was the perfect place to watch for shooting stars, as long as she didn't make too much noise. She could hear her parents downstairs; the chatter of the TV, her mum and dad laughing. Mundane sounds of a normal Saturday night in the Chapel house. Comforting. Safe.

Annabel desperately wanted a puppy for her impending ninth birthday. Her mum had said, *"We'll see."*

When she'd asked her dad, he shrugged. "Well, Bell Pepper" – her Dad always called her Bell Pepper because of her red hair – "we'll see what your mother says."

That usually meant yes, but just to be sure, Annabel decided to watch for a shooting star.

She often stayed up, waiting until her mum and dad were downstairs watching TV. When the coast was clear, she'd creep out of bed and tiptoe over to the window seat so she could hunt for shooting stars. It was the only way to make wishes come true. She felt a little guilty tonight because this wish was kind of selfish – something just for her. Last time, she wished her Year Three teacher, Mrs

Roe, would feel happier. She looked sad when she thought no one was watching. Annabel didn't know why, but felt sure it had something to do with Mr Roe's stomach and how sick he felt.

Annabel often had strong feelings about things and they usually turned out to be right. She called them *feelings,* but it was more like buzzing in her head as if busy worker bees were turning her thoughts over, searching for something important. When the buzzing started, she could almost feel the bees gathering and then suddenly, *snap,* they'd uncover an image. Sometimes the images were fuzzy like a snow globe filled with glitter, but other times, the snapshots were as clear as the photos her mum took on the iPad. Annabel had come to not only trust her feelings, but sort of rely on them.

A week after Annabel's wish, she'd heard her mother telling Mrs Abbey – the woman with the weird eyebrows from the supermarket – that Mrs Roe's husband had something called an ulcer in his stomach and he was going to the city to have an operation. Mrs Roe didn't come to school for a whole week after that, and Annabel felt so worried, *her* stomach hurt. Then Mrs Roe came back and was her old self again, maybe even happier. The whole thing made Annabel both confused and relieved. She wasn't sure why Mrs Roe would be so pleased that her husband had an operation, but she was glad her teacher was no longer sad.

Tonight, Annabel planned to wish for a puppy because sometimes she felt lonely living so far out of town on the apple orchard. A puppy would mean having a friend that could live with her. She had friends at school but she couldn't just ride her bike to their houses and hang out. It took thirty minutes for the school bus to get to her stop and another five minutes' walk to her front door. She pulled her blanket up around her shoulders, letting her toes peek out the bottom. The sky was so black, it almost looked blue. She wondered if the stars were as bright over everyone's house or maybe they were shining just for her. If she had a puppy, she could love it and take it for walks and maybe it could sleep in her bedroom at night.

Annabel reached out and touched the red frilly curtains that framed her window. Red was her favourite colour; the curtains had been a special surprise last Christmas. She looked up at the starry night and yawned. Her eyelids drooped and her head drifted down to her chest. Ready to give up for the night, a flash of light caught her eye. It shot across the sky in a blink, leaving a fiery tail fading in its wake. Annabel closed her eyes and made her secret wish. When she opened them again, she pressed her lips together in a smile. She could see herself down in the backyard playing with her puppy, throwing a ball for it and teaching it to fetch. Looking down across the backyard imagining the scene, she found herself looking at a child standing near her old swing.

Annabel pushed her face close to the window, so close her nose almost touched the glass, fogging it around her mouth. For a moment, it seemed she might be dreaming, but when her nose *did* touch the pane, Annabel gasped at the cold shock. There really was a girl in the yard. Standing under the big jacaranda tree, she had one hand on Annabel's swing as her raggedy dress blew in the breeze.

She must be lost. Why else would she be out alone at night *and* wearing rags? The thought of being lost in the dark seemed like the most horrific thing in the world. Annabel could imagine how scared the girl must be.

Her arms and legs were bare and very thin, like sticks or… bone. *The poor thing, maybe she's hungry.* Annabel's eyes adjusted to the darkness and she saw the details more clearly. Wisps of hair clung to a nearly bald head, and the skin on her arms and legs hung in saggy folds.

Annabel's head snapped back from the glass. It wasn't a little girl at all. She didn't know what it was, but as it tried to move and turn around, its legs jerked stiffly. The skinny body pitched from side to side as it struggled to reposition itself. Annabel's heart jumped into her throat, making her head whoosh with the wild pumping. Her breath came out in little gasps. A monster was in her yard. Her mother told her there was no such thing as monsters, but she was wrong. There was a monster right outside her window... and it wanted her. She pulled the curtains closed with shaky fingers, ready to run.

Something in Annabel, something far wiser than her usual eight-year-old reasoning, made her stop and think. If she ran downstairs and called for help, her dad would rush outside to confront whatever had frightened her. She couldn't risk that. Annabel had a *feeling* that whatever that thing outside was, it wouldn't or *couldn't* come into the house. That's why it'd tried to trick her into coming outside.

Unsure what to do and afraid to go back to bed, Annabel made her wobbly legs move and walked down the stairs. The sounds of TV and laughter, so comforting only moments ago seemed dangerous, as if inviting unwanted visitors.

"Mum, I had a nightmare. Can I sit with you for a while?" She tried to keep the tremble out of her voice.

Her parents' faces turned in unison, her dad still smiling at something funny on the screen and her mum with a frown of concern. They looked so normal, it pulled at her heart. They had no idea about the monster, about what was waiting outside. Annabel couldn't stop herself – tears tumbled down her cheeks and sobs hitched her chest. For the first time since she was four years old, Annabel spent the night in her parents' bed.

Chapter Five

Maggie perched on the edge of the sofa, her hand resting on Tess's shoulder as if keeping the woman anchored in place. They were in Harness's office. It was the first time Maggie had been inside the police station. She wondered how many traumatised people had sat on the same couch and breathed in the smell of stale coffee that hung in the air. Her friend lay quietly, unmoving, eyes open and face devoid of colour. She wasn't sleeping but at least the shaking had stopped.

Harness opened the door, and his eyes fell on Tess. For a moment, he stood in the doorway as if surprised to see the two women in his office.

"Maggie, can I speak to you in the hallway?" He shifted his gaze from Tess. "It's important."

"Yes, okay." Maggie forced herself to stand.

Before leaving the office, she stood over her friend. "I'm just out in the hall. Okay? I'll be right back."

Tess turned her head and stared at Maggie with unfocused eyes. Her mouth was slightly open as if she'd heard her friend's voice but didn't understand the words. Maggie smoothed a strand of hair from Tess's brow before kissing her lightly on the forehead and leaving the room.

"I've called Dr Cole. He's on his way. Has she said anything about what happened?" Harness asked, his business-like tone taking her by surprise.

"Just that Eddie was sick and Ollie, her husband, was driving them into town when something happened." Maggie rubbed her eyes. "From what she's able to tell me, there might have been an accident. I think she panicked and ran all the way into town." She rubbed her hand over her face. "Oh God, Harness. I knew the baby was sick. She called me this morning and told me. I should have been there."

"Don't blame yourself. You couldn't know all this was going to happen." His tone softened. He took her hand, holding it loosely between his fingers. "I need your help. We still have to find her husband and work out what the hell happened."

"I'll do whatever I can."

She slipped her hand out of his grasp. Whatever was or wasn't happening between them would have to wait. She couldn't allow herself to be distracted when Tess needed her. Standing in the hall holding hands with Harness while Ollie was missing and Eddie was dead felt wrong – almost as if she was betraying Tess in some way.

Harness looked like he was about to say something, but instead took a step back, putting some distance between them. His face remained unreadable, but she suspected she'd hurt his feelings.

"Where's Eddie?" Her throat contracted, making it difficult to get the question out.

"He's in the kitchen. When the doctor gets here, he's going to take a look and see what he can tell us."

Maggie nodded and stared at the kitchen door. She didn't want to think about Eddie lying in there all alone, but found it hard to look away.

"The battery on my phone is nearly dead, is there a phone I can use? I need to call Tess's mother and let her know what's happened."

She turned away from the kitchen and tried to focus her mind on what to do next. Harness gestured towards a phone in the main area of the station. She wanted to say something, make him understand why she'd pulled away, but he was already moving across the station, phone pressed to his ear.

* * *

Dr Cole approached the old kitchen table where the tiny form lay draped in a fuzzy blue blanket. Cole put his bag on the table and took out several instruments, placing them next to the blue blanket. He hesitated before unfolding the blanket. The naked bulb above the table cast a harsh yellow light over the dead infant, bringing the scene into jarringly clear focus. Harness flinched and closed his eyes. Molly was older than Eddie when she died, almost three, but the unnatural stillness of a dead child was the same, no matter what the age. He leaned back, letting his spine rest against the cold brick wall and opened his eyes, forcing himself to focus on the examination.

The baby was fully clothed in a pale blue onesie with a white collar; on the left, just below the shoulder was a little yellow duck. Cole undid the top clasp and slid his stethoscope inside. After listening for a few seconds, he puffed out a tired breath and removed the disc. He leaned in and examined the neck before pulling the clothing to one side and pressing his finger on the skin of the shoulder. He shone a small penlight into the baby's lifeless eyes then looked in the mouth and ears. When Cole examined the baby's hands, the tiny fingers were curled inwards, making it look like Eddie was clutching the doctor's finger.

The only sounds in the room came from the ticking of the clock over the sink and the doctor's breathing. Gingerly, Cole turned the small body over and took the baby's temperature.

When he was finished, the doctor fastened the clasps on the onesie with a gentle touch.

"Well?" Harness kept his tone neutral.

"Look, Gibson," Cole said, "I'm not a coroner and I don't want to disturb any evidence by undressing the little fella."

"I get it." Harness waved his hand, gesturing for the doctor to continue. "Just tell me what you think."

"It's difficult to tell on such a young infant because rigor mortis is not readily perceivable, but judging by temperature, post-mortem paleness and lividity, I would say he's been dead about ninety minutes. I can't see any signs of violence or trauma." Cole hesitated.

"Go on," Harness urged.

Tony Cole, a thin grey-haired man in his early sixties, prided himself on being as fit as a man half his age, but at that moment, his shoulders sagged and every line on his face appeared to be etched into his pale skin.

"I would guess a virus. Something nasty, maybe flu-like. This wasn't a natural death. There's blood in his mouth; even without teeth he's clamped down so hard that he's almost bitten through his tongue, and the blood vessels in his eyes have burst." He pointed a finger at the lifeless form. "This baby died a sudden and painful death. With no obvious signs of violence, and the build-up of mucus around the nose together with the colour of his mouth and eyes, I would say an aggressive virus."

* * *

Maggie dialled the number, not allowing herself to think about what she was about to do. If she did, her nerve would go. The ringing sounded hollow and distant, conjuring an image of Sandra bolting out of bed, frightened, unprepared for the horror that was about to engulf her world. Maggie's hand shook. She was about to cause Sandra so much grief, but at the same time, she didn't want the call coming from a stranger.

"Hello?" Sandra sounded sleepy and worried at the same time.

"Sandra, it's Maggie."

"Maggie, is—"

"It's... Something's happened. Sandra, it's Eddie." Maggie paused for a second and drew in a deep breath, wishing she'd slowed down and prepared what she was going to say. Now that the line echoed with silence, she had no choice but to plunge in with the news. "I'm so sorry, but he's died." Once the words were out, everything felt flat. What was left of Maggie's strength drained away. She sat down on the nearby office chair and propped her elbow on the table. There was no sound on the line, and for one horrifying moment, Maggie thought they'd been disconnected. Then Sandra spoke.

"No. No, not the baby..." Sandra's voice, at first anguished and frightened, broke.

"I'm so sorry." The words seemed empty and meaningless. Maggie heard a muffled sob. She closed her eyes and wished she could stop, but she had more misery to deliver.

"Ollie's been in an accident. They were driving into town to get help and... And the police are looking for him."

Maggie knew she wasn't making much sense, but nothing about what had happened made sense.

"Tess?" The word was little more than a whisper. "Is Tess... is she—"

"She's okay," Maggie answered, before realising that *okay* didn't begin to describe Tess's state and quickly adding, "she's safe."

Sandra let out a shuddering breath. "I'm coming. Tell Tess I'm coming. I'll be there in a few hours."

"We're at the police station. It's on Sutton Street, near the general store."

"Okay. I'll find it." She paused. "How... I mean what happened to Eddie?"

What happened to Eddie? Maggie wished she had an answer. The same question kept going around and around in her mind. He was a healthy little baby one day and then gone the next.

"We're not sure. He seemed to be getting sick and then..." Maggie let her voice trail off. What *could* she say? There *were* no answers.

"Okay. I'll be there as quickly as I can."

Maggie hung up, grateful that Sandra hadn't pushed for more. It was close to midnight and what felt like a year since she left home that morning.

An hour ago, Maggie had followed Harness into the unlit building. Small country stations didn't stay open all night unless there was a major problem. In less than an hour, Harness had marshalled Thorn Tree's entire police force, which, including Harness, was three men.

Maggie, lost in thought, watched Constable Mark Leary as he rubbed his pale face, thick fingers working through a shock of red hair still rumpled from sleep. Harness had instructed the younger officer to stay on the radio and answer the phones while sending the town's only other officer out to Tess's house in search of Ollie's car.

Maggie was just about to go back in and sit with Tess when a call came through on the radio.

"Leary? Attwell here. Over." Senior Constable Jason Attwell's voice came over the radio with a robotic crackle.

"Attwell, what's the situation?" Leary asked.

"I think I've found the husband. His car is wrapped around a tree on Maple Road near the turnoff to the Chapel Orchard. He's alive but in bad shape. I'm going to need a medivac here right away. Over."

"Roger. Stand by." Leary pivoted to the phone and began making calls.

Maggie sat near the desk, trying to make sense of what was happening. The tragedy kept unfolding, gathering more and more momentum like the storm that had raged through town the night before. Only now it wasn't smashed windows and fallen trees, but death.

Leary covered the phone with his hand. "Get the sarge." He snapped his fingers to get her attention.

Before Maggie had time to react, the kitchen door swung open and Harness entered followed by Dr Cole. The young constable stopped and waited.

"How long until the chopper gets to them?" Harness asked.

"About thirty-five minutes. It's coming from Perth. It's the only one available."

Harness turned to Cole. "Doc, can you get out to Maple Road and see what you can do?"

"I can be there in fifteen minutes." Cole was already heading for the door.

Harness turned to Maggie. "Did you reach the mother?"

"Yes. She'll be here in a few hours."

"Good." He ran a hand across the back of his neck. "Can you stay with Tess until then? I've got some calls to make."

"Yes, of course." She pushed herself up from the chair. "Is there anything else I can do to help?"

"You can make a list. Full names and any phone numbers for Tess, her mother and the husband. Include the husband's employer if you can. Give the list to Leary." He paused. "Don't tell Tess anything about her husband until we know how he's doing." Harness turned and picked up the nearest phone. Maggie wanted to ask him what the doctor had said about Eddie, but it was clear he didn't have time to talk.

* * *

Maggie hovered at the back of the station house. In an effort to stop herself from staring at the kitchen door, she fixed her gaze on the wall clock and watched the minute hand tick to 1.56 in the morning. A couple of hours ago

37

things had been moving so fast, it seemed the world was spinning. Now time slowed. When the front door of the station house thumped open, Maggie almost let out a yelp of surprise. Tess's mother raced into the small waiting area looking tired and dishevelled. A gust of cold night air flooded the room before the door creaked closed.

Harness stepped up to the counter to meet the woman.

"I'm Senior Sergeant Gibson. Mrs Michaels, I'm very sorry for your loss." His tone was gentle and formal at the same time. Maggie guessed he'd had plenty of experience delivering bad news.

Sandra's back stiffened. "Can you tell me what's happened? Where's my daughter?" Her hair was pulled back in a messy bun and she was wearing a rumpled tracksuit. Maggie could only imagine what must have been going through the woman's mind during the two-hour drive from Perth.

"Your daughter's in my office resting. We have an officer and the town's doctor at the accident scene. They're taking care of your son-in-law. As soon as the medivac team arrives, he'll be air-lifted to the hospital."

Sandra nodded and remained quietly composed. She took a deep breath. "And my grandson?"

"I'm looking after Eddie for now." Harness's voice was gentle, almost soothing.

When her grandson's name was mentioned, the lower half of Sandra's face trembled and her shoulders sagged. Maggie rushed around the counter and took hold of Sandra's arm, leading her to the nearest seat.

"Sandra, sit a moment." Maggie could feel the woman trembling.

"No, I need to see Tess." She sounded breathless, ready to break down. Maggie guided her down onto the seat, then pulled up a chair so that she could sit facing Sandra.

Maggie took both of the woman's hands in hers, noticing the coolness of her skin. "Sandra." Maggie spoke slowly, keeping her tone calm. "In a minute I'm going to take you in to see Tess. She's awake but very confused."

Sandra's eyes were shiny, wide with emotion.

"I think she's in shock. Dr Cole is out helping Ollie, so we need to look after her ourselves." Maggie stopped and waited for Sandra to respond.

"Yes, yes, I'm sorry. It's all been such a shock. I'm all right. Maggie, I need to see my daughter."

Maggie nodded and stood up. Still holding Sandra's hand, she led her into Harness's office.

Chapter Six

The sound of crying dragged Marley Dicks from a deep sleep. She pulled the pillow out from under her and clamped it over her head. *Damn it, the second time in one night.* If only the kid would learn to sleep in and shut up, motherhood would be a lot easier. At least the wailing wasn't as loud as last night. Zoe was nearly eighteen months old with a powerful set of lungs, but today, her cries were softer. *Good, maybe she's finally learning.* Marley tried to tune out the sobs and go back to sleep, but it was no good. As usual, the kid managed to ruin any chance she had to catch up on some rest.

"I'm coming." Marley swung her legs over the side of the bed and scratched her cheek. Her face still stung.

The night came to her in hazy snapshots. A French guy, a backpacker she'd picked up at the pub. He called her *chéri,* his accent making up for acne-scarred cheeks and ratty goatee. He seemed nice, even holding the door open for her as if Marley's dump was some kind of palace. He certainly seemed to be into her, clutching her hair and groaning while she gave him head.

She reached down and picked a bit of lint out from between her toes and flicked it across the bedroom, remembering the way the French guy pushed her away when she tried to kiss him, calling her a *dirty slut* in that snotty accent. *Who the hell did he think he was?* To make matters worse, when she told him to fuck off, he slapped her. Marley had been so shocked when the look on his scarred face changed from mild disgust to anger, she'd fallen back on her ass. Shocked, she was unable to do anything but watch open-mouthed as he snatched up her small bag of weed and left, slamming the door behind him.

The crash of the door shook the flimsy fibro-cement walls, setting off a squall of shrieks from Zoe's room. Still clutching her burning cheek, Marley stomped into her daughter's room to find the child's nappy needed changing. She'd cleaned the kid up and put her back in her cot. Zoe clung to Marley as she put her down, the toddler's sticky fingers clutching at Marley's hair. *All I want is some time to myself. The kid never stops.* She pulled the baby loose and thrust her into the cot. Zoe's face was so red, it looked like she had been scalded.

Now the kid was off again. Marley checked the time on the bedside clock: 3 a.m. If she could get Zoe back to sleep, she might stand a chance of getting a few more hours for herself. Sliding her feet into flip-flops, she shuffled her way to the kitchen and took an unwashed bottle out of the sink. She grabbed the baby paracetamol from the fridge and poured a sizable amount in then added water.

Before she opened the door, Marley screwed her eyes closed and puffed out her cheeks. The constant whimpering set her teeth on edge. It was as if the kid was torturing her. Pushing down her irritation, she opened the door. The baby stood in the cot, snot and dribble covering her nose and mouth. Spotting Marley in the doorway, Zoe stretched out her arms, hands grasping air. Not wanting the kid to latch onto her, Marley handed her the bottle but kept her distance. Zoe grasped the bottle and tucked it into her small mouth, sucking breathlessly on the milky-looking mixture.

I knew the greedy little thing wouldn't be able to resist. Marley yawned and watched her daughter suck back the liquid as tears streamed down her angry red cheeks. In seconds, the baby settled onto her bottom and began twirling a strand of hair in her chubby fist. Marley nodded, pleased to see the girl was learning to settle herself. Making as little sound as possible, Marley edged out of the room and closed the door.

* * *

A snort caught in Marley's throat, jerking her awake. She rolled her head to the side and checked the time: almost 9 a.m. With a sleepy grunt, she tumbled from the bed, pulling sagging track pants up around her sizable hips. On her way down the short hallway, it struck her that the house was unusually quiet. Most mornings the kid was jumping up and down by eight o'clock. By nine o'clock, the screams were enough to wake the dead. A patch of sunlight filtered through the kitchen window and fell on her daughter's door. Marley put her hand on the knob and hesitated, the skin on her arms prickled with gooseflesh. The urge to turn and run welled up in her belly like the acid burn of a dodgy kebab. Marley chewed her thumbnail. At nineteen, running seemed like a viable option. A muffled moan, almost as soft as a whisper, came from the other side of the door. Marley gathered up her courage and entered her daughter's room.

Light shone through the gap in the curtains, landing on the dilapidated cot. Although she was a little spooked by the quiet, some part of Marley still expected to see Zoe standing up, arms outstretched. The unnatural stillness in the room was almost jarring.

Marley approached the cot, noting the smell: dirty nappy mixed with vomit. Peering into the baby's bed, Marley's mouth dropped open. "Oh, fuck."

Zoe lay on her back, a thick bubbly layer of foam covering her nose and mouth. Her eyes were swollen, as if bruised. "Zoe? Zoe, baby!"

Zoe's eyes fluttered, but didn't quite open. Marley ran her hands through her limp sandy hair, trying to decide what to do next. Her small brown eyes darted around the room and came to rest on the empty bottle lying next to the baby. *Could you overdose on paracetamol?* Ignoring her daughter, Marley snatched up the bottle and rushed out of the house. She opened the bin and pushed the bottle as far down into the rubbish as her hand could reach. Unsure what to do next, Marley scurried back inside to check on Zoe.

Once in the baby's room, it was clear Zoe was far from all right. Marley searched the room for something to wrap around the child. She rifled through the pile of dirty washing near the door and found one of the baby's blankets. It smelt of sour milk, but it would do.

"Come on, kiddo," Marley said and lifted Zoe out of the cot and onto her shoulder. The child's limp body draped against her. She shuddered and rubbed Zoe's back. A spark of motherly concern, maybe the first she'd ever experienced, washed over her and tears sprang into her eyes. *What if she dies?* Fear and guilt blotted out the concern almost as quickly as it arose. *They'll blame me.*

Marley pushed the thought away. The kid had been sick plenty of times, but she always got better. She'd take her to the doctor and get some medicine then everything would be all right again.

"It's okay, Zoe. Mummy will take care of you." She trotted through the house, the baby's legs swinging lifelessly as she crouched over the coffee table and grabbed the car keys. Zoe responded with a rattling breath.

Marley laid the child on the back seat, not daring to try fastening her in the baby restraints for fear she'd fall forward and choke.

"Okay. Good, okay."

She jumped into the driver's seat and turned the key. The engine spluttered and died. Swearing under her breath she tried again. This time the car groaned to life. Not giving the old wreck time to cut out, Marley slammed the gears into reverse and pulled out of the driveway.

"It's all right, sweetie. Everything will be all right now. We'll be at the doctor's in a minute." She spoke over her shoulder to the unresponsive toddler as the car bounced over a pothole.

Five minutes later, Marley pulled up in front of the doctor's surgery. Marley bolted from the car and rushed across the narrow strip of lawn, her chest heaving from the excursion. By the time Dr Cole's wife, Mary, wrenched open the car door, Zoe had been dead for three minutes.

Chapter Seven

Maggie climbed the stairs to her bedroom, her shoulders aching with tension and fatigue. She kicked off her shoes, noticing the morning sun creeping across the floor. It felt like a lifetime since she was last in the room. She jerked the curtains closed before stumbling back to the bed. Still wearing last night's clothes, she crawled under the covers. Images of Eddie, face frozen in death, pushed into her mind. The urge to run through the nightmarish events of the previous evening tugged at her thoughts, tempting her to relive the anguish that was building in her chest like a lump of hardened clay. She closed her eyes, expecting to toss and turn, but instead fell into a deep sleep.

Something chased her. Legs pumping, she ran through a carpet of huge, waxy red flowers. She looked back over her shoulder and saw a stick-like figure jerking its body forward with unrelenting determination. She tried to speed up, but her legs pulled and stretched as if made of rubber. Her progress was maddeningly slow.

A drum pounded, faintly at first like a heartbeat. She opened her mouth to scream and felt her vocal cords twanging without sound. The drumming intensified, the flowers pulsating under her feet. Maggie covered her ears and stumbled forward, desperate to avoid the creature rustling through the foliage at her back. The pounding grew louder, deafening.

Maggie woke, eyes wide, the drum still reverberating in her ears. Heart jumping, it took her a moment to realise it wasn't the drumming from her dream, but someone knocking her front door.

Still shaken, she struggled out of bed, bracing herself against the wall as she stumbled down the stairs. She reached the door and hesitated, the stick-like creature from the dream still loomed in her mind, mixing with the memory of Tess stumbling out of the darkness holding her dead infant. It was easy to believe the nightmare might still be playing out. Maggie ran a hand over her face, trying to wipe away the sense of dread, and opened the door.

"What took you so long?" Doug Loggie's friendly smile quickly turned to concern. "Are you okay? You look like you've seen a ghost."

Maggie let out a relieved breath before realising she was still wearing last night's clothes, creased and moulded to her body with sweat. She touched the puffy skin under her eyes. She probably had mascara all over her face too.

"Doug, sorry. I had a rough night. What—"

"I got your message and came over to clear your yard."

"Yes, the storm." Maggie still felt confused but tried to cover. "Yes, okay. I'll leave you to it." She closed the door on his stunned face.

After taking a hot shower and putting on clean clothes, Maggie felt almost normal again. She tied her long auburn hair in a ponytail and caught a glimpse of herself in the mirror over the sink, puffy eyes staring out of a pale face. Outside, a crow squawked and was quickly joined by a chorus of similar cries. Maggie turned away from her reflection and headed downstairs. After making two cups of instant coffee, she opened the back door.

Doug was busy raking up the remnants of Friday night's storm. Three piles of freshly gathered leaves dotted the yard, each one peppered with red flowers. A wheelbarrow sat near the corner of the house laden with small branches and clumps of dried grass.

She watched him carry a stack of fallen branches to the wheelbarrow and toss them in. He fished out a few that were too long and snapped them in half as easily as if they were twigs. He'd probably had countless calls, yet here he was. Her throat constricted and tears pricked her eyes. Doug had become her safe harbour, in many ways filling the void left when her grandfather died. Last night the world had turned upside down, but watching Doug setting her garden straight was an anchor she desperately needed.

"Coffee?" Maggie held up a steaming cup and noticed her hand was shaking.

Doug turned and gave her a grateful smile. "Just what I need. You're a lifesaver."

Maggie handed him the mug and sat down on the steps, setting her cup beside her. Doug stood, one hand on his hip, sipping the hot drink.

After a moment of awkward silence, Maggie spoke. "Doug, I'm sorry about earlier. I practically shut the door in your face… I did shut the door in your face." She tried to laugh, but the sound was forced, shaky. "I– I had a hard night."

Doug took his time answering. "I know. I heard about Ollie and the baby. It's a bad business when tragedy strikes a family twice."

After three years, she was still surprised at how quickly news spread in a small town.

"How did you hear?"

"Half the town heard the sirens last night. Agnes Wells made it her business to find out what was happening. Ran into her at the general store this morning. She was telling anyone who'd listen." Doug shook his head disapprovingly. "That woman loves to spread gossip, especially when it's about someone else's misery."

Maggie rubbed her eyes, trying to wipe away the image of Eddie's lifeless face. She didn't trust herself to speak. Instead, she picked up her cup and took a sip.

"What are all these red flowers called? Do you know?" Maggie asked, searching for something to say.

"Well, there's a Latin name for them, *Floreo pectus*, but my mother called them something else." Doug gestured towards the waxy vines growing up around the back veranda. Even after the storm, flowers and tiny buds still clung stubbornly to the vines. "She said they were so resilient that they could grow out of rock."

Doug finished his coffee and set the cup down on the stairs. "Maureen would know the name. She's good with things like that – names, birthdays – she keeps a record of the little things so that they aren't forgotten." He ran his hand through his bushy white hair and smiled as though he was remembering something sweet.

The way Doug described the flower brought back memories of her grandfather. When she was a little girl, he'd tell her stories about *his* father, Blue Hawk, and the Cherokee people. He once told her that plants, in response to human suffering, made medicine to cure each sickness that entered the world.

"They're pretty in a kind of wild way." She drained the last drops of coffee from her cup. "I was thinking of asking you to cut them down, but they're growing on me."

Doug nodded. "I'm nearly finished here, just a few piles of leaves to clear and I'll be off. Maureen had a difficult night. I think she might be coming down with something. I don't like leaving her for too long after chemo."

Coming down with something?

"How's she doing? I mean with her treatment."

"She's getting through it. Maureen's a strong woman." He nodded. "She'll beat it."

Maggie admired Doug's relationship with his wife. When he spoke of her, there was always affection in his

48

voice, making the elderly man seem younger somehow. Maggie thought of her ex-husband. He'd taken such pleasure in making her feel small. If it wasn't for Doug, she wouldn't be able to believe there were still good men left in the world.

On impulse, Maggie reached out and put her hand over Doug's.

"I know she will." She stood and picked up the empty cups. "Give Maureen my best. I'm going to drive over and check on Tess and her mum, maybe there's some news."

"Tell her I'm praying for her and Ollie. It's a bad business when a baby dies. Maureen and I were never blessed with children. Lost our only baby before it was born. Maureen was six months along and the happiest I'd ever seen her, but then–" He stopped for a second, as if lost in thought. "Then just as suddenly as it came, it went. It's been thirty years now, but that loss still weighs on Maureen. Me too, I suppose."

He got up, gave Maggie a nod and went back to the Floreo pectus and the rest of the yard.

Chapter Eight

Maureen rubbed her hands together, the dull ache in her fingers having made them painful and unresponsive. Her head throbbed, keeping time with her pulsating joints. Chemo was nothing new, its effects familiar – fatigue, the sickness – but this new misery was different.

Earlier, she woke from a dream about a little girl who'd wandered into the backyard. The bedraggled child moved around the garden on unsteady feet. Her small, frail body was shrouded in mist, making it difficult for Maureen to keep track of the child's movements. She seemed to be searching for something; was it her mother? The girl approached a large tree and came to an abrupt stop. Maureen felt herself drawn to the child as if invisible arms were reaching out for her. The girl's bare feet moved across the misty ground, and with each step, the pull of the child's need for her grew stronger. She was searching for someone to love her. If Maureen could just take her hand, everything would be all right. Her chest still ached with loss, all the sorrow bottled and stoppered after Beth's death. *She was so small, not ready for the world.*

The lost child in her dream seemed to be looking up at something in the distance. Maureen turned her head and saw a square shape floating in the blackness; it was filled with light, a light so brilliant it seared Maureen's eyes.

She turned back to the little girl and noticed a swing. It was made of some sort of dark wood but instead of having ropes, it hung from a chain of stiff white sticks. Maureen shuffled forward, desperate to reach the child. If she could just take her hand, then the little girl would know. She'd know that she wasn't alone. Know she was safe.

Maureen reached out to the girl, her fingers stretching as invisible needles pierced her knuckles like knives. Then everything spun backwards. The garden shrank into a whirlpool of mist and leaves. Before it disappeared, Maureen felt cold skin press against her fingertips.

Dreaming of children was not uncommon for Maureen. She supposed it was a commonality in childless women, but last night had been different somehow – *real*.

Waking up, Maureen found her arms crossed over her body, holding tight to a non-existent child. Crows screeched outside her window as the sun broke through the curtains. She'd watched the morning light play across the cheerful floral bedspread that covered her thin frame and allowed herself a few moments before she pushed away the sorrow of losing yet another child, if only in her dreams. She'd promised Doug she was fine, making a big show of eating the scrambled eggs he'd made her for breakfast, only to vomit them up once he left the house. *Ah, Doug*. Even after all these years of marriage, when she thought of her sweetheart, she couldn't help but smile. He worried too much.

Maureen dropped painfully into the rocking chair Doug had made for her when she was pregnant. *So many years ago*. She wrapped a soft wool throw around her shoulders and stared out the window. Concentrating her gaze on the cloudless blue sky, she waited for the aches and pains to recede enough so she could walk to the bedroom and get dressed. Maybe a couple of paracetamol and a glass of water would dull the pain. Wincing, she took hold of the sides of the chair and pushed herself up. The room tilted and her legs shook, giving her no option but to drop back down.

She wished she hadn't been so stubborn and pig-headed, always so sure she could get through whatever life threw at her. She should've told Doug she didn't feel well. He'd have stayed home and she wouldn't be alone. Bowing her hairless head, she lifted aching fingers to her face. Her cheeks were wet.

Icy shudders ripped through her chest, thumping her against the backrest of the rocking chair. She whispered Doug's name over and over until she wasn't sure if her body shook from pain or sorrow. Cold spasms sent darts of lightning up and down her fragile limbs. Maureen closed her eyes and prayed that Doug would come through the front door. But when her eyelids fluttered on her cheeks, blackness swallowed her and dragged her downwards. In the seconds before Maureen's world collapsed, she heard a child's laugh.

Chapter Nine

Maggie watched the ice cubes bob around in the amber liquid, clicking together when Sandra put the two glasses of tea down on the coffee table. The sound reminded Maggie of Agnes's party. It seemed like an old memory of a life uncomplicated by sudden death and grief. Maggie sat facing Sandra. Her usually impeccably made-up face was scrubbed clean, fine lines around her eyes and mouth painfully visible in the morning light.

They were in Tess and Ollie's living room. The last time Maggie had been in the house, it was abuzz with noise and activity. Eddie, fresh from a bath wriggling on the changing mat while Tess dried him with a fluffy towel. Today the place was silent. The smell of baby powder and fabric softener hung in the air. A pile of carefully folded baby clothes sat on the ironing board near the kitchen door. Maggie found her gaze drifting between the clothes and Sandra's face.

"How is she?" Maggie picked up her glass and made herself focus on the liquid.

"I don't know. Last night, when I told her about Ollie, she just stared at me as though she didn't understand," Sandra said. "She's asleep now, I suppose that's good.

When she wakes up, I'm going to drive her back to Perth where I can look after her and be near Ollie."

"And Ollie?" Maggie asked.

"In a coma. They took him to Fremantle Hospital last night." Sandra paused. "Two days ago, everything was perfect. Tess and Ollie were so happy, and we had a beautiful new baby. Now everything's a mess," she said, choking back a sob.

"Oh, Sandra." Maggie got up and sat next to her on the sofa. She placed her arm around Sandra's shoulders. Not sure of what else to do, Maggie let her own tears flow. After a moment or so, Sandra pulled away and took a sip of tea.

"What are we supposed to do now, Maggie?"

This new defeated Sandra was so different from the glamorous, confident woman Maggie knew.

She didn't know what to tell the woman. There were no easy answers. "Focus on Tess and Ollie," Maggie said, swiping at her eyes. "It's all we *can* do now."

Sandra nodded, but looked distracted. "I wish I could make everything all right for Tess, like I used to when she was little."

She paused and took a long shuddering breath as she looked around the room. There were reminders of the new-born's presence in every corner.

"Last night, when I finally got her to bed," Sandra continued, "Tess said her heart hurt and then she closed her eyes and wouldn't speak to me." Sandra stopped and looked at Maggie with red-rimmed eyes. "How do I fix that?"

Maggie searched for something to say. "We concentrate on taking a few steps at a time. Getting through today. Looking after Ollie." She stood and took Sandra's half-empty glass from the coffee table. "I'll tidy up in the kitchen. You go pack some things for Tess and Ollie."

Sandra looked surprised but gave Maggie a weak smile and nodded.

"Good." Maggie continued. "When I'm finished in the kitchen, I'll take your car and fill it up."

* * *

Maggie took Sandra's car and drove into town to get petrol. It was Sunday, so the usually busy main street was quiet. She turned onto Sutton Street just as a police car drove past going in the opposite direction. She craned her neck to see who was driving, but the vehicle sped past in a blur of white and red. *I wonder if it's Harness.* Last night she'd left the station without really speaking to him... What was there to say? She wondered what new tragedy he was dealing with and hoped, for his sake, that it wasn't as bad as last night.

A few moments later, Maggie pulled into the petrol station. Like the rest of town, it was quiet, almost eerily so. She filled the tank and then took the watering can next to the pump and poured water over her hands. A lone crow hopped across the little grassy area at the side of the petrol station. It jumped onto a picnic table then fluttered up to a telephone pole. Maggie gasped. There were crows, maybe two dozen of the things, lining the wires above the pumps. The scene put her in mind of an old movie where birds suddenly started gathering and attacking people. She wiped her hands on the front of her jeans, keeping her eyes on the birds. Had there always been so many crows in Thorn Tree?

She was about to go inside and pay when an old green Jeep pulled in and parked on the other side of the pump. Jackson flung open the door and jumped out. Behind him, the birds squawked and flapped their wings.

"Maggie." He sounded breathless. "I heard about Tess." He stopped, seeming unsure of himself.

"It seems like everyone has heard about Tess." The minute the words were out, she recognised how bitter she sounded and wished she could take it back.

Jackson dropped his head, his dark hair lifting in the breeze. "I'm sorry," he said. "I wasn't gossiping. I just... I don't know. I mean–"

"No. *I'm* sorry, Jackson. I'm just on edge." She glanced up to where the birds were congregated. "I know you care about Tess and Ollie and…" She couldn't bring herself to say Eddie's name aloud.

"That's okay. You're a picnic compared to my mum. My little sister's sick, she's got a temperature and feels fluey. It's got Mum in a flap."

She grabbed his upper arm. "Get her out of town." The words were out before she knew she was going to say them. Suddenly it seemed vital that Jackson get his little sister as far away from Thorn Tree as quickly as possible.

Jackson blinked in surprise, but rather than stepping back, he brought his left hand up and put it over Maggie's, holding her hand in place on his arm. He nodded.

"That's what Gran said. She kept going on about it not being safe for kids here. She wouldn't stop until my mum got so worked up that she's taking my sister to Perth to stay with my aunty. That's why I'm filling up Dad's car."

Maggie was about to ask what his grandmother had meant by *not safe for children* when the distant wailing of an ambulance silenced them both. It drew nearer, following the same route the police car had taken not ten minutes earlier. The wailing sliced through the air and sent the gathering birds into a frenzy of squawking and flapping. Jackson looked up at the crows and laughed nervously, but there was no humour in the sound.

* * *

"I know it's hard, but Ollie needs you." Maggie sat down on the bed next to Tess while Sandra slipped a pair of trainers onto her daughter's feet. "You have to keep going even though you don't want to."

She'd left the petrol station intent on asking Tess what happened when they were driving into town. How had

Ollie, usually a safe driver, ended up in a coma? Nothing made much sense. The roads would have been deserted. How could things have gone so wrong? But whatever questions she had, they'd have to wait. Her friend was not in a state to give answers.

Tess stared at the top of her mother's head. She'd let Maggie and Sandra dress her, cooperating and answering simple questions. But when Sandra explained that they were driving to Perth, her body had stiffened. "No. I can't, it's too much." Her voice was flat, as if it belonged to someone else.

"Ollie's hurt – badly. You can't just let him lie there alone; you're his wife." Maggie knew she sounded harsh, but maybe that's what Tess needed.

Tess tore her gaze away from her mother's head and for the first time since Eddie's death seemed to focus on what was being said. Her eyes were bloodshot and her usually bouncy brown hair hung around her face in lank strings.

"I can't lose Ollie too." There was emotion in her voice now, raw and urgent. "I can't sit in a hospital and watch him slip away from me, just like my..." Tess's voice broke and a shuddering sob shook her body, vibrating through her hand.

Sandra got up from her knees and sat on the other side of Tess, taking her daughter in her arms. "You won't, I promise you won't." She held Tess in firm arms, her own eyes shiny with tears.

Tess wrapped both her arms around her mother. Sandra held her as if she were a child and whispered assurances.

"I'll stay with you. We'll look after Ollie together and we'll make sure the doctors take care of him. He'll get better, I know he will."

Sandra looked at Maggie over her daughter's shoulder. They both knew that she was making promises she didn't know if she could keep. But the desperate look in Sandra's eyes told Maggie she needed to make everything all right for her daughter. *God knows Tess needs hope.*

"Ollie's strong. He's healthy. If he can hear your voice, he'll find his way back," Maggie added. She just prayed she was doing the right thing by encouraging Tess to believe everything would work out.

Tess pulled back from her mother and turned to Maggie. She saw a small flicker of the old Tess, the one that took charge of every situation with a natural confidence, or at least she hoped that's what she saw.

"Yes, I should be there. I should talk to the doctors."

Maggie put the last of the bags in the boot and Sandra slammed the lid.

"Thank you, Maggie." Sandra hesitated, studying the keys in her hand. "Well, we'd better get going." She gave Maggie's shoulder a brief squeeze and headed for the driver's seat.

Maggie walked around the car and rested her forearms on the open window. She leaned in and kissed Tess on the forehead.

"Give that to Ollie for me," she said, sounding much brighter than she felt.

Tess nodded, but continued to stare straight ahead. The little flicker was gone.

"Let me know when there's any news," Maggie said and stood back as the car rolled down the driveway wondering if her friend would ever resurface from the sorrow that engulfed her.

* * *

The twenty-minute drive home seemed like a marathon. She'd been on an emotional rollercoaster for the last twenty-four hours, and, judging by the way her limbs ached and her thoughts ran in circles, it was catching up with her.

She climbed the front steps slowly, taking one at a time. There was a piece of paper, folded and wedged between the frame and the screen door. She grabbed the paper and opened the door.

Dumping her bag and the paper on the coffee table, she headed for the kitchen. So much had happened, there had been no time to really think. To grieve. Even though Eddie wasn't her baby, she'd felt a joy and closeness to both Eddie and Tess through the pregnancy and the birth. For the first time in years, Maggie had been connected to something truly happy and hopeful, but now it was shattered, never to really be whole again. Her throat constricted and her chest tightened as if something were building up inside her, trying to get out. Maggie slumped on a chair and put her elbows on the kitchen table, hands clenched together as if praying.

Doug's words went around in her mind, *"It's been thirty years and that baby still weighs heavily on her."* Maggie wondered how long it would take Tess to come to terms with what happened. *What did happen?* Nothing was clear. None of last night made any sense.

Her mind raced from one thought to another, throwing up images of Tess stumbling down the dark, empty street. Eddie's face, distorted in death. She couldn't rest. She needed to be doing something. She got up and wandered around the kitchen. Ignoring two days' worth of dirty dishes, she chose instead to leaf through a pile of unopened mail on the counter, not really taking anything in. Any way she looked at it, there were unanswered questions. Things just didn't add up. Babies died, she accepted that, but quietly. Eddie's death was different.

Why, she wondered, had Tess and Ollie decided to drive into town? If the baby was that sick, why not call for help? There was no doubt about it, something strange had happened. Maggie felt sure of it.

Chapter Ten

Instead of going home when his shift ended, Harness headed for his old Jeep and sat behind the wheel. Usually content to be alone, tonight the last place he wanted to be was in an empty house. Resting his forearms on the wheel, he leaned forward in the seat, unable to shake off the sense that something was wrong. Death always seemed like an insult to the living, but what happened the night before went deeper. It struck at him in a way that stirred up a hailstorm of memories.

He stared at the darkened windows of his house, knowing if he went inside, he'd fall back into a hole filled with sadness. *Sadness or loneliness?* Was he trying to avoid being alone because thinking about Eddie's death would push him back into despair, or was he looking for an excuse to see Maggie again?

When he first set eyes on her three years ago, she'd been standing on the footpath outside her café talking to Doug Loggie. Harness, sitting in the squad car across the road, glanced over just as she tilted her head to one side and laughed at something Doug had said. Watching her, he found himself smiling and thinking about what it would be like to be close to someone again, to make plans for the future. To do all the ordinary things people did when they were in a relationship. But being close to someone meant taking a risk. He wasn't ready to put his tenuous hold on a steady, if not happy, life on the line.

Three years later and he was still stalled in the same rut he'd carved out for himself when he arrived in Thorn Tree six years ago. In the city, he'd dealt with tragedy on a regular basis. It was a part of the job he'd grown to accept. But when tragedy hit his own life, *his* family, he could no longer compartmentalise the two. Being a cop was all he'd ever known, so he opted for the slow-paced world of country policing. But watching the doctor examine Eddie made him realise he couldn't hide from the world any longer.

He didn't want to let grief into his life, not again. But he'd nursed his wounds for long enough and didn't want to be alone anymore. He thought of Maggie, the way she flushed with embarrassment when he'd pulled her car over. She was smart and funny, somehow managing to be confident and vulnerable at the same time. In the midst of all the chaos last night, he found himself admiring her calmness.

He turned on the engine and reversed out of his driveway. It was almost dark. Clouds the colour of granite were gathering in the sky. Leaving the lights of town behind, he headed west. Harness had no idea what he would say to Maggie when he turned up on her doorstep, but he knew he couldn't wait another three years.

* * *

Dark clouds swallowed the late-afternoon sun, leaving the sky the colour of ashes at the bottom of a long-extinguished fire pit. Maggie pulled the curtains closed. She'd been wandering around the house all afternoon trying to keep busy. With the initial shock subsiding, she was left with an invisible weight pressing down on her shoulders like tired hands. Unable to shake the need for action, she decided to ring Jackson and ask if he could open the café tomorrow – keep things going until she got there. She'd also have to call Cilla. Monday was supposed to be her day off, but Maggie hoped she'd consider working half a day.

Maggie figured she'd call Cilla first and make sure Jackson wouldn't be left alone to cope with the morning coffee rush. She shuffled into the kitchen and grabbed her mobile phone. The pane rattled in the wind. The thought of another storm made her nerves jangle. Turning away from the window, Maggie found Cilla's number and pressed *call*. The line engaged and rang. A hiss of static spurted into Maggie's ear.

"Hello?"

"Hi, Cilla, it's Maggie."

"Maggie, I..." *Static*.

She could barely hear Cilla's voice.

"Cilla, can you work tomorrow?" Maggie waited, not sure if the other woman could hear her.

"Robert..." *Static*... "So sick... sorry."

"Cilla?" The call dropped into dead silence.

Maggie stared at the phone in her hand. Robert, Cilla's nine-year-old son, battled severe asthma. It wasn't unusual for him to be unwell, but she usually left him with her husband rather than miss out on an extra shift. Maggie's fingers hesitated over the phone. First Eddie, then Jackson's sister, now Robert Edgell. Could their illnesses be connected? It was possible. Weird strains of flu popped up everywhere. Thorn Tree was a tourist town, maybe someone carrying a virus... Recalling the moment she opened the fuzzy blue blanket and saw the baby's dead face, her thoughts wavered. She had no real medical knowledge, but it didn't look like the flu killed Eddie.

She called Jackson. The line hissed static into her ear. In the instant before pulling the phone away from her head, the sound changed. The hiss ramped up in volume, spitting out what sounded like a choir of whispers. So many urgent voices, it was impossible to make out any one word. Startled, Maggie dropped the phone on the kitchen table, watching it spin to a slow stop. It had to be the storm interfering with the satellite. *But there's no storm, not really. Just the wind.*

Maggie glanced at the kitchen window, the glass black like a frozen lake. Suddenly the light from the kitchen wasn't enough. She shivered and turned on the lounge room lights. Usually she didn't mind the solitude of living so far outside of town, but without the phone, she felt alone, vulnerable. She knew half the people in town, but except for Tess and Ollie, Doug was the only other person she felt close to.

Thinking about Doug stirred her memory. She paced, eager to latch onto something that might take her mind off the memory of the whispering voices bursting through the static. *It was just static.* She snatched up the piece of paper she'd dropped on the coffee table and unfolded its crumpled edges; just as she'd thought, it was a note from Doug.

> *Dear Maggie,*
> *Your yard's as good as new. $80 should cover it.*
> *I remembered the name of those flowers: Stone Flowers. Hard name for something so pretty.*
> *I'm booked solid for the next few days, but if you get time, pop around on Wednesday after work. Maureen would love to see you.*
> *Take care*
> *Doug*

Maggie reread the note, the familiar scrawl like a lifeline from the outside world reminding her she wasn't completely alone. She thought about flowers that were so resilient they could grow out of stone. Maggie prayed that in the coming days, Tess could be a stone flower. She had a feeling they were all going to need to be stone flowers because lately, the ground felt stony.

Back in the kitchen, Maggie dropped the note on the kitchen table and grabbed a bottle of wine out of the fridge and a glass from the draining board. She sloshed some wine into the glass and took a sip, enjoying the sharp, clean taste as it slipped down her throat. She'd let the storm spook her. *It's not a storm.* Was it any wonder, after what she'd seen over the last few days?

The wind soughed, the sound reminded her of the ocean. Maggie took another sip of wine and frowned. In his note, Doug hadn't mentioned the dead cat. Most likely he'd buried it, not wanting it to upset her. But another possibility crept into her mind. Maybe he didn't see it and it was still out there, fur shredded and bits of flesh tangled amongst the branches. *Maybe the birds carried it away in pieces.*

A *thump* on the front door made Maggie jolt, splashing chardonnay over her hand. There'd been no hiss of tyres or rumble of an engine. Was it possible the wind had blocked out the sound? She put the glass down and without thinking, licked the back of her hand. Another *thump*, this time louder. Maggie took a step towards the living room and hesitated. She ran her hand over her mouth. Was it a good idea to answer the door with no idea who could be out there? Without the phone, she had no way of calling for help.

She moved into the living room, trying to make as little noise as possible. Anyone outside would have seen the lights and known she was home. *What if it's the thing that killed the cat?* Her heart rate kicked up a notch then fluttered

"Maggie?" She heard her name, the voice almost eaten by the wind.

Relieved that it was in fact a human being on her doorstep and not a feral dog trying to get in, Maggie stepped forward and took hold of the doorknob. "Who's there?" Her voice sounded high-pitched, almost childlike.

"It's Harness."

Chapter Eleven

Her mother was worried, Annabel could see and more importantly feel the anxiety. The usually unflappable Lisa Chapel was very much in a flap.

The lights were on, but the darkness pressed in, casting long shadows around the kitchen. Dad was late and Annabel watched as her mother snatched sidelong glances at the clock and kept a constant eye on her phone. A phone that was usually banned from the dinner table, now sat next to her plate.

But it wasn't just seeing her mother on edge that had Annabel concerned, it was feeling the woman's fear. Feeling wasn't exactly the correct word. To Annabel, it was more like having a fish swimming just below the surface of her thoughts. Sometimes it was like bees buzzing, but today, it was a fish sending up bubbles that broke through the water popping out words like *accident*, *crash* and the most frightening – *dead*.

"Okay," her mother said in an overly cheerful voice. "If you've finished, why don't you go upstairs and put on your pyjamas? I'll make us some hot chocolate and then we can watch TV till Dad gets home."

Relieved at no longer having to push the food around her plate while pretending to eat, Annabel sprang up from the table. As she moved, she stole another quick glance at the kitchen window, hoping to see her dad's car's headlights as he pulled up around the back of the house. She could feel the tension coming from her mother, now like an invisible arm reaching across the table and tapping Annabel's forehead. Mum was trying very hard to keep Annabel *and* herself from worrying. Her mother was good at staying calm. She'd been a nurse before Annabel was born. Sometimes she'd tell stories about what it was like to work in a big, busy hospital. Her tales were always funny and would make them both laugh, but Annabel knew her mother was careful to leave out anything gross or sad so that she didn't frighten or upset her daughter.

Annabel loved hearing her mother talk about the hospital, remembering funny patient names and crazy situations. She liked the story about the old lady that wandered out of her room and sat at the nurse's station. While everyone was busy, she started answering calls, telling people that they had reached the prime minister's residence. Her mother's blue eyes sparkled when she laughed. But Annabel could feel the sad memories that her mother kept private, things that she'd never told anyone, not even Annabel's dad.

Annabel looked at her mother's lovely but worried face and forced a smile. "Okay, Mummy. I won't be long," she said and headed out of the room, hesitating in the doorway long enough to see her mother push her plate away and reach for the phone.

Once in her bedroom, Annabel pulled her pyjamas out from under her pillow. She stripped off her clothes, put them in her laundry basket and then shoved her feet into pink pyjama pants. She kept her eyes on what she was doing, determined not to look at the window. The monster was real, or maybe it was a ghost. It didn't matter, she'd seen it with her own eyes. It was doing something to the phone – it brought the storm. She pulled the pyjama pants up and snatched the pink top off the bed, trying to spend as little time alone in her room as possible. It was almost fully dark, the thing would be back, she could feel it. She pulled the pyjama top down over her head and jammed her arms through the sleeves as she moved towards the bedroom door.

A familiar creak, the sound of the swing moving in the wind. Her hand hovered over the light switch. The gale continued to rattle the windows, but now the sound changed into something even and rhythmic – drumming. Annabel found herself turning towards the window even though her instincts screamed at her to run.

In spite of her fear, Annabel felt her body being pulled towards to the very spot she wanted to avoid. She whimpered, curling her fingers, trying to plant her feet as her body responded to the steady pounding. The drumming continued, forcing the beat of her heart to change.

Reaching the window, Annabel saw only blackness. Her face, slick with sweat, drew closer to the pane as her eyes strained to see the backyard. Everything remained black save the swirling leaves that danced in time with the drumming. The moonlight was almost completely blocked by dark storm clouds.

As Annabel's eyes adjusted to the darkness, a shape emerged. The old rope swing rushed forward in a wash of misty, silver light. Something dark perched on the seat – a figure. Not sure if it was really there or a trick of the shadows, she leaned against the pane, cupping her hands around her eyes.

Suddenly the shape lurched as if it felt her touch the glass. Moving fast, shuddering from side to side, it sprang off the swing and came forward – spiderlike and inhuman. Annabel let out a shriek and pulled back from the window.

She covered her mouth, certain the creature could hear her. *I should run. I should run.* She could see its head tilting up, looking at her window, eyes piercing her soul. In a sudden jerky movement, it raised its arm and the drumming amplified, becoming louder and more urgent. Long thin fingers bent back in an unnatural motion — beckoning.

Annabel felt the urge to push her body forward through the glass. Her fingers brushed the sill, fumbling with the latch at the casing. *I should run.* The room faded away until the only things that remained were Annabel, the window and the rhythmic drumming.

The lock popped.

The creature stirred — lurching its body forward one halting step at a time.

Annabel dug her fingers under the stiff frame. Her heart bashed against the insides of her ribs. *I should run.* Her breath steamed the glass as her fingers found purchase. *I should run. I should...* Her breathing slowed to long, deep bursts that matched the pace with the drumming. Her lower lip drooped and her eyelids fluttered.

She raised herself onto the tips of her toes and pulled her right knee up onto the sill. For a second her body swayed and then she drew her left knee up. Balancing on the narrow strip of wood that framed the window, Annabel placed her hands on the pane. Her palms flat against the glass, fingers splayed, she pushed forward. *I should... jump.* The unlocked window caught, then inched open. The monster juddered forward, spreading its stick-like arms. It would catch her and she'd feel its cold breath and be carried away. Away from fear. Away from death. No more pretending to be like the other children.

"Annabel, it's ready." Her mother's voice from downstairs, like an echo from another world, broke through the rhythm.

The drumming lessened. Her breath became her own again. The monster staggered back to the swing. The terrible realisation of what she was about to do gave her a burst of strength. She drew back, pushed her knees off the sill, her feet thumping the floor. Fingers trembling, she whipped the curtains shut.

She wanted to scream and scream until the drumming faded, but all that came was a series of hiccupping shrieks. Instead of running, she crumpled to the floor and drew her knees to her chest. She pushed her fingers through her now damp hair and covered her ears. Gradually the drumming quietened and became an intermittent rattle once more.

After a few moments curled up on the floor, Annabel's heart rate slowed. She uncovered her ears and listened. The gale blew, rustling the trees and shaking the windows, but unlike a few minutes ago, the sound was bland, less urgent. Finding her body more responsive, she shuffled across the floor on her hands and knees. With each slide, the bare wooden floor grazed her palms. Annabel didn't care about the pain, only getting away from the window. She neared the doorway and pushed herself forward, sliding onto the upstairs landing on her bottom. Once out of the bedroom, she bolted to her feet and scrambled down the stairs.

She found her mum waiting in the lounge room, two cups of rapidly cooling hot chocolate on the coffee table. The TV was on and canned laughter filled the room. Lisa Chapel sat in her usual spot on the sofa staring at the screen, blonde hair tucked behind her ears. Annabel slumped against the doorway, grateful for the return to normalcy. In this room, there were no monsters. No grey ghosts that looked like skeletal little girls.

"Hot choc…" Her mother's voice trailed off. She jumped to her feet. "What is it? What happened?"

She swept Annabel up in her arms, hugging her tight.

"You're shaking, love. What's wrong?"

Her mother's voice was husky, as if she might be crying. She smelled like apples and creamy soap, a scent that was sweet and safe. When the tears came, Annabel's body vibrated with emotion.

Her mother helped her to the sofa and knelt in front of her, wiping Annabel's tears away with her fingers.

"Is this about your dad? He's fine. I'm sure of it. He's been late plenty of times before." Her voice was soothing, her hands cool on Annabel's face.

Her mother tucked a stray strand of hair behind Annabel's ear. "You're sweating," she said, touching the scratches on her daughter's palms. "How did this happen?"

Annabel shook her head. "I... I... I just..." They both heard the car pull in at the same time.

Her mother stood. "See? Everything's fine. Dad's home."

She turned to go to the back door, but Annabel shot out a hand.

"No. Don't go out there." She held on to her mother's arm with all the strength she could muster.

Lisa turned back to her daughter, eyes shiny as if holding back her own tears.

"Annabel?" Her voice was low, almost a whisper. "What is it?"

Before Annabel could answer, the back door squealed on its hinges, the sound echoing through the house. Annabel tightened the grip on her mother's arm.

"Sorry I'm so late, girls, but the weirdest thing happened," her father called out.

Annabel relaxed her grip, but wasn't ready to let go.

"We're in here, Rodney," her mother responded as she patted Annabel's hand and sat down next to her on the couch.

Her father entered the room, his hair standing up in wild spikes. Annabel noticed a smudge of grease on his forehead. He looked from his wife to his daughter.

"What is it? Something happened?"

"It's nothing." Lisa touched the corner of her eye. "With the storm and the phones not working." She waved a hand towards her husband. "Then you being so late, I guess we got a little spooked."

"That's not like you, Lisa." Rodney leaned over his wife and gave her a quick kiss on the cheek. "What about you, Bell Pepper? Were you spooked?" he said, planting a big smacker on Annabel's forehead.

Annabel nodded, not trusting herself to speak. Her daddy was home; for some reason that made her want to cry even more. Instead, she stood and laced her arms around his waist, hugging him as tightly as she could.

A few minutes later, the three of them sat at the kitchen table. Rodney Chapel ate his reheated dinner and explained his lateness.

"It was the strangest thing," he said around a mouthful of pasta. "Ollie didn't show up for work this morning, and when I called his mobile, there was no answer. I spent the day ploughed under with work, and then at four o'clock I gave the last group of pickers a lift into town. The storm blew up when I started home." He put down his fork and took a long swig of water.

"I tried to call you but there was only static." Annabel watched her father's hands; they were steady but his voice was a bit shaky. "Then the sky clouded over and I had difficulty seeing the road. I was driving around a bend when" – he paused and shook his head – "well, I thought I saw a child in the middle of the road. I hit the brakes and nearly skidded into the ditch. I got out and looked around, but there was no one there. I even searched a way into the bush on each side of the road. I called and called but nothing."

He looked at his wife. Annabel had seen them do this before, it was as if they were communicating something they didn't want her to know. Neither spoke, but Lisa nodded for him to continue.

"When I got back to the ute, the back tyre was all torn up. I don't know how *that* happened because I couldn't see anything on the road. Well, anyway, by the time I changed the tyre and drove home, it was pretty late. I tried to call a few more times but couldn't break through the static." He paused and looked at his wife. "Sorry if I scared you."

"Oh, Rod. I'm just glad you're okay." Her mother reached over and covered his hand with hers. "What do you think it was on the road? A roo?"

Before he could answer, Annabel spoke. "Did the child look like a little girl?" Her voice was small. She tried to keep the words from running together in a string of sobs.

"Well, yeah. Kind of. How did you..." He stopped, not really needing to ask how she knew. They never talked about it, but Rodney and Lisa knew about their daughter's *gift*.

"She was here." Annabel swallowed. Saying it out loud. Talking about the thing that kept trying to get her to come outside, made it real. If it was real, none of them were safe.

"Wait a minute." Lisa turned in her seat, giving Annabel her full attention. "You saw a little girl?" There was a warning tone in her mother's voice. She didn't like secrets.

Annabel nodded. "It's not a little girl." As the words came out, she was sure the wind howled louder.

Chapter Twelve

Agnes Wells sat at her desk, a glass of whiskey on her right. Blue light from the laptop bathed her face, giving her bony features and bulging eyes a ghoulish appearance. She had a number of accounts, but the one that interested her wasn't in her name. Her knobbly fingers raced over the keys, eyes scanning the numbers, headings and subheadings on the screen until she found what she was looking for. Leaning closer to the screen, she smiled and picked up her glass, then raised it to the empty room as if addressing a banquet of diners.

Apart from the small desk lamp, the ethereal glow of the screen was the only light in the darkened study. Agnes finished her drink then clapped her hands together in childlike glee. *Everything is going beautifully. It won't be long now before all this unpleasant business is over and by then I'll own most of the town.*

Agnes switched off the computer and stood, almost skipping to the display cabinet with a girlish step that belied her sixty-eight years. She danced the empty glass across the room. She opened the bottom door and took out the heavy crystal decanter that she usually produced during business meetings. It made many a man raise an eyebrow. Most of them were surprised that a woman in her position would offer whiskey, let alone drink it herself.

"Bunch of redneck hicks," she said to no one in particular and poured a generous hit. Trailing her hand along the thick satin of the sofa, relishing its rich feel, she inhaled the sharp scent of the liquor before sitting back down at her desk and taking a swig. The whiskey slid down her throat, leaving a warm, smooth trail in its wake. The smell of the whiskey reminded her of her late husband. It had been some time since she'd allowed him to slither into her thoughts. *Fat old slug.* Agnes laughed out loud and then clamped a hand over her mouth, eyes still sparkling with amusement. It had been twenty years since she'd dispatched that piece of garbage and never felt a moment's regret.

Working as a barmaid at The Scraggy Beak in Fremantle, Agnes's curvy twenty-four-year-old body brought her more tips than anyone else on the floor. It was a working man's pub. A dive. Agnes hated the place with all the dirty builders patting her ass and telling her crude jokes, always leering and winking. In those days a woman couldn't cry sexual harassment, not if she wanted to keep her job.

Agnes had the sense to know when to giggle and squeal as the filthy mutts pawed at her with stained hands. At the end of each night she'd count the money in her tip jar. Money that she'd ferret away to one day escape from the dystopic life that The Scraggy Beak represented.

When Stan Wells walked into the pub, Agnes smelled money *and* gullibility. He was with a group of grubby dock workers, but he definitely wasn't one of them. Most of the men in The Scraggy Beak were fat, but hardened by years of manual labour. Stan had the soft look of a chubby schoolgirl with clean nails, delicate hands and neat clothes. Stan Wells was a loud and confident forty-year-old fuck, buying drinks for his friends who smiled, hanging on his every word as long as the free booze flowed.

Agnes had never been pretty, but she was young and slim; she knew how to smile and flutter her eyelashes at a voracious old git like Stan. When she'd turned her full attention on him, it wasn't long before he bought her a drink. A few hours later, Agnes was naked in his hotel room.

That first night, she realised Stan Wells had some unusual sexual tastes. At first, he was hesitant and tentative about the things he wanted her to do, afraid that she'd recoil in horror, but Agnes was more than willing to accommodate his every desire, moaning enthusiastically and gasping with feigned pleasure. By morning, Stan proclaimed his undying love and they were married three weeks later.

Now, forty-five years later, Agnes knew how to do a little dirty work. She wouldn't have come this far if she was the sort of woman who shied away from dark deeds.

Dark deeds. She immediately thought of her new business partner and the smirk vanished. Just thinking of the woman made her nervous, almost paranoid to the point where she felt the woman could hear her thoughts. Without thinking, Agnes glanced over her shoulder as if half-expecting her to be standing in the shadows, lips stretched in that unnaturally wide smile.

Agnes shuddered and poured herself another drink. She leaned against the desk and looked towards the window. The smack of the wind rattled the pane and jolted her into the present. Whatever happened now was none of her concern. She was a businesswoman, Thorn Tree was her town, and by the time her business was completed, she'd own most of it. Agnes sank back into her chair and sipped her drink. *Sometimes dark deeds are a necessary evil.*

Chapter Thirteen

Maggie made herself take a deep breath and rub her damp palms together before opening the door. She'd almost convinced herself that a feral animal was on her doorstep. While the idea seemed crazy, she still couldn't shake the feeling that something was lurking in the storm.

"Hi." Harness cocked his head to one side. "Can I come in?"

The relief she'd felt only moments ago was engulfed by concern. He looked like a changed man. Dark shadows scored the skin under his blue eyes, and his clothes were rumpled as if he'd been in them for days.

"Harness, come in. Are you okay?" Maggie moved aside and held the door for him.

He stepped into the house and stopped. For a second, Maggie thought he was going to hug her, but instead, he turned and walked into the living room. Without waiting to be asked, he sat on the couch. Maggie closed the door. Not quite sure what to do next, she followed him and sat on the armchair nearest the sofa.

He leaned forward and stared at his hands while outside the gale whistled through the trees like claws tearing through fabric. Maggie bit the inside of her cheek, squashing the need to fill the silence with awkward babble. She watched the side of his face, noticing the way the muscles in his jaw rippled as he clenched his teeth. There was something on his mind. He could have waited until the phones were working and called her, but instead he'd driven out of town in what felt like the beginning of a major storm.

"I'm sorry about what happened to your friend and her baby."

He seemed to want to say more, so Maggie waited.

"I know it seems crazy, me just showing up here, but I had to see you." He looked up and held her gaze.

His eyes were raw, tired-looking. "Something happened. Something *is* happening, and it just made me realise that I needed to see you."

"What is it, Harness? Is it Tess? What's going on?"

She tried to keep her emotions under control, but the need to know, even if it was bad news, stretched her already jangling nerves.

"It's not about Tess... or maybe it is. I'm not sure."

He stopped speaking and put his head in his hands. Maggie leaned forward and touched his forearm, the skin warm under her fingers.

"Tell me?" She spoke softly, ready for the worst.

He looked up. "Since last night, four more people have died." His voice was flat – exhausted.

Maggie let go of his arm and shook her head. Whatever she'd been expecting, it wasn't this. "What do you mean? Has there been an accident?" Even as she asked, she knew it made no sense.

"No. It's like the baby... Eddie. They're just getting sick and dying. Three children and an old lady."

Maggie thought of the sirens she'd heard back in town and a cold finger touched the base of her spine. While she was getting petrol and talking to Jackson, people were dying. *Children* were dying.

"What does Dr Cole think? Does he have any idea what's causing this sickness?"

Harness leaned back on the couch and rubbed his brow. "Not really. He thinks it looks a bit like flu, but it's killing people too fast." He stopped and looked at Maggie again. It was more than weariness that cast a shadow around his eyes. At first, she'd assumed the look was exhaustion, but now she thought it was sadness.

The two sat silently as the storm howled, windows creaking as if threatening to break. There were so many questions. So many things she wanted to ask. How could four people just get sick and die within hours of each other? And why was he telling *her* all this? She wanted to ask but couldn't bring herself to fire questions at him.

"Have you eaten anything today?"

He gave her a tired but relieved look and shook his head.

"All right. I'll make us something."

Maggie didn't wait for an answer. She left him sitting on the couch and hurried to the kitchen.

Going about the mundane task of making sandwiches gave her something to do with her hands while she tried to make sense of the situation. Grabbing the bread out of the cupboard and ham and cheese from the fridge, she began assembling the sandwiches.

What could make people so sick so quickly and why here? Why Eddie? Then there was Harness. She wasn't sure why he'd come to her, but the haunted look in his eyes told her he needed her help in some way. She hadn't known him long, but Harness Gibson didn't strike her as the vulnerable type. It was clear that seeing those children had taken its toll.

Maggie took a quick sip from her wine glass and then returned to the lounge room with two plates. She placed one on the coffee table in front of Harness.

"I hope you like ham and cheese."

"Yes. Thanks." He pulled the plate onto his lap, but just stared at the food.

Maggie sat down and put her plate on the table. She didn't feel particularly hungry but forced herself to take a bite.

"What happens now? I mean, if something is making people sick, shouldn't you notify someone?"

"Yes. Dr Cole called the Health Department." He rubbed his chin. "They're sending someone tomorrow. The lab results on Eddie won't be ready for a few days, but the doc's been to the coroner's office in Perth trying to hurry things up. When Eddie seemed like an isolated case, there was no rush."

Maggie stopped eating and stared at him. He registered her shock and stopped.

"No. It's okay, Harness. I know what you mean. No one thought… I don't think anyone thought others would get sick too."

"Yeah, but now things have changed. Whatever this is, it's killed four people in twenty-four hours. Tomorrow we'll have to close the school and any other place where people gather. Sorry, Maggie, but that includes your café."

She nodded. "You think this thing's going to spread?"

"I'm not taking any chances." As he spoke, he picked up the sandwich and took a bite. "Nice," he said around a mouthful.

He'd braved the storm to be with her. Maybe like her, he needed someone to turn to. She thought of the way he'd slipped his hand around her waist and kissed her. The hint of lemon-scented soap and the rasp of his stubble against her cheek. Only last night they'd been on the verge of something, she wasn't sure what, but for a while it seemed full of promise. Now they were talking about how many children had died. The cold finger that touched her spine earlier crawled its way up her back.

Harness stuffed the last morsel of bread in his mouth then Maggie cleared away the plates. A few minutes later she returned from the kitchen to find him trying to use his mobile.

"I think the storm is interfering with the phones. I gave Jackson a ring just before you showed up, nothing but static," she said.

"Look, Maggie, I'm probably needed back in town. The station could be trying to reach me. I can't afford to drop off the radar during a crisis." He shrugged. "Sorry."

Maggie knew he was right, but couldn't help feeling disappointed. She wanted him to stay, but what she needed would have to wait.

"That's okay. You go and do what you have to do, but... be careful."

Already heading for the door, her words stopped him. He turned as if to speak, but instead placed his hands on her shoulders. For a second, the intensity and fatigue vanished from his features and dimples appeared. He leaned down and kissed her, his lips touching hers for the briefest of seconds.

"There's a town meeting tomorrow at noon in the church hall. Can you be there?"

"Yes, of course." She was surprised at his sudden change of direction.

"Okay, good. I'll see you there. Make sure you lock up when I go."

Maggie stood at the door and watched him hurry down the drive with the wind whipping his clothes. As he pulled out, he gave a wave before his taillights disappeared into the night. With the warmth of his kiss still tingling her lips, Maggie stared out into the darkness and had the distinct feeling something sinister was looking back.

* * *

With the exception of a few blossoms here and there, the stone flower vines were stripped bare. Another morning revealed the aftermath of a stormy night. Only *storm* wasn't the right word for the recent weather, not really. It was more like nightly gales that blew up out of nowhere, battering Thorn Tree with growing intensity. This time, Maggie didn't venture further than the deck, worried that whatever killed the cat had been back in the night. She remembered the way she'd felt watching Harness drive away. The almost physical sensation of eyes crawling over her skin. It was as if something was crouched, hidden in the darkness – watching. Maggie wrapped her arms around herself. In spite of the sun, she couldn't shake the chill that seemed to have taken up residence in her bones.

Before going back inside, she glanced at the remaining buds still clinging to the vines. Something about the toughness of those few flowers comforted her, not even the fierceness of the storm could kill them. Surprised by her own sense of whimsy, Maggie grabbed her cup from the table and went inside.

She needed to reach Jackson before he left for work to let him know the café would be closed. Setting the now cool mug on the counter, she picked up her mobile. Remarkably, there was no trace of static on the line.

When Jackson answered, his voice was clear as a bell. "Maggie, are you okay?" She couldn't help being touched by the concern in his voice.

"I'm fine. I just want to let you know that the Hawk's Nest won't be open today. Sorry about the short notice, but I couldn't get through last night."

"I thought as much. I heard about those kids *and* Mrs Loggie." He took a breath. "This is getting weird."

"Wait. What do you mean, Mrs Loggie? What's happened?" For a second, there was silence, and Maggie thought the line had gone dead.

"She died yesterday." There was a rustle, as if he were moving the phone from one ear to the other. "I'm not sure of the details, but with all those kids dying I guess they think whatever killed them might have got Mrs Loggie too."

"*Got* Mrs Loggie?" She heard herself repeating his words, not really able to take in their meaning.

"Yeah. My dad wanted to leave town and meet up with Mom and Asha, but Gran refused to budge. Said she won't run away. This whole thing is making her a bit crazy. She's kind of freaking me out." He sounded jittery, almost out of breath.

"Jackson, I'm coming into town to sort a few things out. There's a meeting at twelve, about the... deaths. Can I come over and talk to your gran when I'm finished?"

It was an odd request, as she'd only ever seen his gran a few times and had been struck by how dark and traditionally Indian the woman looked in comparison to the rest of her family.

She expected Jackson to laugh and ask why; instead, he simply said, "Hang on, I'll ask."

There was a long pause. Maggie could hear a door opening and the echo of distant voices.

When Jackson returned, he sounded calmer. "She says to come at one o'clock and wear red."

"Did you say to wear red?"

"Yep. Wear red." He gave an embarrassed chuckle. "Don't ask. It's better to just go along with it."

Maggie hung up, not really sure what she hoped to achieve by talking to Jackson's grandmother. The idea was spur of the moment, but maybe the old lady could shed some light on what was happening. After all, she'd been the first person to know something was wrong... That morning, after the first storm, Jackson said his grandmother was worried about his little sister. If the old lady knew what was killing people, Maggie owed it to Eddie to find out.

Before going upstairs to get ready, she made another call. The phone rang for what seemed like an eternity. Just as Maggie was about to hang up, a voice answered.

"Yes?" It was a man. Maggie guessed it was Cilla's husband. She'd met him a few times when he dropped by the café to speak to Cilla, but she couldn't think of his name.

"Hi, is Cilla there?" she asked.

"Who's this?" His voice was hoarse, almost gruff.

"It's Maggie. I just wanted to let her know that the café is closed and I'm not sure when we are going to be able to reopen. Sorry it's so last minute, but..." She paused, not really sure how to explain.

"Okay."

Maggie waited, but he didn't continue.

"Is Cilla okay?" Maggie wasn't sure why she asked, only that there was something off in the man's voice, as though he wasn't really listening to what she was telling him.

"No. It's Robert." His voice caught, as if he was having trouble speaking. "He... He died." A sob, painfully clear. The rawness reminded Maggie of the way Tess sounded when she held out her dead baby in the street the other night.

"I'm so sorry—"

"I have to go."

The line went dead. Maggie stared at the phone as if it were something alien sitting in her hand. *He died.* The words rang in her head. Then, for some reason, her mind threw up the man's name. Shane. Shane Edgell. She thought of calling back and asking if there was anything she could do to help, but didn't think she could bear to hear another of Shane's sobs. Not when all she could think of was Eddie and how his little lifeless body felt in her arms. She wondered when he would be released for burial and her mind conjured up the image of a tiny white coffin. When they should be marvelling at his first real smile, they'd be burying him. Maggie put the phone in her handbag and went upstairs to get ready.

Maggie turned on the shower and waited until it was running hot before tossing her pyjamas on the floor and stepping in. Harness said three children and an old lady – Maureen – died. Was Robert one of the children he'd mentioned last night? *No*, Maggie spoke to Cilla moments before Harness arrived, so whatever happened to the boy came later. With Robert, that made five dead in less than three days. She tipped shampoo into her hand and lathered her hair, raking her nails back and forth over her scalp. She didn't know much about viruses, but this one was attacking the most susceptible and killing fast.

She rinsed her hair and then began scrubbing her body with a washcloth. Eddie was a new-born, Robert had severe asthma, and Mrs Loggie was undergoing chemotherapy for cancer. *Maybe the other children were also vulnerable in some way?*

Maggie stepped out of the shower and towelled herself dry. Her skin tingled from all the scrubbing but her mind felt clearer. She thought about Jackson's strange request to wear red and slipped on jeans and a red T-shirt. As she was dressing, it occurred to her that, as far as she knew, no one had let Ollie's boss know what was happening. She didn't have the Chapels' number in her phone, but she was sure Tess had given it to her when she was pregnant so she could let his employer know if Tess went into labour or to get hold of Ollie if his phone wasn't working. *Tess was good like that, she thought of everything*. Maggie shut her eyes for a moment and took a deep breath. Her chest was tight with the build-up of emotion; the temptation to give in to despair beckoned. It would be easy to crawl back into bed and wallow in grief. *If it's like this for me, how must Tess feel?*

Maggie forced herself to keep moving. She found the number on a yellow Post-it Note sticky-taped into her address book. But when she rang, the call went straight to voicemail. Leaving recorded messages was a pet hate, an act that always felt stilted and uncomfortable. Not sure what to say, she stumbled out a message and left her number.

* * *

The drive into town was uneventful. Clear sky was visible between tall stands of gum trees, the road scattered with fallen leaves and small branches. Except for the now ever-present crows dancing along the bitumen, the countryside had a deserted feel that reminded Maggie of a movie about the end of the world. She watched a bird swoop low, almost crossing in front of the car before settling on the twisted branch of a wattle tree. It was as if the creatures were gathering in Thorn Tree. Maybe they sensed death?

Two storms in three nights, both times people – children – became sick or died. Could it be a coincidence? The dream she'd had the night Eddie died came to mind. She remembered the frightening grey figure, the way it jerked towards her. As impossible as it seemed, the storms, the dream and the deaths all felt connected somehow.

As she neared town, fields and bushland gave way to houses and rainwater tanks. Homes on the outskirts of town sat on larger blocks than those in the town proper. Many properties had cows, sheep, or even ducks roaming freely on grassy fields. Others were alive with plants, vegetables and fruit trees. Maggie loved this part of living in a small town: the expanse of space and the ease at which people and animals intermingled. Things she usually took the time to appreciate seemed isolated and fragile as she tried to make sense of the tragic circumstances enveloping Thorn Tree.

Entering the town, everything appeared surprisingly normal, if a little quiet. It wasn't until she drove along Prosperity Street that the scene shifted. The clear sunny sky was a stark contrast to the flat, mostly empty street. Shops were shut, *closed* signs hanging on almost every door save the pharmacy, where a line of people trailed out onto the pavement. As she passed the small crowd, a woman holding a toddler in her arms turned and stared at Maggie, their eyes making contact. For a brief second, Maggie thought she saw panic in the woman's gaze.

Around the corner, Sutton Street buzzed with movement. The caravan park was alive with people busily packing cars, trailers and campers. Maggie noticed an elderly woman folding deck chairs, a white and blue surgical mask covering the lower half of her face. A pudgy bald man loaded the chairs into a trailer. He, too, wore a surgical mask. A knot of dread twisted in Maggie's stomach, making her grimace and grip the steering wheel.

Cars crawled forward, moving only centimetres before grinding to a halt. After five minutes of tapping the steering wheel and cursing under her breath, she decided it might be quicker to walk. Finding a parking spot was easy when everyone was hell-bent on leaving. Maggie pulled in opposite the library and locked the car. The air thick with the stench of exhaust fumes, Maggie clutched her handbag and crossed the road. A pool of what looked like vomit ran in wet splashes across the pavement in front of the library. Covering her mouth and nose against the sickening smell, Maggie stepped onto the road and picked her way around the mess, trying not to gag.

As she made her way along Sutton Street, Maggie realised the congestion was caused by the queue of vehicles waiting in line at the petrol station. Both bowsers were in use, the one nearest the street blocked by a green four-wheel drive. A skinny man wearing a large straw hat shuffled towards the car, struggling with an armful of snacks. Behind him, the driver of a white pop-top van beeped his horn, the sound shrill and urgent over the hum of engines.

The guy in the straw hat stopped. His mouth moved but the beeping continued, drowning out his words. Grimacing and jutting his neck forward, the man used his free hand to fling a can of cola at the white pop-top van. The impact split the can, cracking the windscreen and sending a spray of brown foam fizzing over the bonnet of the van.

Without realising it, Maggie gasped and stopped walking, watching open-mouthed as the crazy scene unfolded. The beeping ceased. The driver of the pop-top, a stocky bear of a man, jumped out of his vehicle and charged the older guy in the straw hat, driving him into the rear of his 4WD. The straw hat flew off the older man's head, revealing a wisp of fluffy white hair. The bigger man roared something unintelligible and held the now struggling old guy by the throat, jamming him against his vehicle before delivering a sickening punch. Maggie heard a *crack*, almost as loud as the sound of the can hitting the window. The older man's nose pumped blood in a jet of bright splatters covering his mouth and chin.

Pop-top's wife was out of the van screaming, her voice mingling with the older man's wails. Barry, the owner of the petrol station, appeared in the doorway, a cricket bat held out in front of him.

"What the fuck are you doing?" Barry bellowed.

The bigger man released his hold on the smaller man's throat and stepped back, his wife clinging to his bicep. The older man's nose, shiny with blood, looked strangely flat on his face. His eyes were wide as his legs buckled and his butt hit the concrete. Maggie watched horrified as the elderly man licked his bloody lips and dabbed his fingers in the rapidly spreading liquid.

A few people left their cars to gather near the entrance to the petrol station. A chubby girl in a strappy top, shoulders pink with sunburn, held up her phone.

"Look what he did to my car!" the man shouted as his wife pulled him towards their van.

Maggie stepped off the curb, about to cross the road and help the man on the ground, when he scrambled to his feet and staggered, one hand trailing a bloody line along the length of his vehicle.

"Slow down, mate." Barry followed him to the driver's door, still holding the bat. "Are you all right?"

The elderly man swayed slightly.

"I'm gonna sue you."

The words came out in a slushy stream as he climbed behind the wheel. Ignoring Barry's offer of help, he gunned the engine and took off, the 4WD fishtailing to the left as the vehicle bounced out of the petrol station.

Barry turned in a circle, arms up in a gesture of disbelief.

"Get your fuel and get the fuck out of here," he yelled, pointing the bat at the pop-top driver before storming back inside the petrol station.

Maggie retreated to the pavement. The smell of fumes now mingled with something dank and sour. As she turned away and moved towards the corner, another horn began beeping. Maggie picked up her pace, resisting the urge to run.

Chapter Fourteen

Harness stepped up to the lectern and turned on the microphone, wincing at a whine of static from the nearby speaker. A spatter of nervous laughter rose and then dried up in a wave of seat-shifting and whispers. Ancient yellowed ceiling fans hummed overhead, the blades slowly circulating the smell of sweat and coffee.

News of the meeting began circulating at a little after eight o'clock that morning with signs posted in most public areas, but the nearly one hundred concerned residents and local business owners occupying the town hall had likely heard of the gathering through word of mouth.

Not surprisingly, after six years heading the town's police force, Harness recognised most of the faces staring back at him. Only, unlike other meetings and gatherings, the faces looked washed out and shiny with anxiety. They were waiting for an explanation. Something tangible to blame for the sudden rash of deaths. But what could he really offer apart from inane warnings and vague reassurances? Thorn Tree was a town on the verge of panic. Just driving from the station he'd had to stop and break up a fight outside the caravan park. Old men ready to throw punches over a minor fender bender. Would anything he said here make a difference?

As he swallowed and leaned towards the microphone, the side door at the rear of the building opened and Maggie entered the hall. He watched her make her way up the centre aisle and sit in an empty row. She wore red, just as she had the other night, only rather than accentuate her creamy skin, the dim lighting in the hall washed her face in artificial light, making her look pale, almost fragile. The hastily rehearsed speech died on his lips and he found himself struggling to draw breath. He'd never had a panic attack but guessed this was what it felt like. The fans whooshed above his head like a flock of angry birds. He took hold of the lectern and clenched his fingers around the sides. Rows of faces stared up at him, some confused, some impatient. Amongst them was Maggie, clearly shaken by what she'd seen on the streets. They were waiting for him to say something.

Mayor Wells, seated to his left, gave a loud stage cough, intended to signal him to get to business. The other two council members sitting next to her nodded their heads in silent agreement as another agonising second passed. Harness turned back to the crowd and fixed his gaze on Maggie. As if sensing something was off, she gave him a nod of encouragement. It was as if the small movement of her head cut through the confusion that clouded his mind, allowing him to focus. The words he'd carefully put together came rushing back.

He took a breath. "Thanks for coming, everyone." The speakers boomed his voice across the hall. Realising the volume was turned too high, Harness lowered his voice. "Most of you have probably heard that we've had a spate of unexplained deaths. We're not sure of the cause." He hesitated. "At this stage, it looks like it could be viral–"

"Is it SARS?" Cybil Zolts, a woman with a pinched mouth and sagging jowls, said from the front row.

"Why aren't we being given vaccinations?" A man behind her, who Harness recognised as Andy Smithson, a local plumber, barked out the question.

"I can't keep my shop closed or I'll go out of business." This time a voice came from somewhere near the back row.

Harness slammed his hand on the lectern. The sound echoed like a shotgun through the sound system. Everyone stopped talking.

"Let me finish and then you can ask all the questions you want."

It came out harsher than he'd intended, but it had the desired effect.

"Because we don't know what we're dealing with yet, I've asked Principal Mike Tolman to close the school."

Harness pointed to Tolman, who turned in his seat near the front and raised his hand in an awkward salute. Harness nodded and continued.

"We're asking anyone who owns a business where people congregate, to do the same. It will probably only be for a few days, just until we get a handle on this thing."

He stopped and looked around, registering the shock and fear on people's faces. An elderly woman in the third row reached for her husband's hand as if she were watching a horror movie and something was about to jump out of the screen. A situation like this could turn bad fast. People needed to know someone was in control, so he continued before anyone could find their voice to argue.

"We have someone coming from the Department of Health to give us advice on how to proceed. Dr Cole's surgery will be operating as a flu centre, so that means they'll only see people with flu symptoms until further notice."

At the mention of flu, a flurry of whispers broke out, spreading through the gathering like a vocal wave.

"I want everyone to stay calm. Stay home. Don't put yourself in harm's way. Call everyone you can think of and let them know to do the same. Any questions?"

"Is it swine flu?" Cybil Zolts asked, struggling to her feet. "Cause if it's swine flu, we should all be given antibiotics."

"Again, we can't be certain at this stage what we're dealing with, just that it looks viral. When we have more information, we'll let everyone know."

"This bloke from the Health Department, will he be bringing vaccines?" The question came from Andy Smithson.

Harness sighed and tried to keep his voice even.

"As I've said, we are not sure what we're dealing with. At this stage, vaccinations are unlikely."

With the exception of Principal Tolman, Maggie and the elderly couple in the third row, the crowd eyed him with open hostility. They were afraid and looking for someone to blame. It wouldn't be long before tempers flared. Right on cue, Cybil Zolts stood, pushing her chair back with a *thwomp*.

"This isn't good enough. I've got health problems." She planted her fists on her hips and turned to the people behind her. "We should be getting help from Mandurah Hospital. Why isn't the Health Minister here?"

A ripple of agreement spread through the gathering.

"Okay." Harness leaned into the microphone. "Meeting's over. Go home."

"This is a joke."

Andy Smithson jumped to his feet, kicking the chair in front of him and sending it skidding into Cybil Zolts's meaty knees. The woman let out a porcine grunt and staggered to the left, almost landing in Principal Tolman's lap. Tolman, forced to grab the woman's bulky rear end in order to prevent being crushed, reddened with embarrassment. A few people sniggered, but the laughter died as Cybil righted herself and stormed towards the exit.

Harness left the stage and approached Smithson.

"I want you out of here before I arrest you for disorderly conduct." Stepping into the man's space, Harness towered over the burly plumber.

"What did I do?" Smithson asked, giving Harness a wounded look before following the rapidly departing townspeople out of the building.

Harness watched until the last few citizens left, with the intention of following the crowd outside lest anyone decide to cause trouble. He was also eager to find Maggie and grab a few minutes with her before heading back to the station. Before he'd made it halfway across the old hall, Agnes appeared at his shoulder.

"Why didn't you spell it out for them?" Her voice was stony.

"What are you talking about, Agnes?"

He pressed the corners of his eyes with his thumb and forefinger. A wave of exhaustion caught him by surprise.

"Voluntary quarantine. That is what you were asking of them, wasn't it?" She gave a tight smile.

The question took him by surprise, cutting through his weariness and stopping his progress towards the exit. He turned and gave the mayor his full attention. As usual, she wore heavy makeup, bright eye shadow and pink lipstick. The gaudy look was at odds with her conservative grey skirt and white long-sleeved blouse. Even in heels, the elderly woman had to crane her neck to meet his gaze.

"Agnes, if I had used the word *quarantine,* it would have caused a panic." He spoke slowly as if she were a child. He could hear the patronising tone in his voice, but felt too exhausted to care.

"Don't speak down to me, Gibson." She spat the words out, the forced smile vanished and her already round eyes bulged. "I've lived in this town for forty-five years." As she spoke, Agnes moved closer. "I know these people better than a city boy like you. They need to be panicked *and* they need to be shocked, or by tomorrow, everything you told them will be forgotten."

Harness was taken aback by her sudden outburst. He'd know Agnes for years and had never seen her like this. In a matter of seconds, she'd gone from cool to maniacal. He took a step back, not out of fear, but the need to put distance between them.

"Calm down." It came out as a warning.

He didn't want the situation to escalate and he sure as hell didn't want to have to cuff the old lady and throw her in the lockup.

"Listen, Agnes, I'm only going to tell you this once. This is a police matter. You have no authority. I only asked you here as a courtesy. Go home and don't stir up trouble."

Agnes held his gaze, her mouth now a thin, pink, angry line cutting an ugly slash across her face.

"You're making a big mistake, Gibson."

She paused for a second, letting her words sink in before storming across the empty hall, heels clacking like pistons on the old jarrah floor. As she headed for the exit, Agnes pulled her mobile out of her pocket and began punching in numbers.

Probably calling the commissioner. He was anxious to see if Maggie was still around, but forced himself to wait, giving the mayor time to get in her car and hopefully drive away.

Harness turned the fans off and flicked the light switch. When he exited the building, he pulled the door closed and checked that the lock had caught before leaving. To his relief, Maggie had waited for him, leaning her back against his car, arms crossed over her chest. He raised his hand to acknowledge her and she smiled back. Even with her hair tied back and a worry line between her brows, she managed to look striking in red. He smiled, guessing he looked like an idiot with the big goofy grin on his face, but couldn't help it.

"Hi. I'm glad you waited." He wanted to kiss her but he wasn't sure how she'd react.

She continued to lean against the car. "I just wanted to see how you are. Last night, you... well, you seemed a bit upset."

"I was," he said, and ran his thumb over his lower lip. "All those kids. I just needed to get away for a while. Sorry if I worried you."

"Don't be. I want to help." She reached for his hand. Her skin was cool and soft; he could see a light sprinkling of freckles on the back of her hand and fought the urge to kiss them.

He searched for something to say. "Where's your car?"

She let go of his hand and gestured over her shoulder.

"I couldn't get through on Sutton Street so I parked and walked the rest of the way."

"I'd like to ask you out for dinner, but in light of what's happening, would you be interested in a lift back to the station and then I could walk you to your car?"

He tried to sound casual, but was eager to spend a few extra minutes alone with her. She nodded and within minutes they were in his Jeep, heading for the station.

"How do you think the meeting went?" Maggie asked.

"I would have liked a bigger turnout, but you know how this town works. By tonight everyone will have heard what happened anyway. People were scared, I could see that. I expected it. Mayor Wells wasn't happy with how I handled it." He shrugged.

"Why? Did she think it should have been her doing all the talking?" Maggie asked with a note of humour.

"No. But that's always a possibility with Agnes." He frowned. "She thought I should have put the frighteners on everyone. You know, get them worried."

"It doesn't make any sense," she said, turning to look at him. "Panic is the last thing we need. People were acting crazy this morning trying to get out of town. How could it help to stir up more fear?"

"Good question. Maybe she's going a bit batty," he offered.

"Mm." Maggie didn't look convinced.

"Come on," he said, getting out of the Jeep. "I need to check in before I walk you to your car."

Harness led Maggie into the surprisingly quiet station. Mark Leary manned the radio and phones while a couple with a little girl waited at the counter. The man looked familiar, but Harness couldn't quite place him. Leary looked up, relief spreading across the young constable's face.

"Boss, there's a message for you from Dr Cole."

He held a piece of paper up as if to prove the message really existed. He nodded towards the couple.

"These people are the Chapels, they've been asking to speak to you."

Harness was eager to find out what the doctor had to tell him, but decided to deal with the Chapels first. Out of habit, he walked around behind the counter before he addressed the couple. To his surprise, they both turned to Maggie.

"I got your message. Is there any more news on Ollie?" the man asked.

"No, I'm waiting to hear from Sandra, Tess's mother, but nothing yet."

"When you hear from her, let her know that we're thinking of them and if they need anything, anything at all, we want to help."

"Thanks, Lisa." Maggie touched the woman's shoulder. "I'll pass that on."

It was obvious they all knew each other. It took Harness a second to make the connection. Rodney Chapel was Ollie Becks's boss and the owner of the Chapel Orchard.

"Was there something you wanted to see me about?" Harness broke in, hoping to move the meeting along so that he could find out what the doctor wanted.

"Yes," Rodney answered.

"Okay, but we'll have to make it quick." Harness didn't think he needed to explain why. "Come into my office." Rodney nodded and asked if his little girl could wait at the counter. Harness hesitated.

"I'll wait with her," Maggie offered.

"Thanks, Maggie." Lisa spoke with obvious familiarity before turning to her daughter. "I want you to wait here with Maggie while we go and talk to the police officer. And don't worry, everything will be okay." She ran her fingers over one of her daughter's pigtails.

Harness wondered what the little girl had to worry about as he led the couple to his office. He held the door and motioned for them to sit. As he closed it, he heard the little girl's voice as she spoke to Maggie.

"He really likes you!"

Hoping the parents hadn't heard, he settled himself on the other side of the desk. Experience had taught him that it was better to let people speak in their own time: let them fill the silence and often say more than they had intended.

Rodney spoke first. "This is a bit awkward. I mean, I know you're busy, but we just thought you should know." He glanced at his wife and she responded with a nod, as if urging him to continue.

"I'm pretty sure I saw a little girl on the road yesterday evening. I didn't hit her, but she was out in the middle of nowhere during the storm. I swerved to avoid her and nearly rolled the ute."

Lisa Chapel sucked in a breath. Her husband paused and looked down. Harness guessed he hadn't shared the part about nearly rolling the ute with her until that moment.

"What happened then?" Harness prompted.

Rodney ran his hand through his slightly receding sandy hair. He was a sturdy-looking man, well-muscled and tanned from years of outdoor manual work.

"Then she was gone." He sounded mystified by his own words. "I looked everywhere and I couldn't find her. When I got back to the ute, one of the back tyres was all torn up." He stopped and looked at his wife. Harness couldn't be sure, but he thought something passed between them.

Lisa took over. She was younger than her husband, maybe mid-thirties, slim with blonde hair and intelligent blue eyes which she fixed on Harness.

"My daughter, Annabel, she's seen a girl hanging around our property at night and yesterday during the storm."

She stopped and glanced at her husband. Harness could tell they were holding something back or leaving something out. He waited, but it was clear that they'd finished and were waiting for him to speak.

"So, Mrs Chapel..."

"Lisa," she said.

"Lisa, you think there's a lost child wandering around on your property?"

He kept his tone neutral. The Chapels were concerned, and he didn't want to sound dismissive.

"Yes, I do. Or at least someone hanging around that shouldn't be there."

"Okay." Harness picked up his pen. "Can you give me a description?"

This time Rodney answered. "Small, skinny, and wearing a ratty dress."

Harness stopped writing and stared at the couple. He considered himself pretty good at reading people. Over his many years on the force he'd probably had hundreds if not thousands of people stare him in the face and lie, but the Chapels didn't come across as liars *or* nuts – just hardworking people who appeared genuinely worried.

"Look, Lisa, Rodney, I'll send someone out to your place this afternoon to have a look around. I haven't had any reports of a missing girl, but I'll make some calls. That's about all I can do at the moment."

They seemed relieved. After taking their number and promising to let them know if he found anything, Harness led them back to the front of the station.

Maggie sat in the waiting area with the little red-haired girl. It looked to Harness like they were deep in conversation. As he approached, the girl stopped speaking and smiled at him. She made him think of Molly. He wondered what his daughter would've looked like if she'd had the chance to grow from a toddler into a little girl. It was a fleeting thought, but even after all the years, it still came with a stab of pain.

Annabel looked young, about eight, but he wasn't that good with kids' ages. Her long red hair was tied in two bunches held by red ribbons. When she smiled, her nose wrinkled.

"I'm almost nine," she said, as if he'd asked the question.

Harness was a little taken aback, but smiled all the same.

"So, you've got a birthday coming up," he said.

"Yes. I'm hoping for a puppy." She gave her parents a pointed look.

Her mother shook her head. "We'll see."

Rodney shook Harness's hand and thanked him for his time and then ushered his family out of the station. Annabel stared over her shoulder at Harness until the door closed behind her.

"Cute kid," he said, smiling after her.

"Did they tell you about the little girl?" Maggie asked.

She was staring at the door where the family had exited. Harness wondered what Annabel had told her. He decided it wouldn't hurt to tell her about their meeting.

Harness took Maggie's arm and led her to the door. As much as he wanted to learn about the doc's findings, he also wanted to keep his promise to Maggie. "Come on. I'll walk you to your car."

Once they were on the street, he detailed his meeting with the Chapels, ending with, "I think they're keeping something back. How well do you know them?"

"Not very. They came to a few barbeques at Tess and Ollie's. I'd usually chat to Lisa more than Rodney." She shrugged, making the casual movement look elegant. "You know how it is at those things, the men all stand around the barbeque and the women congregate." She thought for a moment. "Lisa pops into the café sometimes with Annabel. They seem like a nice, normal family. Not secretive if that's what you're asking."

"What did Annabel tell you?"

"That a monster pretending to be a little girl keeps coming into her backyard at night. She's really frightened."

Before Maggie could say more, her phone rang. Harness walked on ahead a few steps, giving her some privacy. He stood by the curb and watched the petrol station across the road; Barry Tucker, the owner, was hosing down the forecourt. When he saw Harness watching him, he grinned and waved. Something in the man's demeanour was off, but Harness couldn't quite put his finger on it.

He'd been trying not to listen to Maggie's conversation, but when he heard her mention Ollie, his ears pricked up.

"That's great news." Even with her back turned, he could tell she was smiling.

"What?" Maggie turned around. The smile was gone, replaced by what looked like shock.

"Okay. Thanks, Sandra, I'll call you later."

"What is it?" he asked.

She took a deep, shaky breath before answering. "Ollie's awake and doing much better."

"That's good. Did he say anything about what happened?"

"Yes. On the night Eddie died, he was driving into town. Tess was in the back with the baby... he said a little girl stepped into the road. He swerved. That's when the car rolled."

Chapter Fifteen

As the afternoon sun cast long shadows on the deserted pavements, Maggie drove along Sutton Street, noticing the traffic had dwindled to a few cars and camper vans. Passing the petrol station, she could see the forecourt glistening wet from a recent hose down. The scene looked calm and mundane, as though nothing had happened. She thought of the bloody hand trail along the green 4WD and increased her speed.

By the time she parked in front of Jackson's house, it was ten past one. She left the car and hurried up the driveway toward the brown brick home. On the right of the house, Jackson's old yellow Corolla was parked in a carport.

Steep concrete stairs rose up to a spotless front porch, freshly swept of newly cut grass from the large lawn. The front door was made up of four dimpled panes set in a green wood frame. Hanging on the right-hand side, just under the bell, was a string of blue beads painted to look like little eyes. They were threaded onto a strip of silk that dangled from a silver ring. The strange-looking trinket struck Maggie as creepy.

Sandra's voice jumped into her mind: *a little girl stepped into the road*. Fear twisted like a tight knot in the pit of Maggie's stomach. Annabel was convinced a monster pretending to be a little girl was visiting her at night. Could it be a coincidence that Rodney, Annabel and Ollie had all seen a little girl? She hesitated. Suddenly the last thing she wanted was to talk to Jackson's grandmother. Maggie's gut told her the woman would tell her things she didn't want to know.

She glanced back at her car. For a second, the idea of turning and driving away was almost irresistible. *This is insane. I can't believe I'm letting Annabel's fear of monsters rattle me.* Whatever Jackson's grandmother could tell her about the virus could be helpful. The more they knew, the better their chances of protecting other children from the sickness. Maggie pressed the doorbell, her fingers brushing over the beads, sending them clacking against the glass. The sound reminded her of chattering teeth.

Jackson opened the door wearing jeans and a light blue T-shirt. His hair was damp, suggesting he'd just showered. She wondered if he was going out on a date later.

"Hi, Maggie. Come in."

"Sorry I'm late." She hesitated on the doorstep. "I was at the meeting and then–"

"No problem." Jackson held the door open, waiting for her to enter.

The inside of the house was more modern than the outside suggested, with highly polished jarrah floorboards and latte-coloured walls. They stood in a large hallway. To the right was a half-opened door that led to what Maggie guessed was the lounge room, and to the left was a large cluttered study. A hint of jasmine hung in the air.

"This way," Jackson said, leading her down the hall and through the spacious kitchen.

He spoke over his shoulder as they went, "Gran's been waiting for you. She'll be pleased you wore red."

On the other side of the kitchen was a room that seemed to run almost the entire length of the house. The floor was jarrah and decorated with large colourful rugs. A white cane sofa, two matching chairs and a coffee table sat in the right corner. From midway to ceiling, the back wall was made up of windows, allowing the afternoon sun to bathe the room in comforting warmth.

Jackson's grandmother was seated on a worn brown leather armchair that didn't match the rest of the room. As Maggie and Jackson entered, the older woman stood and came towards them. She was short. Her mostly grey hair, flecked with a few strands of black, was swept back into a tight bun. She wore a calf-length black tunic over coffee-coloured satin pants that narrowed at the ankles. Her eyebrows were surprisingly bushy against a dark face dominated by a sharp hooked nose. She reminded Maggie of the witch in *The Wizard of Oz*.

"Here she is," Jackson said as the small woman swept past him and took Maggie's hand.

She greeted Maggie with a smile that transformed her face from harsh to impish. "Welcome, dear. I'm Manjula Korrapati Palmer, but you must call me Manjula." She led Maggie to the cane sofa. "Sit, sit, sit."

"Thank you for seeing me... ah, Manjula."

Maggie sat on the edge of the sofa. The smell of jasmine was stronger in this room, mixed with something spicy that she couldn't quite identify. There was something exotic and appealing about the combination of odours. Manjula settled in one of the cane chairs so they were facing each other.

"All right. Well, I'll let you two get on with it," Jackson said, looking at his grandmother. He nodded, giving Manjula a pointed look, which she returned with a wink. He seemed pleased, almost relieved by her response, and left the room.

She leaned forward, her dark eyes searching Maggie's face. Now she was in front of the woman, Maggie wasn't sure how to begin. What could the old lady possibly tell her that might help make sense of what was happening in town? She wished she'd rehearsed something on the way over so that she didn't sound too crazy, but Manjula didn't wait for Maggie to speak.

"There is something evil in this town," she said. Her voice was flat, almost matter-of-fact. "You've sensed it too."

The last part was a statement, not a question. Maggie nodded, but didn't speak. She was relieved that Manjula had put her feelings into words so easily.

Manjula continued, "Children are dying and you want answers. Yes?" Her accent was heavy, but her English perfect.

Maggie nodded. "I've been having strange dreams… And there's a little girl… People have seen her."

Maggie wavered. A few dreams and a child. Saying it aloud sounded more than a bit silly. She half-expected Manjula to laugh, but looking into the old lady's eyes, she could see that she was taking her words seriously. Maggie let herself relax.

"Outside of the dreams, have *you* seen the little girl?" she asked.

"No." Maggie shook her head.

Manjula seemed relieved. "Good. Then you are safe… for now. All this, I have seen before… so long ago." Her eyes took on a dreamy look. "I was born in Naghar, a small village located in Bageshwar district in the Indian state of Uttarakhand. It was a farming village in a deep valley near the Pungar River."

Manjula smiled and looked towards the windows as if seeing her village through the glass. When she turned back to face Maggie, her eyes were heavy with unshed tears.

"Forgive me, Maggie. I am eighty-five, but I remember my childhood in Naghar better than I remember last week."

Maggie could feel herself warming to the woman. "Maybe last week isn't worth remembering."

Manjula looked pleased and patted Maggie's hand. "I can see why my grandson likes you so much."

Maggie wasn't sure how to respond. "Jackson's a good friend."

Manjula nodded and continued her story.

"My parents were farmers and I, a child, would spend my days helping my mother to prepare meals or playing in the fields with my best friend Meena. I had no brothers or sisters, but it didn't matter." She touched a finger to her chest. "Meena was my sister." She paused for a moment, as if caught up in the memory.

"Even as a child I knew Meena was gifted. She was a very beautiful little girl, but that wasn't what made her special. She always saw only the good in everyone and she was more... connected than others. It is hard for me to explain, but she was connected to the world in a way that most are not. She felt things!"

Manjula stopped speaking, waiting for Maggie to indicate she understood. Maggie nodded, not sure what else to do. Manjula seemed satisfied enough to continue.

"When I was nine, a terrible sickness came into our peaceful valley. Children died. People were afraid and began to speak of an Acheri."

"Acheri?" Maggie asked. Her stomach gave an unpleasant lurch and the saliva in her mouth evaporated, leaving her tongue dry. The question came out as little more than a croak. "What's that?"

Manjula took her time as though it was a question she didn't want to answer.

"An Acheri is a demon. Some say it is the spirit of a girl that faced a horrible death and has come back to the physical world to torment other children. It seeks only to cause pain and misery."

"So you think this... Acheri is here in Thorn Tree?" Maggie asked.

"I know it's here and so do you." She reached out and placed her finger on Maggie's chest just above her heart. "You feel it. Your people know of this demon, that is why you are here, yes?"

Maggie didn't believe in ghosts or anything supernatural. Her grandfather told her stories of spirits and witches, but she'd always considered them to be like fables, harmless fun. Yet now, if she believed Manjula's story, she would have to allow a shift in what she'd always held true. If she accepted the woman's account of what was happening in Thorn Tree, nothing would ever be black and white again. Was she ready to believe something outside modern science could exist? That evil was a real, tangible thing? The knot in her stomach twisted, this time threatening to push its way up into her chest.

"What happened in your village?" Maggie asked, not willing to answer Manjula's question.

"I don't know. My parents took me away, just as I told my daughter-in-law to take Asha. We walked for twenty-five miles to the nearest train station and then travelled to Delhi. We never returned to Naghar."

"What happened to Meena?" Maggie asked.

"I don't know. I wanted her to come with us, but her mother had been crippled for many years and Meena would not leave her. She told me that the Acheri had come for her in the night. It tried to disguise itself as a little girl, but she saw its true face." Manjula shook her head. "She tried to be brave, but I knew she was frightened."

She stopped talking and reached into one of the deep pockets on her tunic and produced a photograph which she handed to Maggie.

It was a black-and-white shot, faded and creased from years of handling. The background was a dusty field showing rows of overturned earth. In the foreground were two little girls. The children were holding hands, smiling into the camera. The girl on the right was clearly Manjula. Even as a child she had sharp features and a kind smile.

The girl on the left was smaller, very pretty with long dark curls framing her small shoulders. In her free hand, the girl held what looked like a little tin whistle. Her head was cocked slightly to the left as though she were about to laugh.

Maggie put her finger on the photo. "Meena?"

Manjula nodded and took the picture from Maggie. She clearly didn't want to be separated from it. The older woman looked tired, as though talking about Meena and the Acheri had sapped her strength. Maggie had more questions, but didn't want to push.

"Manjula, are you all right?"

"Yes." Her voice was weak and distant.

"Do you want me to call Jackson?"

Maggie didn't like the tremor in the old lady's hands. It was as if her strength was trickling away with each memory.

The old lady shook her head, so Maggie continued.

"Manjula, there's a girl here, her name is Annabel. She told me that she's seen a monster in her garden that is pretending to be a little girl." Before Maggie could continue, Manjula took her hand and squeezed it with surprising strength.

"She's in danger, and now, so are you. Everyone in my village said the Acheri had come to cause misery, but I believe it comes with a purpose. It came for Meena and now it is here looking for someone like her. Maybe this girl, Annabel?"

Maggie thought of the way Annabel described the thing she'd seen in her backyard. In spite of the sunshine streaming through the windows, she felt a chill.

"You said it comes to torment other children." Maggie touched the old lady's arm. "Can it... Can it kill adults too?"

"It is a being born of hatred. It kills as it sees fit. Children are easiest to fool, but it will bring misery to as many as possible."

Manjula's shoulders slumped with exhaustion. Her words were sluggish, as if she were sleepy. She patted Maggie's hand.

"Please call my grandson. I need to rest for a while."

Chapter Sixteen

Agnes paced the study, jabbing numbers into her phone as her heels skimmed the carpet. She'd been told to only use *the number* if someone mentioned the woman by name, but how could she ignore what was going on? The line crackled, the ringing hollow and distant, reminding her of the way the connection echoed on long-distance calls back in the seventies. A click then breathing, heavy and regular, gave Agnes pause. She had no idea what sort of organisation the woman belonged to or what their reasons were for setting up in Thorn Tree. In truth, she didn't care as long as cash flowed her way, but something wasn't right. *I've always known it wasn't right.*

"Hello." Agnes forced the worry out of her voice.

"Yes?" One word, enough to send a sliver of ice down Agnes's spine.

"I want something done about Gibson. Whatever you're doing, he's keeping it quiet. That wasn't part of the deal. You said there'd be panic selling… and prices would drop." Agnes paused, her heart racing. The line hissed, but the woman on the other end remained silent. "You need to hold up your end of the bargain or the deal's off." Agnes's throat constricted with an angry shiver.

The other woman's response was unemotional.

"*We* make the demands; *we* give the orders. *You* listen. The alternative is uninviting." The line crackled then disconnected.

Agnes stared at the phone in her hand, the woman's words echoing in her head. The anger leached out of Agnes's body, leaving her breathless and off balance. For the first time since agreeing to play hostess, Agnes thought of the children. Gibson had hired a refrigerated truck from a rental place in Mandurah. She'd seen the obscene-looking vehicle parked behind the doctor's surgery, powered by a thick black extension cord through the back window of the building. Inside were the bodies of the dead. *Children's bodies.*

She hadn't set foot inside the truck, nor would she. Gibson had explained to her how the bodies were being stored before the meeting today. He'd asked her to keep it to herself. *Always the diplomat*, she thought bitterly.

But now she had bigger concerns. She'd heard about big chemical companies and how they had shadowy employees who handled the wet work. The call had been a mistake – a big one. *Damn Gibson.* She'd allowed his bombastic attitude to get her riled up.

"Damn." What had she been thinking? *I wasn't thinking.*

Agnes continued to pace. There was no way of predicting how the woman would react to Agnes's threats. Her hands clenched into fists, squeezing tighter until her bright pink nails dug into the soft flesh of her palms.

"Now what?" Agnes spoke to the empty room. The idea of running came and just as quickly went. No, this was her town. If the woman came, she'd be ready. She continued pacing while tiny drops of blood fell from her hands, leaving stark red spots on the pristine cream carpet.

Chapter Seventeen

Maggie drove away from Jackson's house, feeling dread twist and grind in the pit of her stomach. The feeling was similar to a bout of food poisoning she'd had the previous summer, only this time the clenching and spiralling in her gut came from fear. A sick feeling churned and nagged at her until a cold sweat broke out on the back of her neck. It was nearly three o'clock. The roads were eerily quiet, allowing her the freedom to drive slowly while her mind raced.

Everything Manjula told her fit with what was happening in Thorn Tree. When she was sitting with the old lady, it had been easy for Maggie to accept the possibility that something supernatural was at play, but now the ordinariness of the suburban streets, the clear blue sky and the pleasant rows of well-maintained houses contradicted that theory. The world looked so normal, it was difficult to believe that something as unbelievable as demons could exist.

Maggie's grandfather had told her stories about evil spirits that tormented the sick and then stole their hearts. He said that they were invisible and only a medicine man could see them. Maggie recalled her father laughing and pointing out that the medicine man probably used the invisible spirit excuse whenever a patient died. She noticed a line of crows perched on the front fence of a run-down fibro-cement house, their black feathers shiny in the sun. So shiny it looked like they'd been dipped in oil. What, she wondered, would her grandfather make of the sudden influx of birds?

Maggie hesitated at the entrance to the back lane, noticing the way the buildings threw jagged shadows across the patchy strip of bitumen. She decided to park on the street and enter through the front.

The café stood in silence, unlit windows dark and empty. The abandoned feel made her skin prickle, yet at the same time, she loved the place. It was more than a business. It symbolised her new life and everything that made Thorn Tree her home. Her marriage was all about Richard and his dreams. His aspirations of becoming a real estate mogul. His feelings. Maggie had been window dressing and an emotional punching bag. She was nothing – hopeless. How many times had he screamed the words in her face? But the café, her house, her friends... they were hers. Hers alone. She pulled the keys out of the ignition and held them in her hand. What did she believe? Was there more to the world than the human eye could see?

She thought of Tess, Ollie, Eddie, Doug, Annabel and finally Harness. Could something evil really be stalking these people? Stalking her? The possibility that Manjula was right, terrified her. Not just because she was afraid of the thing she'd seen in her dreams, but because people she cared for, maybe even loved, could be in danger.

Maggie ran her hand across the back of her neck. Her palm came away wet with sweat. She got out of the car and unlocked the café, letting the front door swing closed behind her. Turning the lights on in the kitchen, she made the decision to tell Harness about the Acheri. What choice did she have? Risk looking like a nut job in front of a man she had feelings for *or* try to handle the situation alone. If she did that and failed, more people might die. *Or maybe I'm going a little bit nuts.* She'd certainly had plenty of experience dealing with the troubled minds of others.

Even before she married Richard, she knew things weren't right. He had mood swings, one minute excited and making plans for the future, the next angry and depressed. She'd kept that side of their relationship a secret, even from her family and friends. She was so convinced that she could fix things and, just by loving him enough, make everything right. *Look how that turned out.*

Maggie pulled her phone out of her bag and dialled Harness's number.

"Hi, Maggie." He sounded pleased to hear from her. It was a good start.

"Harness, I need to talk to you. Can you..." She stumbled, not sure how much to say. "Do you want to come over for dinner tonight?"

"Yes." He answered without hesitation. "But it might not be until about eight. Is everything okay?" Concern edged his voice.

She imagined him standing alongside his Jeep or maybe sitting in his office, the phone to his ear. In her mind, she could see the way the fine lines at the corners of his eyes deepened when he concentrated. The urge to blurt everything out almost got the better of her.

"It's a long story. I'll tell you about it tonight... Okay?"

"Okay." He sounded unsure but agreed.

"Thanks. See you later." She ended the call, not giving him time to push for answers.

Remarkably, she felt relieved. Maybe laying her suspicions out for Harness would help her see things with a clearer mind, make the whole idea of an evil entity stalking the children seem so far-fetched that they'd both laugh. She put the phone away and opened the cool room door, taking out a large tray of lasagne and sliding it onto the workbench. She wanted Harness to convince her she was wrong, point out the insanity of Manjula's story.

Maybe then the niggling dread coating her insides like a greasy aftertaste would evaporate.

She took a large knife from the block and sliced into the lasagne. Cutting a sizable square out of the side, she put it in a take-away container, the rest she re-covered with cling film. She planned on taking the smaller piece to Doug Loggie and keeping the rest for dinner tonight. A tub of lasagne wasn't much, but at least she could let Doug know she was thinking of him. She didn't want to imagine what he must be going through; how raw his pain would be. *So much death.* She shivered, so caught up in her thoughts, she didn't hear the front door open.

Gathering up her bag and the food, Maggie left the kitchen. With the afternoon sun fading and no lights on, the seating area was a spider's web of shadows and angles. Something caught her eye, bringing her to an abrupt stop.

"Maggie, you look like you're on a mission."

The voice was pleasant, almost conversational, but the dark figure behind the counter didn't move. Maggie's heart jumped with a terrifying *thump* that reverberated in her ears.

"We're closed," she said, the words stuttering out sounding shaky and weak.

A chuckle, like dirt shifting at the bottom of a tin bucket. It was the laugh that triggered her memory, not the voice but the throaty snigger that was unforgettable. The travel writer from Agnes's party, the one who'd managed to reduce Maggie to a stumbling wreck with a few carefully chosen words. With recognition came confusion. Why was the woman standing behind the counter in the obviously closed café? Was she looking for money? Instinctively, Maggie glanced at the front door, hoping to spot someone passing on the street.

She inched forward, not sure if she should run or stay while at the same time trying to remember the woman's name. The new angle gave Maggie a better view of the woman's face. Wide mouth stretched into a humourless grin together with angular cheekbones gave her a clown-like appearance. *Prapti – that's her name.* They stood in silence. If Prapti intended to rob her, Maggie wondered why she didn't make some move.

"I'm about to leave, so if you don't mind..." She tried to sound matter-of-fact, but it came out more like a plea.

Prapti ignored her, running her hand over the counter, long yellowed fingernails scraping the shiny metal surface. Maggie swallowed and watched the woman rub her forefinger and thumb together as if finding dirt.

"You really must try to keep this place clean or people might get sick." She spoke slowly, finishing with another chuckle.

Maggie's eyes shifted back to the door. If she ran, it would only take her a few seconds to reach it, but she'd have to pass Prapti, who could easily lunge over the counter. As if reading her mind, Prapti looked at the door and shook her head.

"You're always in a hurry. A hurry to leave me at the party, a hurry to leave the old woman's house." Prapti paused, allowing her words to sink in.

"How do you know about that?" Maggie asked.

She needed to get closer to the door if she had any chance of making it out of the café before the woman tried anything.

"You've been following me?"

Maggie kept talking and half-turned to the nearest table. She didn't like turning her back on the woman, but putting the food down allowed her to take a step closer to the door. There was a flap in the middle of the counter; without warning, Prapti flipped it back, letting it slam against the flat surface with a *crack*. She moved with surprising speed, putting herself between Maggie and the exit. Instinctively, Maggie stepped back and braced herself, certain Prapti was about to grab for her.

"I'm not here to hurt you." Prapti sounded wounded, but the clown smile didn't waver. If possible, the woman's mouth appeared to cover almost the entire lower half of her face.

"What do you want?" Maggie's heart rate kicked up a notch, making it hard to keep her breathing under control.

"To offer my condolences, of course. I heard about your friend and her dead baby. I know squaws grieve hard over dead infants." The whites of her eyes seemed to catch the light, reflecting it back like beacons. "It must be very hard for you."

Up until that point, Maggie's only thought had been escape, but the raw cruelty in Prapti's words triggered something Maggie didn't know she possessed. Rage, cold and sudden, flared up, washing away the fear and pushing her to act. Without realising it, Maggie stepped towards Prapti.

"Get out of here." She spoke through gritted teeth, her hands curled into fists at her sides.

Prapti held up both her hands. "Now, now. I don't want you to go on the war path." Her strangely luminous eyes widened with mock surprise.

Maggie could see the woman enjoyed taunting her, so she forced herself to speak evenly.

"Is that it? Have you finished? Because I have things to do." She glanced at her watch as though bored with the conversation.

It was clearly not the reaction Prapti hoped for. Just for an instant, the edges of her smile shrank. Maggie felt a little spark of satisfaction. Her momentary triumph wasn't lost on Prapti. When she spoke, the mocking tone was gone, replaced by a voice that was deep and thick with anger. She jabbed a finger under Maggie's nose.

"You. You have no concept of what's happening here. Do you really think a savage like you can be anything more than an insect to us? You and the old hag think you know so much." The words were spilling out, her teeth moving like blades on a hacksaw. "You weep over a few dead children, but don't see the beauty in what we do." She paused, stepping towards Maggie.

With the two women only a metre apart, Maggie could smell something sour and musty. The odour filled her mouth and threatened to turn her stomach, but she stood her ground.

"Stay out of this." Prapti's neck jutted forward, and for a second, Maggie thought she might bite her like a savage dog. "Go back to your house with the pretty red flowers and mind your own business. If you do as you're told, your boyfriend might keep his worthless life."

Maggie held the woman's eyes – pitiless black holes of madness.

"Get out," Maggie responded flatly. The anger that raced through her veins like poison only moments earlier was dissipating, seeping away under the barrage of Prapti's hatred. Her knees shook. It wouldn't be long before her legs gave out and she sank to the floor. What then? Would the woman pounce on her?

Prapti shrugged and turned away, walking slowly towards the exit. As soon as the door slammed shut behind her, Maggie pushed off the table and stumbled to it, clicking the lock in place with trembling fingers. For the second time in ten minutes, adrenalin flooded her system, giving her the strength to run through the shop. Sliding across the kitchen, she slammed into the back door, slapping her hands against the wood. The lock was in place, just as she'd left it on Saturday night.

"Jesus." She spoke to the empty room before turning and leaning her back against the door. Her knees gave out, and she allowed herself to sink to the floor.

Prapti hadn't really threatened her. *No, she threatened Harness.* The woman made no move to actually hurt her, yet the possibility of violence felt so real. Maggie rubbed her hands on her jeans, trying to wipe away the clammy sensation that crept over her skin. She needed to think, to collect herself. Why was Prapti following her? Menacing her?

Maggie forced herself to take slow, even breaths, dragging air in through her nose and blowing it out through her mouth. The sound of her own breathing, slow and regular, helped calm her jangling nerves. The kitchen, while dim, looked normal, familiar. *I'm safe, she can't get in.*

The whole encounter had an almost nightmarish quality. She thought of the way the woman laughed and the cruel lilt of her voice. Maggie searched for a way to rationalise what she'd felt when Prapti was in the café. Evil. Maggie drew her knees up to her chest. She felt like she was in the presence of evil.

It took five minutes of calm breathing before she trusted her legs enough to stand. Phoning Harness was her first impulse, but she quickly rejected the idea. If she heard his voice, she'd most likely break down, and right now, she couldn't afford to look like an alarmist. No, she had to be in control when she told him about the Acheri. After all, Prapti hadn't touched her, and until she had her emotions under control, there was no way she could explain to Harness how she knew Prapti was evil, without sounding hysterical.

It occurred to her that she no longer had any doubts about Manjula's story. At least not the part about there being something evil at work in Thorn Tree. The realisation was terrifying and liberating at the same time. Maybe some part of her had always known that the world was a mystical and dangerous place. Darkness had touched her, and in a few hours shattered a lifetime of learned ignorance.

She went back to the shop, her legs more or less steady. Not strong – not yet – but she'd settle for steady. Grabbing the phone out of her bag, Maggie made a call.

Jackson answered on the second ring. "Hello?"

"Where's your grandmother?"

"Still asleep. I think you wore her out." He gave a hesitant laugh.

"Can you go and check on her?"

"Yeah. Why?"

"Just do it." Maggie was too worried to be polite.

"Okay." He sounded hurt, but his feelings would have to wait.

It took a few minutes for him to return.

"Maggie, she's fine. A bit put out because I woke her, but otherwise, she's good," he said.

"Jackson," Maggie continued. "I'm sorry I snapped at you, but there's a woman – I think she might be dangerous. I'm worried about Manjula."

"Is it about the Acheri?"

"Yes, it is." Maggie hesitated. "Did she tell you about it?"

"Yeah, but I only half-believed her." This time there was no trace of humour in his voice.

"Jackson, is your dad home?"

"Not till about five. Why?" he asked.

"Look, when he comes home, tell him... I'm not sure what you should tell him, but be careful. The woman's name is Prapti. She made some threats. Mentioned Manjula, not by name, but I think she followed me to your house." She could hear Jackson's breathing on the end of the line. "She's Indian and… I think she's dangerous. Just be careful. Okay?"

"Okay, Maggie. You too."

Maybe it was the realisation that the things his grandmother had been telling him *could* be true or the possibility that they were all in danger or both, but suddenly Jackson sounded older.

Chapter Eighteen

The Chief Quarantine Officer, Franklin Wooton, arrived at the station at a quarter to two – half an hour late. He introduced himself to Harness and offered no apologies or explanation for his delayed arrival. Wooton, a tall, thin man with a fine, grey comb-over, was immaculately dressed in a blue suit and silver tie. Harness noticed the man's shoes were highly polished, the depth of the shine bouncing light every time he moved. Once the greetings were out of the way, Harness offered the man a coffee.

"No. Thank you. I'd rather we get down to business." Wooton looked at his watch.

"Okay. Come into my office and we can make a start," Harness said, leading the way.

Once they were both seated, Wooton began firing questions.

"When was the first reported case?"

"Saturday night, about ten o'clock. Eddie Becks, a ten-day-old baby."

Wooton nodded dispassionately and took a small notebook and pen out of his breast pocket. The questions continued for about twenty minutes. Harness answered each one, trying, quite successfully, to keep his dwindling patience under control. When it seemed like Wooton had what he needed, he put his notebook back in his pocket and stood up.

"Hang on, Wooton. I've answered your questions, now I have a few of my own."

The man's attitude was starting to grate on his nerves. Wooton was supposed to be here to help, yet Harness had the feeling he was being given a thorough cavity search. Wooton's wispy brown eyebrows shot up in surprise – the first emotion the man had shown throughout the interview. He lowered himself back into the seat, but was clearly unhappy.

"Do you have any results back on Eddie Becks?" Harness asked.

"No. Not yet."

"Have you had any cases like this in any other towns?"

"No." His voice was clipped, mouth puckered in a tight clench.

Harness wanted to reach over the table and grab Wooton by his prissy silver tie. Instead, he smiled and tried a different tact.

"Come on, Wooton, there must be something you can tell me?" Harness spread his hands out in what he hoped was a friendly gesture.

Wooton shook his head. "I'm sorry, Senior Sergeant, but I'm just here to gather information. When that's done, I might have a better idea of what we're dealing with. So, if we could move this along?"

Harness considered persisting, but it was clear either Wooton didn't know anything or was unwilling to share.

"Okay. What now?" Harness asked with a sigh.

Wooton stood up. "I'd like to examine the bodies."

Fifteen minutes later they were standing outside the refrigerated truck that had become the town morgue. Wooton held what looked like a large fold-out toolbox. Harness watched as he took out a thick paper jumpsuit, slowly put it on over his clothes, zipped it up and pulled the hood over his head. He then covered his shoes with paper booties, put on goggles and a surgical mask.

Finally, Wooton closed the box and picked it up and put a gloved hand on the hinged lock on the rear of the truck.

"Wait here." He gave Harness a look that was hard to read through the goggles and mask, perhaps waiting for him to argue. Harness shrugged, more than content to wait outside.

While the Chief Quarantine Officer was in the truck, Harness went back to the squad car. Wooton had wanted to use his nondescript white government car to drive to the makeshift morgue, but Harness had insisted they use the police vehicle – so that he could use the radio to stay in touch with Attwell, the only other officer on duty. Wooton had grudgingly agreed.

Harness had sent Mark Leary home earlier to get some rest, which meant he'd had to lock the station and leave it unmanned while accompanying Wooton. Attwell was out at the Chapels' place checking for any sign of the little girl. Harness knew he could have just as easily gone in Wooton's car and checked in with Attwell on his mobile, but he dug his heels in just to let the smug bastard know who was in charge here. It was petty, but what the hell, it was worth it just to watch Wooton struggling to lift his big toolbox from one car to another.

Harness sat in the squad car and called Attwell on the radio.

"Attwell, Gibson here. Anything to report?"

Attwell came back immediately.

"Nothing, boss. I've had a look around, but the place is huge. We'd need ten men searching all day to be really sure."

Harness was disappointed, but not surprised.

"Okay. If you're done, head back to the station."

Attwell responded that he was on his way. All that was left for Harness to do was wait. He thought about his

124

earlier meeting with the Chapels. He felt sure that it was somehow related to the string of sudden deaths. People had reported seeing a little girl – she could be infected with something. A long shot, but it made sense, especially if the girl had been in contact with any of the dead children. Harness made a mental note to speak to the other victims' families and see if any of the children had mentioned or had contact with a little girl.

Restless, he got out of the car and drummed his fingers on the roof. He doubted Wooton would have much to add, no matter what the man saw inside the truck.

Pulling his phone out, he checked the display. The call he'd received from Maggie just before Wooton arrived played on his mind. There was an edge to her voice, rushed and anxious. Whatever she wanted to tell him, she obviously didn't want to say over the phone. A crow landed on the roof of the car, its claws scraping the metal as it tried to find purchase. Keeping his eyes fixed on the bird, he put the phone back in his pocket. The creature cocked its head to the side, one beady white eye locked on Harness's movements. He remembered reading somewhere that crows would sometimes kill and eat new-born lambs or scavenged the afterbirth as the sheep gave birth. A ripple of revulsion churned in his stomach. As if sensing his thoughts, the creature opened its sharp black beak and squawked.

Harness slapped his palm on the roof of the car, sending the bird flapping into the air. He watched it swoop low over the patch of weedy bitumen and come to rest on top of the truck. At least ten other crows were scattered on the truck's roof like ticks on a mangy dog. The birds hadn't been there when they arrived, he was sure of it. Could they smell the dead? He didn't think so; the seal on the truck was airtight. *Maybe they sense death*. The mobile morgue had to be at least fifteen metres away from the car, but even at this distance, Harness could smell the birds – coppery and cloying, like something damp left to mildew in the darkness. At least he hoped the stench came from the birds.

Harness swiped his arm across his forehead; it came away damp with sweat. The four cups of coffee he'd drunk since waking up roiled in his gut, threatening to spew up into his throat. It occurred to him that at this distance, he could probably shoot the birds. He rested his hands on his hips, fingers loosely touching the grip of his gun.

The truck's rear door slammed open. Wooton stumbled down the two steps, pulling off his goggles and mask. Harness shook his head. *What the fuck was I thinking?* For a moment, he'd been seriously considering taking pot shots at the birds. Shaking off the dreamlike moment, he pulled his gaze away from the birds and watched Wooton shuffle across the bitumen.

The freezing air inside the truck had turned the man's face from pink to blue, giving his skin a translucent tinge.

"I have the samples, so I'm finished here for now."

There was a tremor to his voice. Blinking eyes punctuated each word. Harness wondered if seeing so many dead children lined up in body bags had finally broken through the man's business-like veneer.

"So, you looked at the bodies?" Harness asked.

Wooton nodded but didn't speak.

Harness couldn't blame the man for being affected by what he'd seen. Even in thick black bags, it was clear the small frames inside were those of children. He remembered the feel of the plastic bags, almost weightless, as he helped the two constables carry the bodies into the mobile morgue. He didn't envy Wooton's job of opening each bag and touching the cold little bodies.

Wooton pulled a bag from his toolbox and unrolled it with trembling hands. He pulled off his white overalls and stowed them in the bag. Harness noted it was marked *Hazardous Waste*.

"What now?" Harness asked. He could feel the impatience building again.

"If you wouldn't mind driving me back to my car, I'll take the samples back to Perth."

Harness ran his hand across his forehead and looked up at the cloudless sky. Wooton was obviously shaken up by his experience in the truck, but upset or not, he wasn't giving anything away. The stab of sympathy Harness felt for the man was starting to wear thin.

"I mean, what do you think? You saw the bodies; do you have any idea what killed them?"

Wooton seemed about to say something, but stopped and shook his head. He looked at the ground as if studying something.

"I'm sorry, Senior Sergeant. I can't say I've seen anything like this before. I'll know more when I've processed these samples." He nodded towards the toolbox, his almost bare scalp a shiny pink circle in the afternoon sun.

Harness was about to push Wooton on the results when the back door of the surgery opened and Dr Cole's wife stepped out. Mary Cole, a trained nurse, acted as the town doctor's receptionist. A slim woman in her mid-fifties with an easy-going disposition, Mary knew almost everyone in town by their first name *and* after years of answering the phone in the surgery, could recognise most people's voices before they had time to identify themselves – a very handy skill when taking appointments all day.

"Harness, we need your help. Can you come inside?" Mary's usually tanned face was bleached of colour.

He nodded and turned to Wooton. "You'd better wait here."

Harness crossed the patch of bitumen and followed Mary through the back door without hearing Wooton's reply.

Before they entered the waiting area at the front of the surgery, Harness heard sobbing and Dr Cole's voice.

"In here." Mary pushed open the door.

A woman was crouched on the floor in the middle of the room. Dr Cole squatted next to the woman, holding her arm. It was only when Harness spotted the small legs dangling from the woman's lap that the scene made sense.

Cole looked up as they entered. Twin spots of red sat high on his cheeks and his usually neat white hair stood in messy spikes. "Mary, draw up a sedative."

Mary nodded and darted into the consulting room.

Harness looked around and noticed that a young woman sitting on a chair in the far corner was holding a toddler on her lap. The child had a runny nose but otherwise seemed fine. He wriggled in his mother's arms and tried to get down, but the woman held him tightly, trying to press his face against her chest. She watched the woman on the floor with wide, terrified eyes as unchecked tears ran down her cheeks.

Harness walked over to the young woman and took her arm, pulling her out of the chair. She didn't resist as he propelled her towards the door.

"Wait outside." He opened the door and pushed her out onto the front steps. When he turned back, the doctor was talking to the woman in a gentle, controlled voice.

"Just let me have a look at James? I won't take him away. I just want to help him." He spoke softly, making no move to touch the child.

"Nooooo!" The woman threw her head back and let out a primordial wail. The sound seemed to bounce off the walls and ring inside Harness's head at the same time. He wished he could be far away from the awful scene unfolding, but couldn't tear his eyes away from the two little legs dangling lifelessly from the woman's lap. On one foot was a little yellow Croc, the other shoe lay abandoned on the floor. Harness stared at the discarded shoe and wondered if the child had been sick when the shoes were put on his feet or if he'd been ready to go outside to play when it struck. Cole's voice brought him out of his reverie.

"Harness, help me."

Mary returned and handed the doctor a syringe. The woman on the floor was trying to crawl away, the child still clamped to her chest. Harness knew what the doctor wanted him to do. Without hesitating, he crossed the room and grabbed the woman by the shoulders. Her head snapped up, teeth bared in a look of such vicious desperation that he almost lost his resolve and let her go.

"Hold her steady." Cole's voice remained calm.

The woman's shoulders felt small and fragile under his hands. Harness didn't want to hurt her, but she moved with surprising strength, making it necessary for him to apply more force than he intended. He felt her bones move under his hands and winced. Finally, Cole administered the injection and nodded for Harness to let go. He released his grip just as the fight left the woman's body. She slumped to the side still holding her child, but loosely as if he was suddenly too heavy for her.

Mary sat down on the floor and let the woman lean against her.

"It's okay, Cathy. Just relax." Mary wrapped her arm around the woman's shoulders.

She wasn't unconscious, but her eyelids drooped. As she leaned back against Mary, Harness was able to see the child fully. The little boy wore a yellow T-shirt with a crocodile on the front and tiny denim shorts. He had black curly hair that was a little long for a boy. Eyes that had probably sparkled with mischief were now covered in a milky film, staring vacantly at the ceiling. The boy's lips were black, swollen and caked with white foam. It was clear that the child was dead. Before he looked away, Harness noticed that one of the boy's chubby little hands was curled around a small toy police car.

He'd been crouching near the woman, but now sat back on the floor and let his head drop into his hands. In spite of the warm air, a chill worked its way through his body, filling his bones until his limbs were numb. In the distance a bird cried, the sound lonely and filled with hopelessness. The four of them stayed on the floor in the middle of the waiting room. The woman, Cathy, slumped against Mary; Dr Cole nearby watched the mother and child; and Harness held his head. Four people, all helpless.

Chapter Nineteen

Even with the study door closed, Mike Tolman could hear his wife clanging pots and slamming drawers. Each *bang* jarred his already raw nerves until the urge to barrel down the hall and silence the woman was almost overpowering. The school would be closed tomorrow, not that he cared one way or another. It was what he'd left there that gnawed at his mind.

The school's locked. No matter how many times he told himself it was safe, he couldn't get the image of the little red thumb drive out of his head. He placed his hands on the desk in front of him, fingers splayed. There was no reason for anyone to access his office. The thumb drive would be safe until the school reopened. He was the principal, after all – no one would dare enter the office without contacting him. He stared at his fingers, the neatly trimmed nails clean of grime or stain. *I can wait.* But could he?

It would be easy to turn on the computer, a few clicks and he'd find what he needed. *Just a couple of minutes.* A quick look, no lingering, just enough to put him in a better mood. *Bam.* He jumped in his seat. His fingers curled into fists. Oh God, how he'd love to grab Linda's scrawny neck and squeeze. Beads of sweat popped out on the back of his neck just above his collar as the beginnings of a migraine prickled the back of his eyes.

He couldn't risk using his home computer; it would be too easy for them to find out. Mike wasn't quite sure who *them* was, the police or maybe the school board. It didn't really matter. If they found any trace on the hard drive, he'd be finished. His job, his career, all gone. The thumb drive was different, he could say he found it, they couldn't make him admit it was his.

The thumb drive – if he could just hold it, his head would stop pounding. *Yes*. Yes, that was all he needed. He was the principal, he had every reason to be at the school. He *should* go in and check that everything was locked up. Nodding, he pushed back his chair and slipped his arms into his suit jacket. *It's part of my job to make sure the school's secure*. Already rehearsing his lines, Mike headed for the kitchen to let Linda know he had to pop out.

* * *

Harness rubbed his eyes and refocused on the screen, working his way through the two hours of paperwork that went along with a sudden death. The last thing he wanted was to think about what happened at the surgery, but as usual, police procedure required him to commit every grim detail to paper. Typing out the report usually helped him separate from the event itself, as if reducing the people and actions to clinical terms lessened the impact. Today, it wasn't working for him.

His mind kept coming back to the little boy's mother, *Cathy*. From experience, he knew that her life would never be the same. That moment in the doctor's waiting room had changed her life and the lives of everyone who loved her and her little boy. In time, Cathy would begin functioning again – maybe. She would look the same and sound the same, but that happy, optimistic and hopeful part of her, the thing that sprang to life when she became a parent, had died today, and however good her life was in the future, she would always live under the shadow of death.

He thought of Molly, and a familiar stab of grief pushed its way into his mind. He'd had her in his life for a little over two years, but her absence hollowed every day since. He stopped typing and leaned back in his chair, deciding the paperwork could wait. Attwell hadn't found any trace of the girl at the Chapels', but that didn't mean she wasn't there. He'd go and take a look for himself. Anything was better than staring at the screen.

The sky was a muddy grey, cut through with purple streaks that bled into orange just above the treetops. Thick bush crowded each side of the narrow road leading to the Chapels' property. Harness reduced speed and drove carefully as dusk crept towards darkness. Even though the squad car was fitted with a titanium bull bar, he intended to be ready if a roo jumped into the road. Breaking at high speed or hitting a kangaroo on this type of loose gravel could send the car into a spin that would roll the vehicle.

After travelling at a steady speed for five minutes, he passed the turnoff for the orchard and considered driving out there to take a look around. He decided it might be better to check around the house and take a quick look at the orchard on his way out. He was also eager to talk to Rodney again, prod him for more information on the little girl. Sometimes witnesses saw more than they thought. With the right questions, Rodney Chapel might be able to give a better description of the child. If she was the key to this whole mess, he intended to find out.

Was it possible that there could be a child somewhere in or around Thorn Tree who was carrying a disease, spreading it through the town's children? A long shot, but at this point any lead was better than sitting in his office filling out paperwork.

The road gradually widened and ended at a bitumen driveway leading up to a large two-storey farmhouse.

Harness had visited many rural properties and noted that the Chapels' had all the usual fixtures: rainwater tank, satellite dish and a couple of large workshops. The house itself was surprisingly picturesque with a traditional steep corrugated roof and a wraparound veranda held up with red chamfered posts and decorated with wrought iron lacework, also painted red.

Harness parked behind an orange Hyundai four-wheel drive. He doubted orange was Rodney's colour, so he guessed the car belonged to Lisa. Continuing his survey of the property, he exited the car and walked to the house. There was an old-fashioned bell hanging next to the front door; he rang it and waited. Almost instantly, as if she'd been standing nearby waiting, Annabel swung the door open.

"Hi, Annabel. Is your mum or dad around?"

Annabel nodded, her nose wrinkled as a smile lit up her face, but before she could speak, Lisa Chapel appeared in the hallway.

"Sergeant Gibson, is everything all right?" She held a tea towel, her brow furrowed with worry.

"Yes. Everything's fine. I just wanted to have a follow-up conversation with you and your husband. Is he here?"

"Yes, he's outside in the shed. Come through to the kitchen."

Harness stepped over the threshold and followed Annabel and Lisa. She gestured for him to sit at the table and then turned to her daughter.

"Annabel, go out and ask your dad to come inside."

"Okay." The little girl glanced at Harness and darted for the back door.

"Wait." Her mother stopped her. "When you've done that, I want you to go and check on the chooks. Give them some fresh water and see if there are any more eggs."

Annabel looked disappointed, but nodded and left.

Harness remained standing during the exchange, noticing the faint smell of apples and cinnamon in the air.

When Lisa turned to him, she was smiling. Her eyes flicked to the .38 Police Special on his belt and the smile faded. Harness couldn't blame the woman for being unnerved. City people, country people, it made no difference – most felt uneasy at the sight of a handgun in their homes. For some reason it didn't bother them as much when officers were on the street, but walk into someone's house and suddenly it became all too real.

Harness took a seat at the table, being sure to position himself so that he faced the back door. He wanted a few minutes alone with the woman before her husband arrived; facing the door would allow him to spot Rodney as he approached the house.

"Would you like a cup of coffee?" Lisa began filling the kettle at the sink.

He'd had too much coffee already, but it looked like the woman wanted to be doing something.

"Yes. Thanks. White, no sugar."

"I'm a bit surprised to see you. Constable Attwell was out here earlier. He spent quite a while looking around and I kind of thought if he found anything, he would've told us." She kept her back to Harness as she spoke, busying herself with the coffee.

Harness got straight to business. "I had the feeling you were holding something back this morning."

"What?" Her shoulders stiffened but she didn't turn around.

"When you and Rodney came to see me, you talked about a little girl, but I had a feeling you weren't telling me everything." He stopped talking and gave her time to respond.

Harness watched Lisa's back. She stopped filling the cups and turned around. For a moment, she merely stared at him as though looking for something. Harness could see the woman wrestling with something, perhaps trying to decide if she should confide in him.

"Mrs Chapel, another child died today." He spoke flatly, letting the words sink in, watching the pain register on her face. He didn't like what he was doing, but if shocking her into telling him what he needed to know would help save another child from dying, he was more than prepared to do it.

"Call me Lisa," she said almost absentmindedly as she came over to the table. They sat opposite each other, Lisa looking down at her hands and Harness waiting for her to speak.

"It's Annabel. She's... I don't know, a little bit special." She hesitated and looked up at him, seeming almost embarrassed as she continued. "She's special in a good way. Sensitive. Ever since she was very little, she's sort of *known* things. You know, like if someone is upset or even what they are thinking before they say it. That sort of thing."

She stopped and looked at Harness, waiting for him to respond. Not sure how to react to what she was saying, he nodded. It seemed to be enough for her to continue.

"Rodney and I don't really talk about it. It's just a part of Annabel – who she is. I suppose we're so used to it, we hardly even notice. If she tells us that her friend's mother is worried that she might have a baby in her tummy, we just accept that she's right." She paused and laughed before adding, "She told me today that you wanted to kiss Maggie Hawkbetter, but you were sad about someone named Molly."

Harness felt himself blushing with both shock and embarrassment. He'd never told anyone in the town about his daughter; maybe his feelings for Maggie were more obvious than he realised, but how would she know his daughter's name?

"How did you know about Molly?" The question came out too quickly.

Lisa blinked, but held his gaze.

"I'm sorry. I didn't mean to upset you. I'm just trying to make you understand."

"Understand what?" He could hear the anger in his voice and immediately regretted it. It was out of character for him to lose control in an interview, but hearing Molly's name mentioned so unexpectedly caught him off balance. Lisa was staring at him now, arms wrapped around her body. He'd frightened her.

"Look, I'm sorry, Lisa. You didn't upset me. I'm just... surprised. I know you're trying to help. Just tell me what you know about the little girl."

Before she could answer, the back door opened and Rodney walked in. He looked at his wife and then at Harness.

"What's going on?" He planted his hands on his hips. "Why's my wife upset?"

Lisa stood and put her hand on her husband's arm, but Rodney's gaze locked on Harness.

"Rodney, it's okay." She spoke with unexpected force, making both men turn and look at her. "I'm telling him about Annabel." She gave her husband a pointed look. Rodney looked like he wanted to protest but nodded and sat down across from Harness.

"Mr Chapel, *you* came to me this morning. You asked for my help. For that to happen, you need to tell me everything." Harness spoke calmly, but at the same time making it clear that he was in charge. He waited for the man to respond.

He sighed and nodded. "Call me Rodney."

For the next ten minutes Rodney and Lisa told Harness everything they knew about the little girl. This time they included the things their daughter had told them about the girl being a monster. By the time they finished, three things were clear: one, they both believed their daughter was telling them the truth; two, they were afraid for their child; and three, Harness was convinced that the mysterious *little girl* was connected to the sudden deaths.

It was almost dark when Lisa went to check on Annabel, leaving Harness and Rodney alone in the kitchen.

"I'll need to talk to Annabel."

"Why? We've told you everything." Rodney was understandably alarmed.

"Look, Rodney, I understand your reservations, but I've got six dead children in town and I need to know anything that might help stop a seventh from dying."

"Jesus, Gibson. She's only eight. I don't want her any more frightened than she already is."

Harness held up his hands. "I won't frighten her, but I need to ask her a few questions." When Rodney didn't respond, Harness continued, "A four-year-old boy died in his mother's arms today and I couldn't do anything but watch." His voice shook with emotion. "I can't stop what's happening if I don't have all the facts."

"Okay, okay, but I'll have to check with Lisa."

Moments later, Lisa returned with Annabel. She held the back door open for her daughter, who was using her T-shirt as a makeshift basket to carry eggs.

"You were right, Mum. There were three more eggs in there when I checked."

Annabel struggled to put the eggs on the table, not quick enough to stop one rolling off the edge. Harness reached out and caught it halfway between table and floor.

"Whoa. Good catch." Annabel laughed.

"Thanks." Harness held the egg between his fingers for her to see. "I used to play cricket."

"My dad's good at cricket too, you should play with him." She gave him a shy smile.

"Maybe I will," Harness answered, smiling back.

"Okay. Go and wash your hands and then you can watch TV until dinnertime." Lisa put her hands on her daughter's shoulders and moved her daughter towards the kitchen door. Harness waited for Annabel to leave the room.

"I want to ask Annabel a few questions." He braced himself for an argument, but to his surprise, Lisa nodded.

Chapter Twenty

The light was dying, washing the blue out of the sky and coating the school in dreary grey. Mike got out of his car and hurried up the steps to his office, noticing a row of silent crows perched on the gutters above the entrance. He unlocked the main door to what passed for an administration building in a town as small as Thorn Tree and punched numbers into the alarm pad as the door swung closed behind him.

The air inside the building carried a hint of something earthy.

"Damn. Fucking leaky roof."

The budget was tight enough without having to fork out more money to fix the old roof, but from the smell of things, something was mouldering in the office. Mike rubbed his temples. The tingling behind his eye was turning into a pulsing. If he didn't calm down, he'd be seeing spots. Once he had the thumb drive in his hand, the edges would smooth out and he'd be back to normal.

Just thinking about the images contained on the tiny miracle of modern technology made his penis twitch with anticipation. Without thinking, he rubbed his crotch, feeling the hardness growing beneath the fabric. Could he risk turning on the computer in his office and taking a quick look? Mike licked his lips. The school was empty, there'd be no one to disturb him.

Temptation burned his skin like a heat rash, leaving him almost powerless to resist. "Just this once." The words came out in a rush of air.

With the decision made, the pressure behind his eyes eased. Mike moved towards his office, passing the reinforced glass door leading to the junior classrooms. A flash of movement caught his eye and brought him to an abrupt halt.

"Fuck." He puffed out an angry breath.

Schools were like a magnet for bored kids. Kids whose parents didn't give a damn where they went *or* how much damage they caused. He clamped his teeth together and headed for the door.

Turning the latch, Mike flung the door open and stepped through to the covered bitumen area. Amongst a set of bench seats and tables he noticed more birds. Large black creatures, almost invisible in the dusk light, danced between the lunch tables, unperturbed by his presence. The odour, rotten and mildewed, was stronger here, almost sickening. He hesitated, torn between finding something to throw at the birds or hunting down the kid he'd seen through the door.

A giggle, girlish and faint, echoed through the empty school, the sound carried on a sudden gust of wind. Forgetting the birds, Mike stalked along the cement walkway leading to the classrooms. He could be in his office right now, feeling the heat and excitement wash over him. A few minutes, not much to ask. Out of the question now, all because some brainless girl wanted to hang around the school.

"Un-fucking-believable."

Wasn't it enough that he spent every working day wading through the shitstorm of school life? Another giggle, this time accompanied by a scrape. Mike stopped, head cocked to the side. He'd heard that sound a million times over the years. A school chair gouging a classroom floor. *The little bitch is in one of the classrooms.*

Anger bubbled up in his throat; like sour bile it filled his mouth. With no one around to witness his actions, he'd give the girl the fright of her life. Maybe a couple of sharp smacks thrown in for good measure. *Oh no, Sergeant Gibson, I merely held the child until you arrived. Yes, I would like to press charges.* Mike nodded, but then another thought occurred to him, one so tantalising he slowed his pace and let his mouth drop open. She'd be so scared, she'd agree to anything.

The scenario running in his mind shifted, taking on images that were much more satisfying. He saw himself standing over the girl, her eyes cervine with fear. *I won't call the police this time, but first you have to show me how sorry you are. Show me…* His thoughts came to an abrupt halt as the sound of drumming rang out from the Year Three room. Mike smiled. He was going to enjoy this.

The classroom door stood ajar. Mike made a clicking sound with his tongue. How many times had he reminded Angela to lock the classroom when she left? The silly old cow was barely capable of dressing herself, let alone looking after a class of eight-year-olds. Lucky he came along when he did. If things went well, he'd be more than happy to forgive the teacher's forgetfulness.

Fingers resting on the handle, Mike inched the door open. He planned on surprising the girl, blocking the exit. If she tried to push past him, all the better. The door creaked and swung inwards, letting out a blast of air. The smell hit him before he noticed the faint glow of the screen.

Mike sucked in a sharp breath, the stench of rot caught in the back of his throat. He grabbed for the door handle, meaning to steady himself, and slipped forward, almost losing his balance. It was only then that he realised the

Smartboard was on, shedding eerie coloured light across the first few rows of desks.

The girl sat in the second row, her back to the door. Bathed in the reflection of the images on the screen, her skin appeared multicoloured, like a shifting rainbow. Barely taking in the child's appearance, Mike's attention fixed on the screen and the photos displayed there. His private collection, stark and huge on the big screen: a slideshow of flat-eyed children forced into obscene poses.

"How? How…" Mike clamped a hand over his mouth and stumbled forward.

It was then that he noticed the girl's hair, tangled wisps barely covering an oversized head. Her arm unfolded like a bat's wing, thin fingers ending in sharp curved nails. The nails drew a line along the desk to her right, gouging tracks through the hardened plastic as if it were as soft as butter.

Mike's heart gave a painful jolt, almost sending him to his knees. The door slammed behind him as a gust of wind slapped his back.

"Holy Christ." His voice sounded small and childish as the wind whistled around the room, throwing up papers and books as if the class itself were caught in a cyclone.

Drumming filled his head, jarring his brain with rhythmic pulsing. Mike backpedalled, but his legs were rubbery and unresponsive. The thing in the chair – it wasn't a girl but something inhuman – turned its head. Mike shrieked, a high-pitched sound heavy with fear and revulsion. His heart gave another jolt, this one more painful. He clutched his chest, desperate to get to the door and out of the school before the thing turned around, some part of him knowing if he saw the creature's face, he'd be lost.

Hand reaching around desperate for purchase, his back thumped the door. The thing's head moved, craning at an unnatural angle and all the while the photos slipped from one frame to the next.

"Please. No… Please." Mike's throat constricted with terror and pain as another jolt squeezed his chest.

Its face, when it came into view, was every nightmare come to life. Skull-like features, dark sockets with eyes burning like twin orbs of hell. Mike lost control of his bladder, barely noticing the warm liquid trickling down his leg and staining the front of his suit pants.

The creature unfurled itself from the chair with jerky, disjointed movements. Like a puppet it came forward, slowly at first, but then in a blur of shudders it was almost upon him. Mike screamed, his fingers finally latching on to the door handle and pushing down.

The girl-creature's jaw unhinged, revealing a nest of sharp yellowed teeth; it roared into Mike's face. A spray of spittle hit him as the rancid breath worked its way down his throat. The thing's breath took on a life of its own, filling his head with whispers. Something tore at his arm as he fell backwards out of the classroom.

His back hit the cement, his elbow connecting with the ground with an audible *crack*. Mike cycled his legs, pushing himself across the walkway, sliding on his butt, trying to put as much distance between himself and the creature as possible. Not waiting to see if the thing followed, he scrambled to his feet and ran.

When he reached the undercover lunch area, the light was almost non-existent, turning the tables into dark, hulking shapes. He was sweating now, heat burning his skin while chills racked his bones. He had to get to the admin building, lock himself in and call for help.

The door was barely visible. Why hadn't he turned on the lights? Only a few more steps and he'd be safe. Mike's heart gave another jolt, this one more like a contraction that seized his entire chest. A stab of pain in the back of his neck was followed by tearing at his skin. Clattering, like a million teeth snapping the air. Above the whispering in his mind, a flutter of wings, the smell, *oh God, the smell*. Beaks stabbed at his face and neck, pulling his flesh. Mike batted at the birds, grabbing a fistful of feathers, but still the attack continued.

He was on his knees now, blood blurring his vision. The pressure in his chest was powerful enough to suck the air from his lungs. Something sharp pierced his left eye. Mike managed one last shriek before pitching forward. His head slammed into the bitumen with a wet *crunch*. In his mind, voices, childish and petulant, whispered a chorus of accusations. Their voices followed him into the blackness.

Chapter Twenty-one

Annabel sat between her mother and father, facing Sergeant Gibson across the kitchen table. She was nervous. She'd never spoken to a policeman before, except for the time Constable Leary came to her school and spoke to her class about bicycle safety, but this was different – more serious. She liked Sergeant Gibson and was glad he was here to help her, but it still felt weird to be sitting in her kitchen talking to a policeman.

He started out by telling her that she wasn't in trouble and that he just wanted to talk to her. Then he asked her about school and about her favourite TV shows.

"Tell me about the girl?" His voice changed, got quieter.

"It's not a little girl." Annabel's face felt hot, her voice was too loud.

"It's okay." Sergeant Gibson nodded. "You just tell me what you saw."

She looked at her mother, who also nodded for her to continue.

"The first time I saw it, it was in the backyard standing near my swing. I thought it was a little girl... You know, lost or something, but then I saw it was a monster." She could feel that Sergeant Gibson didn't believe her – not about the monster part. A wave of disappointment swept over her, and tears formed in the corners of her eyes.

"You don't believe me," Annabel said.

She looked down at the table, not wanting him to see her cry. If he didn't believe her, how could he stop the thing from coming back and getting her?

"I do believe you think you saw a monster, but if you tell me everything you saw, well, it might help me understand a bit better."

He spoke in a very kind and patient voice. Annabel felt mean for being so disappointed in him. The feeling only added to her misery, making it hard for her to speak.

"Okay." She kept her eyes on the table. "It was wearing a sort of raggedy dress and had awful grey skin and a scary, jerky way of walking."

When she looked up, Sergeant Gibson was leaning forward, frowning as if he was thinking about something. Her mind buzzed and a word popped into her head. *Virus.* Annabel had no idea what the word meant.

"It wanted to come in, but couldn't. I could feel it wanting to, it was angry because it couldn't get in." She looked at her mother.

"It's okay, love." Lisa spoke softly and put her arm around her.

Annabel looked back at Sergeant Gibson.

"Did you see it again after that night?" he asked.

"Yes. It came back last night and it tried to force me to come outside." She hung her head – she hadn't told her parents about that part. Her mother's body tensed against her. She didn't need the buzzing to tell her that her mother was upset.

"You mean the girl spoke to you?" he asked.

"No." She shook her head, trying to explain. "It did this." She put her hand up and made a beckoning gesture to show him what she meant.

"Okay. Is there anything else you can tell me, Annabel?"

Annabel thought for a moment and then decided to tell him everything – not even her parents knew everything...

"It wants to kill me. It likes killing children." The words came out in a rush as if she had to say them quickly or risk never getting them out.

Her mother gasped. Her fingers tightened around Annabel's shoulders. She'd frightened her mother. Hurting her was worse than hurting herself, but she couldn't stop.

"It will keep coming back until it finds a way to get me and it won't stop killing children until it does." Tears ran down her face. She didn't bother to wipe them away.

"That's enough!" Her mother's voice was angry, hard in a way Annabel had never heard before. She was staring at Sergeant Gibson. For a moment no one spoke. The awkward silence continued until her father finally broke it.

"You can do whatever you think is best, Sergeant Gibson, but I want you to know that we believe our daughter. If she says that that thing out there is dangerous, then we believe her and I'm prepared to do whatever it takes to protect my family."

Annabel brushed her tears away and sat up straighter in her seat. She wanted to jump up and hug her father, but didn't want to look like a baby in front of the sergeant. Instead, she leaned against the comforting warmth of her mother and waited for him to speak.

"Okay." Sergeant Gibson nodded. "I'm going to take a look around outside and then drive out to the orchard and see if I can find any trace of this..." He hesitated and then continued, "This, whatever it is. I'll leave you my card. If it comes back, I want you to call me, day or night." As he spoke, he reached into his shirt pocket, pulled out a card, and passed it to her father. Annabel noticed he called the thing *it*, not *she*. He got up to leave, but stopped and turned back to Annabel.

"You've been very brave," he said. "If it comes back, get your dad to call me and I'll come straight away. Okay?"

Annabel looked into his confused blue eyes. He knew she was telling the truth and it scared him. He was waiting for her to respond, so she nodded and tried to smile. It seemed to be enough. He smiled back, turned and walked towards the front of the house.

Her father got up and followed him. She could hear them speaking at the front door, but couldn't make out what they were saying, so she gave up listening and turned to her mother.

"I'm sorry, Mum. I didn't mean to upset you." A fresh stream of tears ran down her cheeks.

"I'm very proud of you." Lisa smiled, but there were tears in her eyes.

Annabel's mind buzzed. She hadn't just upset her mother, she'd terrified her. For the first time in her life, Annabel wished she was different. She didn't want to feel her mother's fear. Knowing the strongest person in her world was terrified made Annabel sick with fear and guilt. She'd caused this. It now occurred to her that maybe she *was* the bad one because she knew things about people that she wasn't supposed to. Maybe her knowing those things had brought the monster. Now people were dying.

She closed her eyes and let her mother hug her, wishing she could turn off the thoughts in her head.

Chapter Twenty-two

Maggie tried to focus on the road, but couldn't help checking the mirrors every few seconds to make sure no one was following her. She turned on the radio, hoping to distract herself, but the harsh, annoying pop music only intensified her anxiety. She wanted to drive home as fast as she could. Instead, she headed to Doug's house. He'd be suffering. She had to let him know that he wasn't alone – that meant putting her own fears aside, at least for a while.

After five minutes of knocking on his door, it became clear that either Doug was out or he wasn't answering. With no other choice, Maggie decided to leave the lasagne on his front porch with a note:

> *Dear Doug,*
> *I'm so sorry.*
> *If you need anything, call me or come by. If I don't hear from you before, I'll be back again tomorrow.*
> *Eat something.*
> *X, Maggie*

The torn sheet of note paper tucked under the plastic tub didn't seem like much. She thought of knocking again, but decided to let him be.

* * *

Turning all the lights on from the front door to the kitchen, Maggie walked through the house. It would be dark soon, and the constant maelstrom of fears and questions wouldn't leave her alone. She put the second lasagne in the fridge, to be heated up later, and dumped her bag on the counter. A glass of wine would help steady her nerves, but keeping a clear head when she saw Harness was more important. She needed to convince him of things that *she* was still struggling to fully understand. To do that, she needed to be completely sober... at least until she'd finished her story.

With plenty of time to kill before preparing dinner, Maggie made herself a cup of instant coffee and went outside to sit on the back veranda. She usually sat on the back steps looking at the garden, enjoying the smell of clean country air. Tonight felt different, as if the world had changed. She chose to sit on one of the wooden outdoor chairs she'd bought shortly after moving in.

The chair was part of a set of two, and a small table. She'd bought it with plans to sit outside in the summer, eating her meals and watching the sun fade. In reality, she'd only used it a few times, opting for the convenience of eating inside with a plate on her lap. Now, sitting at the little table for two, she realised the reason she avoided the spot was more about loneliness than convenience.

Maggie watched the creamy liquid cooling in the cup and thought of Harness, picturing the little lines that appeared around his eyes when he smiled. She wanted to see him, and not just because she needed to tell him about Manjula and the Acheri. She had feelings for him... strong feelings. Being with him felt right somehow, like that was where she was supposed to be. It didn't make much sense, but two nights ago they left Agnes's party together and since then everything had changed. The world shifted from normal to terrifying and she wanted to hear Harness's deep, steady voice, look into his clear blue eyes and know he believed her.

Her thoughts jolted back to Prapti. Unable to ignore the chill creeping up her spine, Maggie looked over her shoulder and then out into the fading sky. In the distance, dark shapes swirled, creating a black funnel that appeared to be moving. It took her a few seconds to make sense of what she was seeing – birds, hundreds of them circling the town. In spite of the temperate evening air, she shivered and sipped her coffee, grateful for the warmth of the cup in her hands.

Chapter Twenty-three

Looking down, Agnes realised she was naked and clamped her arms over her breasts. Dim, sickly light exposed her location: the upstairs hallway of the house she'd shared with Stan. The *old* house she'd demolished fifteen years earlier to make way for the modern, angular brick and glass structure where she now lived. Impossible, yet somehow, she was back in the building that housed her grim past. Inside the very walls that witnessed her darkest hours.

A nightmare. She'd had many of those over the years. But even as her mind rationalised what was happening, her body felt alive with terror. Turning to run, the bones and muscles in her legs refused to move. Her feet shifted of their own accord, taking her forward. *It's not real... None of it's real.* Yet the malevolence oozing out of every brick and timber felt all too real. The hallway was decorated in faded yellow and brown flowered wallpaper. The gaudy blooms curling off the walls took on a life of their own, brushing against her naked flesh. She stumbled forward, trying to avoid their touch, and found herself facing the doorway to the room she'd once shared with Stan.

The door pulsated; with each *thump* the wood swelled in and out like the brown lung of a heavy smoker. The door shuddered and flew inwards, revealing the bedroom. Agnes struggled to turn away, desperate to avoid seeing what was inside the room. Thrashing and resisting as the invisible force only propelled her closer to the doorway.

She recognised the thing on the bed and shrieked! Stan Wells lay on filthy sheets drumming his feet against the footboard. With each *thump*, his naked body shuddered. His grey skin was mottled with black spots. Greenish fluid leaked from lesions on his face and stomach.

Stan's milky eyes shifted to Agnes. A sly smile spread across his face. A knowing smile that made Agnes lace her fingers through her hair and pull as if she were losing her mind. *Maybe I am.* The Stan-thing's mouth flopped open, revealing a blackened tongue. Agnes whimpered. She pushed backwards with her feet and grabbed at the doorframe, desperate to escape the hideous thing on the bed.

Her fingers found purchase on the wood. She turned to drag her possessed body backwards. The bedsprings creaked. Agnes looked over her shoulder. Stan sat up, his blackened penis clearly erect and impossibly large between his fleshy legs.

"Please, God, no." She shook her head. A long, thin hand snaked around the door from inside the room and clasped Agnes's wrist, sharp nails piercing her skin. The hand burned as if alive with fire, blistering Agnes's flesh. Excruciating pain, too real to be a nightmare, seared her skin. *I'm in hell.*

Agnes let out a sob as her body moved towards the bed. Turning her head, she saw the creature that held her – a twisted monster, eyes burning with hatred. A scream built in her chest, but when she opened her mouth, all that escaped was a defeated rush of air. The monster pulled her towards the bed where Stan waited with open arms.

Agnes woke shrieking and lunged forward, knocking the empty whiskey glass to the floor. It bounced on the cream-coloured carpet and rolled under the desk. She grasped the edge of the table, grateful for something to hold onto, and looked around the study. *A nightmare. Only a nightmare, it can't hurt me.*

The light in the room was dim, but enough for Agnes to recognise her surroundings. She sat at the desk in her perfect study, clutching the sides of the table. The horrors of the dream still swirling in her brain, body feverish and racked with aches, she broke down.

It had been forty years since she'd cried. The sensation of tears was alien on her skin. Lifting her hand to wipe her face, she winced with pain. Angry red welts encircled her right wrist, in some places the skin blistered and raw. Agnes held her arm out as if distancing herself from the limb. A panicked shriek built up in her throat, spilling out in a series of sobs.

Head pounding and body racked with aches, she thought about getting up and pouring herself another drink.

"Steady my nerves." She spoke to the empty room in a voice that was barely recognisable.

Halfway out of the chair, she stopped. Dampness between her legs —she'd wet herself. Agnes fell back into the chair, eyes wide, and stared at the window where the last weak rays of sun were battling the coming night. A blur of black hit the pane, splintering the glass. The *crack* jolted Agnes back in her seat. Another *crunch* as a second bird hit the glass. Agnes cradled her head and whimpered.

Chapter Twenty-four

Just before 8.30, Maggie heard Harness's Jeep crunch over the driveway. Taking a deep breath, she opened the door and stepped aside to let him in.

"Sorry, I didn't have time to go home and change," he said as he followed Maggie through to the kitchen.

"Hard day?"

"The hardest." He didn't need to say any more, by now she knew he meant there'd been another death. For a moment, they were silent, the weight of his words hanging in the air.

"You look nice," he said, changing the subject.

Maggie smiled. She'd chosen a simple blue summer dress and sandals. Wearing her hair down and only a little makeup, she hoped that the overall effect was nice without looking like she was trying too hard.

"Thanks. I hope you're hungry."

They ate outside on the small deck. Maggie went against her better judgement and poured herself a glass of red wine. Harness opted for a beer.

"This looks great. You feeding me is becoming a regular thing." He held her gaze for a moment before continuing. His eyes were unreadable, stony. "When you called me today and asked me to come over, I had a feeling you wanted to tell me something. Don't get me wrong, I'm glad you invited me, it's just that you sounded like something was on your mind."

Maggie could tell he was waiting for her to fill in the blanks.

"I do need to tell you something, a lot in fact, but not yet." She hesitated, not quite ready to tell her story. "Let's eat first, okay?"

Maggie was relieved when he nodded and picked up his knife and fork. They ate in silence for a few minutes, a silence that felt comfortable.

The veranda lights bathed the yard in a soft yellow glow that reflected off the waxy green leaves covering the railings and stairs. The night was alive with soft noises from chirping insects and cooing birds. Maggie leaned back in her seat and sipped her wine, watching Harness lift the beer bottle to his mouth and take a long, thirsty gulp. The wine tasted sweet. The tension coiled in her muscles began to melt away.

Leaning forward, she put her glass on the table.

"There is something I want to ask."

He raised his eyebrows, and the lines at the corners of his eyes vanished. "Okay. Go ahead."

"Your name." Maggie bit her lip, trying not to laugh. "It's... unusual. I just wondered–"

"No, I wasn't named after something a horse wears." He sounded wounded, but he was smiling, dimples creasing his stubbly cheeks.

"Well, you've got to admit, it's not your average name."

Maybe it was the wine, but suddenly she couldn't stop herself from laughing. It felt good – liberating, as if she were stepping out from under something heavy.

"Okay." He put down his knife and fork and held up his hands in surrender. "I don't usually tell people, but for you, I'll make an exception."

Maggie rolled her hand in a hurry-up motion and tried to suppress another bout of laughter.

"It was the seventies."

For some reason, that was enough to make her giggle.

"Why is that funny?" he asked, laughing along with her.

Not trusting herself to speak, Maggie clamped her lips together and nodded for him to continue.

"Like I said, it was the seventies and my parents, Harriet and Nestor–"

"Oooh." Maggie picked up her glass. "I get it now."

"What are all those red flowers?" He used his fork to point towards the trees and sheds, still smiling but obviously keen to change the subject. "They're everywhere. It makes the place look sort of tropical."

"They're called stone flowers. I was going to try and cut them down, but I've decided I like them so I'm letting them go wild."

"Good choice." He grinned and gave an approving nod.

Maggie noticed the slight dimple in his left cheek – her stomach fluttered. Suddenly off balance, she searched for something to say.

"I stopped by Doug Loggie's today. I wanted to check on him, but he didn't answer the door. He's the one who told me... I mean about the flowers – what they're called."

She stopped. At the mention of Doug's name, Harness's expression changed. He probably had to attend when Maureen died. She wished she hadn't said anything, but realised she might as well continue.

"I think I know something about what's happening to the children." She paused.

When he responded, his face was unreadable. "Tell me."

"I went to see a friend of mine today, Jackson, he works for me at the café. I spoke to his grandmother. She's seen something like this before."

Maggie hesitated and then recounted her conversation with Manjula. Without pausing, she told him about her run-in with Prapti at the café. By the time she finished, she realised that he hadn't spoken, just listened and nodded. She almost expected him to laugh or get up and make an excuse to leave. Instead, he took a long drink from his beer.

"I spent the afternoon with the Chapels. They're convinced that there's a monster out there that looks like a little girl. Annabel told me it's killing the children."

It wasn't the response Maggie had expected. There was no trace of humour or sarcasm in his voice. *Does this mean he believes me? Do I believe me?* She knew what Annabel believed, but she was surprised the Chapels believed it too. Their insistence that something supernatural was at work added weight to Maggie's story. She should have been pleased, but all she felt was a dread crawling up from the pit of her stomach.

"What do *you* think?" She was surprised by how much she wanted him to believe her.

"A week ago, I would've said you were all crazy, but now…"

He shrugged and looked off into the backyard. Except for the moon and the veranda light, they were surrounded by darkness, wrapped in its shadows.

"Now, I'm not so sure what I think."

Maggie followed his gaze, noticing the silence. *When did the insects stop chirping?* Beyond the circle of light, the trees stood like inky fingers against the sky. She thought of the flock of birds she'd seen circling the town and her skin prickled.

"Will you help me bring the dinner things in?"

Harness nodded and began stacking the dishes. He helped Maggie carry the plates and utensils inside and pile them into the sink.

"I'm going to have another drink; do you want one?" she asked.

"I'll take another beer."

Maggie poured herself more wine as Harness started on his second beer. They settled in on the couch, almost touching but not quite.

"Tell me again about Prapti?" he asked, continuing the conversation.

"She's... I don't know how to describe it – strange. She came across as menacing. When I think about the things she said–" Maggie paused and shook her head.

Reliving the encounter brought back the sense of fear and outrage she'd experienced in the café. The label *squaw* reverberated in her mind.

"You think she's connected to the girl, the one Annabel and Ollie saw?"

"I'm sure of it." Maggie answered with a degree of conviction she didn't know she felt until the words were out of her mouth.

"Okay. Well, tomorrow I need to find Prapti and question her about this lost girl and the threats she made. What else do you know about her?"

"Not much." Maggie took a sip of her wine. "Agnes introduced her to me at the party the other night. Said she was a writer." Maggie thought for a moment, trying to recall the conversation. "Yes, I remember now. A travel writer."

"Did she say who she writes for or where she's staying?"

Maggie looked at him and felt a little confused.

"You heard the conversation, right? You said you would have told her to go fuck herself if she had spoken to you that way. Remember?"

Harness scratched his head. "I didn't really hear anything Agnes said. I was too busy watching you."

"Oh." It was all she could think to say.

After an awkward silence, Harness spoke.

"I'll go see Agnes tomorrow and find out what she knows. That'll be the first step in locating Prapti and making some sense of what's going on."

She could see he was excited by the idea of having something concrete to do.

"So, you believe me?"

"I'm getting there."

He took her hand and turned it over, as if studying the lines on her palm. Maggie felt a little jolt of pleasure run up her arm as he brought her hand up to his mouth and kissed the skin just above her wrist. He paused for a moment, then leaned in and caught her lips with his. The kiss, soft at first, became urgent. Maggie drew away, looking into his clear blue eyes. She wasn't sure what she was searching for – maybe some sort of promise that he wouldn't hurt her. She saw her face reflected in his pupils. Her reflection and longing – a need for contact, a need she shared.

He was about to speak when she turned and in one fluid movement positioned herself so she was facing him, straddling his lap. Whatever was happening between them felt real. Maggie didn't care if it was the wine or the sense that life was fleeting. She wanted to be close to him. Without taking her eyes off his, she reached down and pulled her dress over her head, letting it drop to the floor. Harness looked surprised, hesitating then running his hands over her naked skin. Leaning down, he kissed the valley between her breasts, his lips warm on her skin. She ran her fingers over his face, letting all other thoughts and images slip from her mind.

They made love a second time, upstairs in Maggie's bed. Moonlight filtered through the half-open curtains, casting a bluish tint over their bodies. When he held her, she felt his heart beating, strong and steady. His breath on her neck deep and regular, the moment sublimely intimate.

Later, relaxed and sleepy, Maggie lay on her side watching Harness stare up at the ceiling through half-closed eyes.

"What made you move to Thorn Tree?" His voice pulled her back from the edge of sleep.

The question caught her off guard; she had to think before answering. *Why did I come here? To start a new life?* Or was she running away...

"The short answer is I needed a fresh start and Thorn Tree is a great town."

A moment ago, wrapped in the warmth of their body heat, she'd felt completely happy. Dredging up the details of her failed marriage was the last thing she wanted to talk about.

"What's the long answer?" he asked, shadows bathing his face, making it difficult for her to see his expression.

"After I left my husband, I... I had to get away. I came here to rewrite my life." When she said the words out loud, her voice shook.

He leaned in and kissed her on the shoulder.

"It's not easy to start again."

It sounded like he was speaking from experience. He moved his head to her pillow and ran his hand over her stomach. A shiver of excitement travelled her body.

"I want to come with you tomorrow, when you go see Agnes."

Even in the dim light she could see he was unhappy.

"No. I don't think that's a good idea." His voice was flat.

"Why? Because this is police business?" She didn't wait for him to reply. "Well, it's not. I don't know what it *is*. What's going on is way outside of police business." She tried to keep the indignation out of her voice, but wasn't having much success.

"No. That's not why." He reached up and brushed a strand of hair from her forehead. His fingers lingered, holding a strand then slowly sliding down the length of her hair. "I just don't want you anywhere near Prapti or whatever is making people sick."

Maggie put her hand on his chest, his bare skin warm under her palm. She understood his reasoning, even felt a flicker of pleasure over his need to protect her. But the people dying weren't strangers on the news, they were her friends and neighbours. She wasn't going to be put off.

"Ness, I'm already involved in this. I'm not going to sit by and do nothing."

"I like it when you call me Ness," he responded with a smile, and in spite of the seriousness of the conversation, Maggie found herself smiling back.

"Okay," she said, "but I'm coming with you tomorrow."

Chapter Twenty-five

Thomas woke with a start, a drumming still echoing in his head. The girl in his dreams was replaced by the dark lines of his small bedroom. She'd called him to follow her along a path through the bush. The details were blurry, but he remembered how pretty she was, skipping through the moonlight, dark curls bouncing against the back of her white dress. Like him, she was hungry. The drumming was kind of scary, but following her made him feel warm. If he didn't need to pee so badly, he'd go back to sleep and see if he could find her again.

He pushed himself to the edge of the mattress, wincing at the pain in his bruised hip. He knew dreams didn't really work that way, once they were gone, they were gone for good. He stood and scurried out of the room, thin arms wrapped around his bare chest. Pausing in the darkened hallway, he cocked his head to one side. The sound of regular snoring told him Aunty Liv and her boyfriend were asleep. Thomas let out a breath and relaxed his hunched shoulders.

No longer worried about making a noise, he padded to the bathroom and flicked on the light. The green-tiled room smelled like cigarettes. Drops of pee dotted the toilet seat. Picking his way around a puddle of something damp on the cracked tiles, he pulled down his underpants and relieved himself.

On his way back to bed, Thomas peeked his head into Aunty Liv's room. She wasn't his real aunty, just his foster mum. He'd had three since he turned seven. Next to her, Tyson shifted and let out a fart that reminded Thomas of the sound a paper bag made when you blew it up and busted it.

Satisfied that Tyson wasn't going to sneak up on him, Thomas padded down the hall into the kitchen. His stomach gave an angry snarl. The last thing he'd eaten was a piece of cold pizza at lunchtime. Just thinking about the cheesy topping made his mouth water. He snatched a quick look over his shoulder just to make sure Tyson hadn't been tricking him in the bedroom. He was clever like that, always catching Thomas out. Pretending to be watching the footy, his hand snaking out and grabbing Thomas's wrist when he reached for a piece of popcorn. Or like earlier this afternoon, when Tyson had been lying on the couch tossing the football in the air with a cigarette dangling from his lips.

"Hey, mate. Wanna catch?"

"No... I mean, no thanks. I just wh–wh..."

Aunty Liv was sitting in the armchair, legs spread wide, thick fingers clamped around her phone. She didn't look up.

"You just wh–wh... What?"

Tyson tossed the ball above his head and caught it with a *whack* that made Thomas jump.

"Come on, don't be a wuss."

Auntie Liv was still jabbing away at her phone.

"I... okay."

"Good on ya."

Tyson waggled his thick eyebrows and hand-balled the football in Thomas's direction, a gentle toss that was easy to catch.

"Don't break anything," Aunty Liv said, finally paying attention. He'd caught the ball and Liv was watching. Tyson never did much in front of her.

"Okay. Toss it back now, dummy."

Thomas passed the ball across the room, but just as it came within catching range, Tyson dipped to the right and elbowed the footy sideways. Thomas let out a puff of air, knowing what was coming even before the ball hit the side table and knocked Liv's open bottle of nail polish onto the carpet.

"Jesus, Tyson." Liv's voice rang out like an angry magpie. "I told you not to break anything."

Tyson jumped to his feet.

"Don't blame me." He pointed a nicotine-stained finger in Thomas's direction. "He's the one who can't throw a ball."

Before Liv had the chance to answer, Tyson crossed the room and landed a kick on Thomas's hip.

In the darkened kitchen, Thomas rubbed at his leg remembering the bolt of pain he felt when Tyson's shoe hit Thomas's leg.

"You clumsy little shit. Get in ya room before I belt you one."

"Hey." Liv was screaming something, but Thomas didn't hang around to hear the rest.

When he reached his room, tears were running down his cheeks. The last thing he heard was Liv's voice, high and breathless.

"If someone at school sees a bruise, they'll—"

Thomas closed the door. Now, alone in the kitchen, he thought back to earlier and how he'd spent the rest of the day curled up on the bed, crying at first but then flicking through an old comic. His thoughts were on Aunty Liv more than Tyson. Tyson made no bones about disliking Thomas, but Liv was supposed to be looking after him. She could have brought him something to eat at dinnertime at least, instead of letting him cry in his room while the tantalising smell of burgers filled the house.

Thomas sniffed and opened the fridge. The solitary light cast a creepy glow on the worn linoleum. A row of beer cans, a crusty-looking tub of cottage cheese and squeezy bottle of tomato sauce. His stomach gurgled. Grabbing the sauce, he squirted a glop into his palm. He sniffed the liquid then lapped at it, swallowing the runny sauce in a few licks. He repeated the process three times before deciding he'd better leave some or Liv might get upset.

His stomach continued to burble, the sauce only waking up his hunger. Snatching a quick glance over his shoulder, just to be sure no one was watching, he tiptoed to the sink. There was a box of cornflakes in the cupboard next to the sink, he'd seen it there a few weeks ago. Since they never had any milk, Thomas was pretty sure the box would still be on the shelf.

A smile lit up his gaunt face. The open box stood alone on the shelf, the curly red label smudged with something yellow, maybe mustard. "Yeah." The word came out louder than he intended.

He forced himself to stop and wait, counting in his head. If he made it to twenty and didn't hear anyone coming down the hall, he was okay to eat. The seconds ticked by slowly, his gut groaning with anticipation. When he reached twenty, Thomas grabbed the box.

Squatting on the floor, he scooped out a handful of flakes and pushed them into his mouth. They were a bit stale, but he gobbled them up so quickly, he bit his tongue. The taste of blood mixed with flakes made him grimace, but didn't slow him down. Even with the metallic taste of blood thrown in, the cornflakes stirred a memory. Honey Joys, that was what his mother called them. Crunchy sticky treats made with cornflakes and honey, probably a bunch of other stuff, but that's all he could taste. She used to make them when she was feeling sweet. *I'm feeling sweet today, I'm going to make you something special.* He could almost hear her voice, feel her hand brushing the hair off his forehead.

Thomas set down the box and looked around the dark kitchen. *Why'd she have to go and get sick again?* A fresh stream of tears ran down his cheeks, cutting a trail through the sauce and cornflake crumbs. It was then that he noticed the back door was open. He scampered across the room and stood in front of the door. The moon was out, painting a silvery trail on the long grass leading to the trees.

It occurred to him that he hadn't noticed the door was open when he entered the room, but the thought was fleeting, washed away by the way the grass wavered in the slight breeze. His eyelids drooped. Drumming, deep and soothing, made him sleepy. Something moved through the grass. His eyes shot open. The girl, the one from his dream. *She's real.*

He stepped through the door, a small voice in his head telling him that dreams weren't real swallowed by the drumming and the whispers. *Happier, playing forever – hold my hand.* Thomas followed the moonlight, barely noticing the chill in the air or the way the long grass scratched at his bruised arms.

He could see her head, bobbing amongst the weeds. All he had to do was catch up and they'd be together. A line of sweat popped out on his forehead. His arms and legs shuddered. Hesitating, Thomas looked back towards the house. It seemed so far away, as if he were on the sea and the tide had carried him for miles. The back door was now only a small rectangle in the distance.

Something touched his fingers; the girl's hand closed around his. He thought she'd be warm, but the hand felt as cold as a popsicle. His teeth chattered. He tried to pull back but the girl's grip tightened. The drumming shook the ground, he could no longer hear anything else. His heart twisted and the girl's face came into view. He should have been afraid, but he felt only relief as the creature pulled him into her embrace. Thomas's mind registered the taste of Honey Joys on his tongue, then blackness.

Chapter Twenty-six

Harness jolted from sleep, the shrill ringing alerting and disorienting him at the same time. His surroundings were unfamiliar. Not until he heard Maggie's soft sleepy voice beside him, did he become grounded in what was happening.

"Ness?" A *click* and light flooded the room. As Harness blinked past the sudden blindness, he saw Maggie's hand hover near the bedside lamp. He quickly located his trousers on the floor and pulled the phone out of the pocket.

"Gibson here." Static crackled. "Hello?" Another hiss of static. He pulled the phone away from his ear, ready to hang up when he caught Rodney's voice.

"It's... back... saw it... closer..." Then dead silence.

Harness hung up, still blinking as his eyes adjusted to the light. He dialled the Chapels' number. Again, a burst of crackling followed by a hiss that sounded more like whispering than static. He checked his watch – 3.45 in the morning.

"What's happened, Ness?" Maggie watched him pull on his clothes.

"That was Rodney. I couldn't make out much, but I think that thing's back. I've got to go."

He leaned down and planted a kiss on her lips before she could object. He was almost at the bedroom door when she called out.

"Wait. I'll come with you." She was half out of bed, the sheet pooling around her naked body.

"No." It came out a fraction too loud. He registered the shock on her face and immediately regretted it.

"I'm sorry, I shouldn't have raised my voice, but I don't want you anywhere near the Chapels." She opened her mouth to argue but he beat her to it. "Not until I've checked things out."

Maggie looked hurt, but nodded.

"I'll come back when I'm done, okay?"

"Okay, but if it's there…"

Long copper hair covered her pale shoulders. He wanted nothing more than to climb back into bed and rest his head against her neck and let the scent of citrus and honey soothe him back to sleep.

"Don't get close to it." She frowned, mouth slightly open.

He wasn't sure how to answer. If the girl, or whatever it was, *was* there then he intended to get close. Close enough to stop it. He could see Maggie waiting for a response. Harness turned back to the bed and kissed her again, then left.

* * *

Driving slowly, lights on full beam, it took nearly half an hour to reach the turnoff for the Chapels' property. Even with the moonlight, the roads were dark, a faint mist adding to the gloom. He started off with the windows down, hoping the night air would sharpen his senses, clear away the fog left over from sleep. Within minutes a sudden drop in temperature forced him to close the windows and flick on the heater.

He made the turn onto the gravel road leading to the Chapels' house at a crawl. A few seconds later, a herd of kangaroos sprang in front of the vehicle. Harness braked hard, swerving left. The car slid sideways and skidded to a stop, spraying gravel at the roos. He let out a long breath, forcing his fingers to ease their grip on the wheel and his shoulders to relax.

He waited, watching the herd bounce through the mist, listening to the thumping of their powerful legs springing off the gravel. His nerves were jangling from the close call, but something about the scene bothered him. There had to be at least eight roos jumping at a frantic speed within inches of his car. He couldn't remember ever seeing that many crossing the road at one time except during a bush fire.

He put the car in park and opened the door. A shock of frigid night air hit him as he stepped on the road. The headlights lit up the bitumen ahead where one lone kangaroo, a large grey male by the look of it, stopped. A tall, solitary figure surrounded by mist, its pale fur gave it a ghostlike appearance. Head up, his ears twitched as it looked back towards the other side of the road. The animal didn't seem to notice Harness or the lights. He followed the roo's gaze back into the tangle of dark bush but saw nothing.

There was no tell-tale smell of burning, no crackle of fire coming from the bush. The usual night-time chorus of insects and nocturnal creatures was missing, the scene eerily silent. He looked back at the kangaroo, wondering what had spooked the herd. The animal's ears twitched once more before it too disappeared into the thick bush.

Casting one more glance towards the trees, Harness returned to the car. Once inside, he snapped the switch and engaged the central locking. Goosebumps prickled the skin on his arms and neck. He had the sense that someone was watching him, but a glance in the rear-view mirror revealed nothing but blackness. He drummed his fingers on the steering wheel for a second then pulled back onto the road.

He thought about what Maggie had said: *the Acheri is a demon who looks like a little girl.* He wished, not for the first time, he was back in the warmth of her bed. After tonight, he had no more doubts. He wanted to be with her. To do that, he'd have to tell her about his past: the leukaemia that took his daughter and his wife's suicide. Grief had been locked inside him for so long, it had become like a second skin. If he could open up to Maggie, maybe he could begin to chip away at the layer of pain that kept him separated from the rest of the world.

He watched the trees fly past, their dark shapes like hulking figures crowding the road. The memory of Maggie's warm body against his seemed distant, a wisp of smoke vanishing – just out of reach. He couldn't shake the feeling that something was pulling him away from her. *God, I've really got to get a grip.* He chuckled to himself, but in the empty car, his voice sounded hollow.

The Chapels' house came into view, a glowing beacon at the end of a long driveway. The lights spilling from the many windows, a stark contrast against the huge expanse of darkness, only served to make the dwelling look more isolated, as though it was the only house on Earth. With at least twenty kilometres between the Chapels and their closest neighbour, Harness supposed they may as well be the last people on Earth – anything could happen out here with no one to see or hear.

He parked the car and opened the door. Wind, violent and sudden, caught him by surprise, almost snatching the breath from his lungs. The gust blew with surprising force, hard enough to make the trees and bushes tremble, the sound like voices whispering in the night. The gale beat against his bare face and arms. It struck Harness as strange that when he'd stepped out of the car a few kilometres up the road the night air felt cold, but exceptionally still.

He pulled his equipment belt from the passenger seat and secured it around his waist. The belt held his gun, handcuffs, baton and torch, making it far too bulky to wear while driving. Harness slid the torch off the belt and held it at his side as he approached the house.

As he climbed onto the porch, the front door opened. Rodney Chapel stepped onto the veranda, hair standing in wild clumps. He wore a pair of faded track pants and a T-shirt. Harness guessed that the man had been asleep shortly before making the call to Harness.

Rodney waited until Harness was close before speaking in a hushed voice. He gestured towards a large tree.

"I wasn't sure if you heard me before the line went dead. It was around there, near the swing. Annabel screamed for me and Lisa. When we got to her room, I looked out the window and… and I saw it. It was coming towards the house."

Rodney raked his fingers through his hair, only adding to the disarray.

"Jesus." He drew out the word, hitting both syllables. "It was the scariest-looking thing. Moving slowly, sort of jerking. I wasn't sure what to do… I banged on the window. It went towards the shed." He spoke quickly, a tremor in his voice.

"Okay. Go back inside and I'll take a look."

"I'll come with you. You know… just in case." Rodney swallowed. Harness could tell the man was scared, but the offer was genuine.

"No, mate. It's better if you stay with your wife and daughter. I'll yell if I need help."

"I've got my shotgun inside. If you call for help, I'll come running."

Harness was grateful but unnerved by the prospect of Rodney charging around in the dark firing his shotgun.

"If I do call for help, promise me you won't come out shooting? I don't want to get my head blown off while you're trying to help," he said without a trace of humour.

Rodney gave a grimace that could have passed for an uncomfortable grin then nodded. He entered the house, stopping before closing the door.

"Be careful, that… thing… looks dangerous."

Harness nodded. He had every intention of being careful. Very careful. Alone on the porch, he descended the steps and walked around to the back of the house.

He spotted the swing, a homemade job – two lengths of rope and a plank of wood hung from a thick branch on a very large jacaranda tree. Harness turned and looked up at the second storey of the house where a lighted window faced the backyard. From this distance, he could make out a set of red curtains.

He looked back towards the swing, moving back and forth in the wind. The lights from the house extended as far as the tree, but beyond was saturated in nearly complete darkness. Harness noted the silhouettes of the two large sheds, the ones he'd seen earlier that day. Swathed in moonlight, the buildings looked like one huge structure. His earlier inspection of the sheds told him they were built about two metres apart, making the narrow space the likeliest place for someone, or something, to hide.

He clicked on the torch and held it above his shoulder, moving the beam back and forth between the tree and the first shed. Overgrown grass near the side of the green galvanised iron wall blocked Harness's sightline. He moved towards the structure, listening for any movement, but above the howling wind, he could hear only his own footsteps crunching over on the fallen leaves.

Playing the light over the front of the building, he noticed the doors were closed and secured with a padlock, making it impossible for whatever Annabel and Rodney had seen to have entered the shed.

He moved around towards the back of the building. The grass was longer, almost up to his knees, with thick bushes growing wild and uncultivated surrounding the rear of the shed. Harness stopped and ran the light over the area. It could have been his imagination, but the air felt colder now, almost icy. Without a closer look, it was impossible to see if anyone was crouched in the bushes between the buildings.

At the back of the sheds, the tangled foliage was higher, almost level with his shoulders and completely blocking the entrance to the gap between the two structures. He shone the torch around, spotting a gap in the thicket. The grass was crushed, branches broken and bent as if something had pushed its way through the bushes. Harness crouched to examine the spot, noticing his breath steaming against the cold air. The branches were bent in towards the gap between the two sheds. A few were snapped off completely. An odour hung in the air, rotten and damp. The ground beneath the shrubbery was tattered with vicious scratches. It looked like something had torn its way through.

Harness moved to stand when a faint sound caught his attention, almost like his own pulse beating in his ears. He stopped moving, holding the beam on the gap. The noise grew louder, becoming more distinct. His already chilled skin broke out in goosebumps. The drumming intensified, seeming to come from everywhere and nowhere at the same time. The sound, too regular and rhythmical to be a trapped animal, set his teeth on edge.

Unclipping his holster, he let his fingers brush the butt of his gun. He couldn't discount the possibility that the *monster* was nothing more than a lost child hiding in the dark. He considered going back and moving the squad car. If he parked it in front of the sheds, the headlights would flood the area. He dismissed the idea, knowing in the minutes it would take him to bring the vehicle around, whatever was hiding might get away.

Harness looked back towards the house. The lights were on in the kitchen. He wondered how long it would take Rodney to get out the door and across the yard. Probably less than a minute. *Will that be quick enough?*

The drumming continued its rhythmic throb. No animal in nature produced that sound. He had no option but to try and get a look between the gap. Shivering, he lowered himself so he was lying on his side. His breath produced clouds of steam as it left his mouth, confirming another swift drop in temperature.

Struggling, fingers numb with the cold, Harness shone the light through the gap. His hands were trembling and not because of the cold. He was scared. Scared in a way he hadn't experienced in a very long time. He'd never believed places or buildings held an atmosphere, but he sure felt something now. Almost like a taste hanging in the air. Not just the putrid smell but something else, cold mixed with electricity. If he had to describe it, he'd say it was evil.

The torch illuminated the bush, painting the thicket in wintery light. Shrubs were torn, jagged branches leading into the darkness between the two buildings. Something had definitely pushed through the area. Something strong. Thudding, his heart matching the beat of the drumming. It made him think of a rabbit warren, only this one was big and appeared to have been created by something with sharp claws. He held the torch close to his cheek, straining to see. He made out shapes, pipes and lengths of timber stored along the ground. The two sheds had to be at least eight metres long, making it almost impossible for him to see the far end.

Ignoring the broken branches as they clawed his face, he pushed further into the gap. The light landed on what looked like a mound of building debris. Harness angled the torch, trying to get a better look. The beam ended about thirty centimetres short of the pile.

"Shit." The word came out bathed in mist. It was no good, he'd have to think of another way.

He shifted backwards, ready to pull himself out of the bushes when the pile moved. It jerked to the left. Harness opened his mouth, intending to call out a warning, when something leapt towards him, covering the eight-metre distance with unnatural speed.

Instinctively, he pulled back. Before he could get himself free of the bushes, a face plunged into the gap only centimetres from his own. He saw it for less than a second. Long enough for him to take in a skull-like form covered with grey skin and yellow eyes lined with black above a jagged mass of cruel fangs. The creature – not a child, but something unnatural and ghastly – roared, spraying Harness's face and open mouth with hot, wet breath.

He clamped his mouth shut, swallowing the foul scent of the thing's breath. Scrambling back, branches like razor-sharp fingers tore at his shirt. He dropped the torch. Rolling right, he stumbled to his feet, drawing his gun. The drumming neared deafening, making it impossible to hear the creature's movements.

The urge to run was strong, almost overwhelming, but he resisted. Instead he planted his feet at shoulder width and aimed the gun at the gap in the bushes. He had to keep himself between the creature and the house.

Waiting, muscles tense and ears pounding, he kept his eyes glued on the bushes. The thing moved fast, but he intended to get a few shots into it before it was on top of him.

Minutes ticked past. The drumming lessened to a faint echo resounding inside his head. Not certain if the danger had passed, Harness edged backwards towards the house, eyes fixed on the torn thicket.

When he was within metres of the back door, he turned and cleared the steps in one jump, landing almost at the door. Turning back towards the sheds, he could see the torch, the beam illuminating the ground beneath the swing; beyond that, the sheds were cloaked in darkness. Keeping his back to the door and still watching the yard for any sign of movement, he raised an elbow, meaning to pound on the wood. The door swung inwards before he had the chance to knock.

Rodney stood in the doorway holding a shotgun, both barrels trained on him like huge dark tunnels. Harness lowered his firearm as Rodney stepped aside for him to enter.

"Did you see it?" Rodney still had the shotgun on his shoulder.

Harness closed the door and bolted it without speaking. Moving to the window, he looked out into the yard. When he was sure nothing was following, he turned to Rodney and took hold of the shotgun's barrels, pushing downwards so they were pointed at the floor.

"I want you to get Lisa and Annabel. I'm taking you to town."

"You saw it, didn't you?" Rodney asked.

"Yes." Harness nodded his head. "I saw it. I don't know what the fuck it is, but you can't stay here."

"What do you *think* it is?" Rodney asked, holding the shotgun at his side.

"Maggie said it's a demon." Harness knew how crazy it sounded even as he was saying it, but after what he'd just seen, he didn't care.

"Yeah. That sounds about right." Rodney's voice was husky. "I'll tell Lisa we're going."

Harness holstered his gun and followed Rodney into the lounge room where Lisa sat on the couch with Annabel curled up next to her. The woman and child were pale, their eyes wide. The sight of them reminded Harness of times when he'd given bad news to people in the middle of the night. They always had the same shell-shocked look on their faces. A look that came from the realisation that their world – the warm safe place they were used to – had been wiped away. If he could see his own expression, it would probably hold the same look of shock and terror.

When Rodney told his wife and daughter they were leaving, Lisa disentangled herself from Annabel so she could go upstairs and grab a few things. Before she went, Lisa kissed her daughter on top of the head.

"Be back in a minute." She rubbed the girl's arm as if reluctant to let her go.

Annabel nodded but didn't speak. While they waited, Harness moved around the room checking the windows. He noticed the wind had dropped, but saw no signs of movement.

Ten minutes later, the four of them left the house. Harness went first, the gun held at his side. Lisa followed, holding Annabel's hand. Rodney came last, carrying an overnight bag in one hand, the shotgun in the other. He pulled the door shut behind them before following Harness and the family to the squad car.

No one spoke while Harness turned on the motor, made a U-turn, and drove away from the house. After a few minutes, Annabel broke the silence.

"Did it touch you?" Her voice was small from the darkness of the back seat.

He could still hear the drumming, now pulsing inside his head. Still feel the demon's hot breath on his skin.

"No, it didn't touch me."

He didn't know why he lied. Maybe because his bones were aching and his skin burned like he'd been scaled. Or maybe he was afraid that when the creature breathed on him, its evil had contaminated him. Either way, Harness kept his gaze on the road, not wanting to look up and see the little girl's knowing eyes in the rear-view mirror.

Chapter Twenty-seven

Sitting at the kitchen table, a cup of coffee cradled in her hand, Maggie watched the window, waiting for the first rays of light. She checked her phone, listening to the dial tone echo in the empty house. He'd be at the Chapels' now. A small part of her still clung to the fading hope that Harness would find a little girl. A long shot, but no stranger than the alternative.

She'd spent most of her married life drowning in a sense of helplessness, and could feel the all too familiar waters of anxiety lapping at her thoughts. Her mind kept coming back to Prapti and the encounter in the café. The woman's threats weren't random, but specifically aimed at Harness. Was it possible he was walking into a trap? The more she thought about it, the more sense it made.

The Acheri shows up at the Chapels', hanging around long enough for Rodney to call Harness. The whole thing engineered to manoeuvre him into the creature's arms. And why the Chapels? The questions just kept piling up until she couldn't think straight.

She pushed the coffee away and slid her laptop across the table. If the phone was working, she'd be able to access the Internet. She turned on the computer, taking a few seconds to grab a notepad and pen from the drawer next to the sink while the screen came to life.

Hands poised over the keyboard, Maggie hesitated, not really sure what she hoped to find. "Simple is best." She spoke to the screen and typed the word *Acheri* into the search bar.

Almost forty-seven thousand hits. Maggie puffed out a breath and scrolled through the first page, finding a number of images, mostly drawings. She clicked on one, watching the stark etching fill the screen. In shades of grey and black, what looked like a half-naked skeletal creature with empty eyes and sharp teeth stood on a crudely drawn hill. Maggie clicked on the next image. This one was similar to the first, using the same colours and style of the previous drawing. Maggie guessed that both images were created by the same artist. Both renderings showed the same hideous face, only in the second image, the Acheri was depicted as a disembodied head floating over an isolated house.

Maggie stared at the image and couldn't help thinking of the Chapels' house. She'd been there once with Tess and Ollie for a barbeque. The home she'd visited was different to the one in the drawing, bigger and more modern, but just as lonely and isolated. Although only a drawing, the skull-like face managed to look knowing and cruel at the same time. She quickly clicked off the pictures and onto a site related to a book where the author claimed to have had a real-life encounter with an Acheri.

The site offered a few paragraphs of information and cited Zachary Chandler as the author. Maggie scanned through the information. According to Chandler, an Acheri was a demonic spirit that originated in both the eastern and western hemispheres.

Native American legend also included mention of the Acheri. Both Native American and Indian cultures believed that an Acheri was the result of a girl that died a horrible, untimely death. Once dead, the girl returned from the spirit world to torment others, mainly children. The Acheri sought to make her victims suffer as she did, resulting in their deaths. Japan also had a similar legend about a demon called Ju-On.

Maggie stopped reading, recalling something Manjula had said: *your people know of this demon*. Did Manjula mean Native Americans? Maggie scrawled the question on her notepad, intending to ask Manjula about it.

The next paragraph sent a shiver up Maggie's spine.

> *The creature will single out children as victims and poison them by casting its shadow over them. The very contact of the Acheri's shadow is like the breath of a person carrying a highly communicable disease; infection occurs instantly. The disease can take many forms and generally manifests as a mysterious wasting sickness that is ultimately fatal.*

The similarities between the article and what was happening in Thorn Tree were startling. As Maggie read the next part, panic gnawed at her gut.

> *She is known to sing and dance in human settlements, sometimes drumming. It is said that hearing her song is a sign of impending illness or death.*

During the dream – only a few nights ago, but already almost forgotten – Maggie was sure she heard drumming. The images came to her in misty snapshots. Someone chasing her while a drum beat out a rhythm. Did that mean she was going to get sick too? No, she felt fine, and until that changed, she refused to believe her fate was sealed. What she needed was answers. But so far, there was nothing about how to stop the demon.

She read the rest of the article, finding only one line that suggested wearing red or crimson could offer defence against the creature. It wasn't much, but better than nothing. Maggie wrote the word *red* on the notepad and underlined it. After a few wasted minutes looking for a way to contact the author, she gave up.

Maggie looked over her notes, writing *drumming* in the centre of the page. Staring at the word, she tapped a finger against her lips. When nothing clicked, she decided it was time for a break. More for something to do than out of hunger, she made herself a cup of coffee and a piece of toast. It was still dark, only the faint hint of light penetrating the blackness. The display on the microwave shifted to 5.15.

Not daring to sit outside before the sun came up, she took her coffee and toast into the lounge room. Nibbling the bread while the coffee sat untouched, she let herself think of Harness. Being with him was intense. The smart thing would be to take it slow, but with so much death and confusion, there seemed to be no time to waste. She wanted to be with him and had to believe he felt the same. Harness didn't strike her as the sort of man who played games. She knew in her gut that what had happened between them was real. But would it last? When things settled down, would their need for each other be as urgent? *Will we both survive this nightmare?*

Her eyes stung from lack of sleep, so she closed them and leaned back, trying to clear her mind of thoughts and questions. *Gautam.* The name clicked into her head like a neon sign over a bar. Maggie could almost hear Agnes's voice, loud and excited, loving the role of hostess. *Prapti Gautam, she's a writer.*

Maggie sat forward with a jolt as if caffeine had replaced the blood in her veins. She got up and went back to the laptop. The name gave her a place to start. She typed it into the search engine and waited. In less than a second she had a thousand hits for Prapti Gautam. It was clear that Prapti – or whoever she was – was using a name that, in India, was as common as Smith.

Maggie let her head fall into her hands. *Damn.* It was frustrating, but made sense. Prapti was dangerous, crazy even, but not stupid. The woman had all but admitted that she was connected to the deaths of eight people, so she'd have to be covering her tracks.

There had to be something else – something she was missing. Maggie grimaced and ran her finger in a line between her eyebrows. A will-o-the-wisp memory danced maddeningly just beyond her reach.

Her grandfather told her so many stories, things his father, Blue Hawk, had passed on to his children. One of his tales frightened her, so much so, she'd pushed it to the back of her mind. She couldn't shake the feeling that her grandfather's story had some significance. Frustrated, she stood up and went to the window. Blackness had turned to murky grey. Day and night were separated by a thin veil. *Veil.*

The word tripped along a series of images in her mind until another word – *handmaiden* – materialised. Maggie gazed out the window, not seeing the watery light hitting the trees, revealing rows of birds perched in silent lines. Her grandfather once told her a chilling tale about a woman who looked normal but was secretly working for an evil spirit. She had special powers given to her by the unholy creature. He explained that the spirit's handmaiden was like a witch's familiar and could act as a go-between for the human and the spirit world. As an eight-year-old, Maggie had been terrified by the idea that someone could look normal but be working for a witch. Witches and spirits all jumbled in her head, she'd had nightmares for months.

Back at the laptop, she tried searching *Demon's Familiar.* Bombarded with thousands of hits, Maggie spent the next hour jumping from site to site reading everything she could about legends that included familiars. Most sites were about witches and animal familiars, but there were a few that linked a human with a demon. Of those sites, she found some few similar beliefs.

Maggie made a list of the most common reoccurring elements attributed to a demon's familiar. After another half hour she'd compiled a list of four main characteristics: One, a familiar was a sort of demi-supernatural creature with some mystical powers. Two, they were thought to use their powers to spy on humans and wreak havoc for their demon. Three, they survived by drinking the blood of the demon they served, and four, probably the most disturbing yet, was the belief that the familiar was considered to be almost as dangerous as the demon it served.

Maggie stared at the list. She wasn't sure what to make of the blood drinking or supernatural powers, but the rest made sense. Prapti seemed to know about Maggie's movements, so it was easy to believe that she had been watching her. She thought about the scene she'd witnessed at the petrol station and decided that whether it was caused by Prapti or the Acheri, the fear spreading through town definitely qualified as havoc. Finally, there was her encounter with the woman. Remembering the way Prapti's eyes seemed to glow in the shadows, Maggie suppressed a shiver. Alone with the woman, Maggie felt a real and imminent threat, leaving her with no doubt Prapti was dangerous.

She read over her notes. After wading through pages of nonsense, she'd gleaned a few startling bits of information. Stories that mirrored what was happening in Thorn Tree too closely to be ignored. Satisfied with what she'd found, Maggie leaned back and stretched. Tiny particles drifted in the sunlight spilling through the kitchen window. She'd been so engrossed with the research that she hadn't noticed the sun had come up.

The microwave flashed 7.45.

"Shit!" Maggie reached for the phone. Time had gotten away from her. She needed to speak to Jackson, but her first priority was Harness. He'd said he'd come back when he was done. Whatever was going on at the Chapels' couldn't have taken this long. Something was wrong, she could feel it in the marrow of her bones.

About to call him, she hesitated. *Maybe last night didn't mean as much as I thought? Maybe it was just a way for him to take his mind off all the horror he's been through over the last few days?* Part of her almost welcomed the moment of self-doubt. Better to believe he was a selfish prick than accept the alternative – something had happened to him. Something bad enough to prevent him contacting her.

Maggie sent the call, her fingers shaking as she touched the screen. It felt like a lifetime before he answered.

"Hello?" His voice was barely a whisper.

"Ness, you okay?" Her voice was shaking as badly as her hands. For a second there was silence.

"I saw it." His usually deep voice sounded strange, almost breathless.

"The… Acheri?" She knew what he was talking about, but still had to ask. Had to know for certain.

"Yeah. It's real. Like something out of a fucking nightmare." The last part came out as a humourless laugh that turned into a cough.

"Ness?"

"I'm here."

"Did it touch you?" She closed her eyes, not really wanting to hear his reply.

"It breathed on me… In my face. Jesus, Maggie, I think I'm sick."

Maggie could hear the desperate edge he was trying to keep out of his voice. Her thoughts turned to Prapti – her warning. *Stay out of this. Go back to your house with the pretty red flowers and mind your own business. If you do as you are told, your boyfriend might live through the week.*

Even as she wondered if telling Harness about the Acheri had brought about what was happening to him, another thought occurred, but it was something she would need to ask Manjula about.

187

"Where are you?" she asked.

"At home, but it might be safer if you stayed away."

"I'm coming." She disconnected the call before he could argue.

Maggie tore the pages containing her notes off the pad and shoved them in her handbag along with her phone, then ran upstairs. Flinging open her wardrobe, she rummaged around on the top shelf until she found what she wanted. With a tug, the red silk scarf tumbled off the shelf, bringing a pile of jumpers along with it. Ignoring the mound of clothes, Maggie wrapped the scarf around her neck and tied it at her throat.

Next, she moved onto the landing, tearing open the linen cupboard door and pulling out sheets and towels until the walkway looked like a crime scene.

"Come on." She tossed a rolled-up rug over her shoulder, letting it flutter over the banister.

It took a few more seconds before she spotted the threadbare red towel. For once, ignoring household jobs like cleaning out the cupboards paid off. Slinging the towel over her shoulder, she headed downstairs. Maggie guessed Harness had a few more hours. He was stronger than the children and Maureen, so that gave him the advantage. Even so, there was no time to waste.

On her way to the car, she called Dr Cole. After a few rings, it went through to a recorded message, instructing callers to go to the emergency department of Mandurah District Hospital if in need of urgent help. Realising it was still too early for the surgery to be open, Maggie hung up and called the police station. Mark Leary answered on the second ring. Maggie wasn't sure how to explain so she just launched into it.

"This is Maggie Hawkbetter. I've just spoken to Senior Sergeant Gibson and he's sick. I've tried the doctor but the surgery isn't open. Can you get Dr Cole to Harness's house as soon as possible?"

"What? You want me to take the doctor to the sarge's house? I can't do that without—"

Maggie didn't have time to argue with the young constable. "Listen. Harness has what killed the kids." She put as much force as possible into her voice. "Don't argue with me, just do it!"

"Are you sure? How do you know? Maybe I should call Attwell?" He was still uncertain.

"I'm sure. I just spoke to the sergeant. You can call whoever you want *after* you get the doctor." Maggie tried not to drive the car off the road as she negotiated a bend.

"Okay." He hesitated. "I'll go now, but if the sarge—"

"Good. I'll be there in ten minutes." Maggie ended the call before Leary could ask any more questions.

Maggie tossed the phone onto the passenger seat and put her foot down. Eight minutes later, she pulled up in front of Harness's house, noticing a car parked behind his Jeep. Scrawny-looking crows dotted the front lawn, their feathers almost green in the sunlight. Maggie leaped out of the car and jogged to the front door. It was open, Constable Leary standing just inside, shoulders and head down. A breath, sharp and cold, caught in Maggie's throat. She was too late. Prapti warned her to keep Harness out of this. Why hadn't she listened?

Leary must have heard her enter. "You were right. He *is* sick. The doctor's with him now."

She tried to respond, but couldn't drag her eyes away from the man's mouth, watching his lips move up and down trying to sort out what he was telling her.

Harness is still alive.

Maggie's eyes blurred and her heartbeat slowed as her body caught up with her mind. Still not quite able to speak, she pushed past Leary and headed towards the rear of the house. She'd never been inside Harness's home and realised she had no idea where his bedroom was.

Leary stopped her with a hand on her arm.

"Better let the doctor finish seeing him first."

His voice was gentle, but Maggie had the urge to slap the young constable. Instead, she let her eyes travel from his hand, still clamped on her arm, to his face.

The young man blushed and quickly removed his grip. She wanted to see Harness for herself, let him know she was here, but stopped herself.

"I called the doc on my way here. He came straight over," Leary said, looking relieved that Maggie was doing as he asked.

"How did Harness look?"

"I only saw him for a second, but sort of like he has a bad case of the flu. The doctor told me to stay out of the room so I backed up pretty fast."

He paused looking down at his shoes. Maggie felt a wave of pity for the young officer. He couldn't be more than twenty-two and had probably seen a lot of dead children over the past few days. Now his boss was sick and on top of everything, he had her charging in like a madwoman.

She searched for something comforting to say, but came up blank. They both knew it was more serious than the flu. After a few moments of awkward silence, Dr Cole appeared in the hallway dressed in a shirt and tie. He must have been getting ready to open the surgery when the call came through. He walked towards Maggie and Leary, pulling his phone out of his pocket.

"It looks the same as the other cases." His voice was tired. "Are you his um..." He looked at Maggie and let his voice trail off.

"I'm his friend." Maggie held the doctor's gaze.

He nodded and continued. "I'm going to call Mary and get her to bring a few things over so I can get him on a drip. I've given him an antiviral injection that may help—"

"Shouldn't he be in a hospital?" Maggie asked.

"Yes, he should, but he's refused to go." Cole's tone went from tired to irritable before turning away and using his phone.

Maggie waited long enough to hear him talking to his wife before she headed towards the bedroom. Cole must have noticed what she was doing. He reacted fast, grabbing her shoulder just before she reached the door.

"You shouldn't go in there. He's contagious," Cole whispered, trying to steer her away.

Maggie jerked out of his grip.

"You're not stopping me."

She tried to keep her voice even, resisting the urge to scream in the doctor's face. Whatever was happening to Harness had nothing to do with the man's understanding of diseases.

"I can't risk anyone else getting infected," Cole continued. "As it is, I should be quarantining Leary." He nodded to the constable, who was listening to the exchange from his position near the front door. Leary's face was the colour of wet newspaper, his hand hovering over the cuffs dangling from his belt.

Maggie eased herself out of the doctor's grip. It was no use trying to explain what was really going on. If she started talking about demons, she'd probably find herself handcuffed to the nearest chair.

"I understand." She let the words out slowly, hoping she sounded calm. "But I've already been exposed." She could see Leary relaxing, but Cole still looked dubious. "I... I was with Harness last night."

Leary turned and seemed intent on examining the doorframe, a burst of colour now filling his cheeks. The doctor nodded. She couldn't tell if he accepted her reasoning or didn't have the energy to argue, but he stepped away from the door and let her pass.

Maggie opened the bedroom door, noticing the scent of something sharp in the air. Harness was slumped, half-sitting in the middle of a queen-size bed. His breathing was loud and heavy as if he were sleeping. As she approached the bed, she was startled by the change in his appearance. His cheeks were slightly sunken and his skin, tanned and healthy-looking only hours before, was now pallid with an absence of colour save a bluish tint to his lips.

Maggie closed her eyes, willing herself to remain composed. When she opened then, Harness was looking at her.

"You look nice." He sounded sleepy.

Not trusting herself to speak, she forced a smile and took his hand. His skin felt cold against hers, his fingers limp. His hand was twice the size of hers. She held it gently, rubbing his palm.

"That's nice." His voice was thick as if he were on the verge of sleep.

"You need to go to the hospital, Ness."

It was as if her words jolted him out of a dream. He pulled his hand away and sat up.

"I'm not going anywhere. Not while that thing is still out there." The last word caught in his throat, setting off a bout of coughing. "The doctor gave me an injection." He wiped at his mouth. "Once I get some fluids, I'm going back out there and stopping it like I should have done last night."

Maggie watched him struggle to stay upright, his breathing rapid and laboured. She didn't want to risk getting him more agitated.

"Okay. You're right. I'm going to go see Agnes and find out where Prapti lives, then I'll come back and we'll decide what to do. Okay?"

Her words had the desired effect. He relaxed and sank back into the pillows. She watched him for another minute until his breathing evened out. Leaning over, she pressed her lips to his forehead. His skin felt clammy and feverish against her mouth. She was about to straighten up when he spoke in a thick, dreamy voice.

"Be careful, Maggie… I love you."

Maggie kissed him again. "I love you, Ness." But when she stood, he was already asleep.

Chapter Twenty-eight

At almost 9.30, the sun was shining in a cloudless sky, promising an Indian summer that might stretch as far as April. Maggie pulled up in front of Agnes's monstrosity of a house and swiped her arm across her forehead. Leaving Harness had been agonising. Not knowing if he'd last until she returned almost paralysed her. But time was running out, she could feel it, the dread clinging to her like the sweat covering her face and neck. With every minute that passed, the Acheri's poison worked its way further into Harness's body.

The garage door was down, making it impossible to tell if Agnes was home. Maggie snatched a quick look around, noting the empty street before stepping out of the car. There were more crows, lines of them standing sentinel along the sharp edges of the modern structure. She couldn't recall ever seeing so many crows. Over the last few days, they'd been everywhere she turned, *almost as if...* She stopped walking and gazed up at the birds. *Almost as if they're watching.* Perhaps sensing her discomfort, the creatures stopped moving, their beady eyes trained on her. Was she becoming paranoid? Seeing spectres everywhere? She didn't think so.

Maggie hurried towards the front door, handbag clutched to her side. She couldn't shake the feeling that the birds were watching – waiting. But the certainty that Agnes was connected to Prapti and the Acheri pushed her on. Agnes had introduced Prapti as a travel writer, indicating she had some knowledge of what the woman was doing in Thorn Tree. Then there was the mayor's strange behaviour at the town meeting. Maybe Maggie was grasping at air, but she was sure Agnes was the key to finding Prapti *and* the demon. What she'd do when she found them depended largely on Manjula, and what she could tell Maggie about stopping the demon.

She pressed the doorbell, listening to its chime echo inside the building. After a slight pause she pressed the bell again, then knocked on one of the glass panels decorating the double-door entry. Nothing. If the mayor was home, she wasn't answering.

She stopped knocking and waited a few seconds before stepping back and surveying the front of the house. Her eyes landed on the stone bench in the front garden where she and Harness had sat on Saturday night, now home to two crows. The house had been lit up with thousands of fairy lights, the place alive with music and voices. Maggie thought about the party and realised that she'd never been to Agnes's house for any other reason *but* a party; nor had she ever entered through the front door – guests always came through the side gate and used the bathroom in the pool house.

Sticking close to the building, Maggie slipped across the front yard. She took a quick look around to make sure no one was watching. *No one human.* Then she opened the gate and walked through to the rear of the property.

She hadn't planned on breaking into Agnes's place, but now Maggie decided it might be the only way to get the information she needed. She didn't have Agnes's number stored in her mobile and she wasn't prepared to waste time trying to track her down. Her gut told her she'd find the answers she needed inside the mayor's house.

Maggie moved along the side of the house, looking for an easy way in. Just before the building ended and opened up to the backyard and pool area, she spotted a single glass-panelled door, most likely the laundry exit. She jerked the handle, not surprised to find it locked. Maggie cursed and looked around.

Her only option was to break in. She thought of Harness. If she backed out now, he didn't stand a chance.

"Okay. I can do this." It occurred to her that burglars didn't usually have conversations with themselves when they were trying to be stealthy. The thought almost made her laugh, more with nervous energy than amusement.

She scanned the area, looking for something heavy to break one of the door's glass panels. A garden bed ran along the side fence filled with dark purple petunias, the earth held in place by a row of white rocks. Maggie grabbed for one, and after a slight struggle, managed to pull it out of the earth.

The rock was about as big as her fist and weighty. Pulse racing and hands sweaty, she hit the rock against the panel nearest the door handle. Glass exploded, shattering with a stark *crash* that cut through the mid-morning tranquillity like a thunderclap. Maggie waited a few seconds, half-expecting to hear angry shouts from the neighbours. When nothing happened, she let out a breath and put her hand through the broken pane, careful to avoid the shards. Her fingers found a small lever which she clicked, unlocking the door.

A jolt of fear mixed with excitement sent a not altogether unpleasant ripple through her stomach. Maggie snatched a quick look back at the gate before entering the house. *I'm actually breaking into someone's house!* Her shoes crunched on the broken glass as she made her way through the laundry room. It was a large house, but surely if Agnes was home, she'd have heard the noise by now. *What if she did hear me and is calling the police?* Leary's face came to mind. With the havoc spreading through town, Maggie doubted a burglary would be his first priority.

Just to be safe, she turned and untucked her T-shirt, using it to wipe the door handle. The laundry room led into a spotless kitchen, gleaming with stainless steel appliances that looked untouched by human hands. There was an odour in the air, something floral mixed with another scent, maybe cleaning products.

She moved farther into the house, looking for an office or study where Agnes might keep phone numbers or records. She entered a large sitting and entertainment room decorated with white furnishings and cream walls. It was hard to imagine Agnes sitting in this house relaxing, watching a movie or reading.

It occurred to Maggie that she knew very little about the mayor of Thorn Tree. She'd often talk to her at fêtes and various other town events, and of course there were the parties, but she didn't know the woman on a personal level. She'd heard rumours about the woman's husband. Loretta Vernhouse, the woman who ran the gift shop on Prosperity Street, went to school with the man. She'd once told Maggie in a stage whisper that Agnes had killed her husband. A fact Loretta swore everyone knew but could never prove. Maggie didn't know if she believed Agnes was a murderer, but there was something about the woman she didn't like. The mayor was always polite, friendly even, but there was an empty quality to her that reminded Maggie of an old toothpaste commercial – all fake smiles and brittle chalk. *Yet here I am creeping about Agnes's empty house about to go through her personal belongings like a thief.* Maggie felt another little shiver. She wondered what that said about her as a person, but decided to leave the self-analysis for another day.

At the far end of the sitting room stood a staircase and another hallway. Maggie decided to head towards the hallway and check upstairs last. As she moved through the room, she kept her eyes on the stairs, watching and listening for any sign of movement. Maggie's right foot hit the leg of the coffee table. The blow knocked the table forward, displacing a glass statue. The heavy piece rolled off the table and bounced onto the thick carpet with an audible *thud*.

Maggie sucked in a breath and froze.

Then she heard a voice, "Please!" The sound was more a wheeze than a word.

Maggie turned back to the kitchen, intending to make a run for the laundry.

"Please, help me!"

Something in the voice, desperation, was so clear, it made Maggie stop. It had to be Agnes. *If she thinks I'm a burglar, she might be pleading with me to leave.* The thought of trying to explain herself to Leary or worse, spend hours at the police station, got Maggie moving. Almost reaching the kitchen, another sound echoed through the house, this time stopping her in her tracks. Coughing, wet and harsh. Realisation struck her. Agnes was sick, that's why she didn't answer the door or come to investigate the sound of breaking glass.

Without realising it, her fingers touched the red scarf tied at her throat. She was right about one thing, Agnes *had* been in contact with the demon. Maggie backtracked, heading through the sitting room.

"Agnes? It's Maggie. Where are you?" She entered the hall, not sure which direction to take.

"Please..."

Maggie followed the voice, noticing an unpleasant acidic aroma hanging in the air. The white walls and pale floors seemed stark, more like an abandoned hospital than a home. Another moan led her to an open doorway where Agnes lay sprawled on the floor. Spotting Maggie in the doorway, the mayor attempted to raise herself on one scrawny elbow, a string of white foam hanging from the corner of her mouth. Maggie grimaced and resisted the urge to back away.

"It's okay, Agnes." She tried to sound reassuring, but stepping around a pool of yellow vomit, it was all Maggie could do not to gag.

Agnes grabbed the leg of Maggie's jeans, her nails rasping on the thick fabric. Maggie wanted to pull away, but instead leaned down and grasped Agnes under the arms.

"I'm going to stand you up, but you need to help me," Maggie said, trying to ignore the pungent smell of urine mixed with whiskey-soaked vomit.

Agnes gave a pained moan which Maggie took for a yes.

The mayor wasn't a large woman; her small stature made Maggie's job a little easier as she struggled to pull the woman to her feet. It took a few attempts, but Maggie finally got her up.

They stood for a moment while Maggie positioned Agnes's arm around her neck and put her own arm around the woman's waist.

"I'm going to walk you through to the sitting room. Okay?"

"Yes." The word came out in a rush of sickly-smelling breath.

At a halting pace, it took almost five minutes to reach the sitting room. By the time Maggie sat Agnes on one of the white couches, both women were drenched in sweat.

Maggie made sure Agnes was seated securely and then hurried into the kitchen to get her a glass of water. When she returned, Agnes was still sitting up, which Maggie took as a good sign. She offered Agnes the glass, but it quickly became clear that she was too weak and shaky to hold it herself. Maggie held the glass to Agnes's lips and watched with a mixture of pity and disgust as she sucked down the liquid.

"Don't drink it too fast, Agnes; you might vomit," Maggie warned.

When the mayor finished drinking, Maggie put the glass down on the floor. Instead of phoning for help or sitting on the couch, Maggie positioned herself on the coffee table directly in front of the woman. She leaned forward so their knees were almost touching. Agnes's eyes were closed as if she was drifting off to asleep. Somewhere in the huge house, a clock ticked.

Maggie thought of Harness, his skin bleached of colour, almost translucent, and his eyes ringed with dark smudges. A flicker of anger swallowed up any pity she felt for the woman. Maggie was certain the mayor was involved with Prapti and the deaths of all the children. As far as she was concerned, that made Agnes as guilty as the demon.

She tapped Agnes on her left knee, but the woman's eyes remained closed.

"Where's Prapti?" Maggie snapped off the words, her voice loud and flat.

Agnes's eyes blinked open and rolled up to Maggie's face. The whites of the woman's eyes were tinged with yellow, the colour matching the splashes of vomit staining her nightie. She regarded Maggie blankly, making no attempt to answer. Maggie searched her mind, trying to decide what her next move should be when Agnes spoke.

"Call an ambulance. I need to get to the hospital. Can't you see how sick I am?" Agnes's voice was breathless, but still carried the same *I'm in charge here* tone she used at town meetings.

"No." Maggie let the word hang in the air, watching the defiance run out of the mayor's sickly face. She needed answers and didn't intend to waste time playing games.

"Tell me where Prapti is or I'll pull the phone out of the wall, throw your mobile in the pool. I'll lock the doors when I leave, you'll be dead before anyone finds you."

Maggie felt a ripple of grim satisfaction as the mayor winced in fear. Outside of disgust and anger, Maggie realised she felt nothing for the woman. She'd made the threat hoping to scare Agnes into spilling her guts, but now the words were out, Maggie knew she was more than capable of leaving the woman to die, just like Eddie had died before he'd had the chance to experience his first laugh. The realisation should have frightened her but, once more, she felt nothing but anger. Maggie waited, letting her words sink in before continuing.

"I think you know all about Prapti and what she's doing in Thorn Tree. *And* I think you know exactly where she's hiding."

Maggie paused, keeping her gaze fixed on Agnes's face. Just for an instant, something flickered in the old woman's eyes. It could have been guilt or maybe just a trick of the light, but Maggie took it as a crack in the woman's resolve. She stood.

"Suit yourself." Maggie shrugged, ready to turn away.

"I didn't." When Agnes finally spoke, her voice was thick, halting, as if her throat was constricted. "I didn't hurt anyone."

Maggie supposed she should feel sympathy for the mayor. Anyone willing to sell out their friends and neighbours for a few dollars or whatever Prapti used to buy Agnes's compliance deserved pity. But instead, Maggie wanted to shake her until the old woman's bulging eyes rolled around like marbles.

"Just tell me where she is."

"There's an old... shearer's cottage... on... a dirt... road." Agnes paused, struggling for each breath. "It's off... Knoll Road. Goes up... to the hills—"

A savage coughing spell cut off her words. Maggie watched unmoved as Agnes wrapped her frail arms around her body as if trying to hold herself together. After a minute or so the hacking subsided to short gurgles. Maggie picked up the glass and held it to Agnes's lips. She took a small sip and then pushed Maggie's hand away with less strength than a kitten.

"I'm going to call Dr Cole now and tell him you need help." Maggie picked up her bag, preparing to leave.

"No… An ambulance. I need to get to the hospital." Agnes let her head tip back against the couch.

Maggie held the phone. She had the information. It would be easy to just turn her back and leave the mayor to die. *God knows she deserves it*. In that moment, Maggie saw herself leaving the house, driving away without a backward glance. No one would ever know what she'd done. *I'll know*. Would a moment's satisfaction be worth the remorse? In the end it was the realisation that she *wouldn't* feel remorse that convinced her to make the call. The cold, empty void in her heart would be worse than guilt.

Dr Cole answered instead of Mary, explaining that his wife was still with Harness. She told him why she was calling and relayed Agnes's request for an ambulance. Before hanging up, Maggie walked into the kitchen so Agnes wouldn't hear her.

"How's he doing?" She gripped the phone, not sure she wanted to hear the answer.

"He seems to have improved a bit, but he really should be in the hospital. If you are… um, close to him, you should try to convince him to go in the ambulance with Agnes. He might listen to you."

"I can't. I've got something I have to do."

It sounded lame and selfish, but how could she explain what she didn't really understand herself?

"Oh… yes. Well, I just thought… never mind." He sounded anything but understanding.

"Dr Cole, I think I know what's causing all this and I'm going to try to stop it. If you don't hear from me by tonight, tell Leary and Attwell to search the old shearer's cottage off Knoll Road." Maggie was about to hang up when the doctor's voice stopped her.

"I think I know what you're talking about. Harness has been saying things… About a demon child. He said it breathed on him. Is that what all this is about?"

Maggie was surprised by the question. She couldn't tell if he believed any of it or not. But what did she have to lose by telling him?

"Yes. It is. You don't have to believe it, just send the police if you don't hear from me by the time it gets dark." She waited, but he didn't respond. "Please, Dr Cole?"

"Yes. I'll send them," he said, and hung up.

Maggie walked back into the sitting room.

"I'll leave the front door open for the doctor and ambulance." She was on her way to the front of the house when Agnes spoke.

"She'll kill you." It was a statement, not a warning.

Maggie paused, about to say something smart, but the retort died on her lips.

"You might be right."

Chapter Twenty-nine

She could feel the woman's fury growing and with it her strength. She would be an admirable adversary, but she, like many others before her, would perish. Prapti had sensed Maggie's strength and powerful spirit that first night at the party. She thought of Agnes, but the image was fleeting and of no importance. Agnes was unworthy of the great honour that had been bestowed upon her. She was an unclean spirit who was useful for ensuring the safety of the Devi, but now her usefulness had come to an end.

Prapti's thoughts turned to the Devi – she felt the familiar rush of anticipation. Soon their work here would be complete and the Devi would allow Prapti to drink her sacred blood. Blood that was Shakti, divine and most powerful. It gave Prapti strength and knowledge. It filled her and nourished her as it had done for many lifetimes.

Prapti stepped out of her clothes and stood naked before the altar. She ran her hands over her breasts and closed her eyes. The first time she'd tasted the dark blood of the Devi she'd been a child herself, alone and abandoned to sleep in the filthy lanes of her village.

She ran her hands over her abdomen, raking her nails across the scarred skin. Her days and nights were filled with hunger and misery, begging for scraps and offering herself to anyone with food or a few coins to spare. When a terrible plague swept through the village and the children began to die, Prapti believed it would soon be her turn to perish. The thought brought comfort.

One night, as she lay huddled in a doorway, the song of the Devi called to her with its dark sweetness. That night she'd walked out of her village and up into the hills where the Devi waited to embrace her. She drank the blood of the Goddess and was reborn. The Devi was her saviour and together they had travelled the world.

The Devi had many names: Demon, Acheri, even Devil. The simple-minded people who gave her these names knew nothing about her glory. She was the Devi, *the Goddess* – she brought balance to the world.

Prapti moved her hips back and forth, anticipating the thrill of the Devi's powerful blood washing over her mouth and face. With Prapti's help, the Devi would rid the world of the ones who would bring about change and hope. The children with a special light in their souls were dangerous to the delicate balance that kept the world from straining to be more than it should.

Prapti opened her eyes and looked at the altar. Tonight, the Devi would visit the little girl that had brought them to this place. Now that they were out of their red-lined house, there would be nothing to stop the Goddess from finishing her work. Prapti continued to caress herself until she sank to her knees before the altar. Eyes glazed and teeth bared, she let out a cry of ecstasy.

Chapter Thirty

She parked the car on the road at the front of the house and hurried up the walkway. As soon as Jackson opened the door, Maggie could tell he'd been crying. Instead of apologising for turning up without calling, she gripped his arm.

"What's wrong?"

"Gran died," he said flatly, stepping aside for Maggie to enter.

She followed Jackson, mind reeling as he led her through to the kitchen. He slumped into a chair. The house was silent save for the distant cry of birds. Maggie sat without being asked and reached across the table to take Jackson's hand. Questions tumbled around in her mind, but she waited, giving him time to gather himself.

"Last night, after I spoke to you, she seemed a bit tired... She gets like that sometimes." He shrugged and continued. "While Dad was watching TV, Gran and I, we talked for a while. She went to bed at her usual time." The muscles in his face twitched as if he was struggling to control his emotions. "When she didn't come out for breakfast, Dad went to check on her." His voice wavered and he looked down at Maggie's hand holding his.

Maggie squeezed it and waited.

"She just went to sleep and never woke up."

"I'm so sorry, Jackson. I know you were close to your gran." She wanted to comfort him but didn't know what else to say.

Before either of them could speak again, Jackson's father appeared in the doorway. He looked at Maggie, but didn't really see her. He was tall and skinny with slightly stooped shoulders, an older version of Jackson only darker. His hair was dishevelled, eyes red and puffy. He'd missed a button when putting on his shirt, giving his body a lopsided appearance.

"Oh. I thought it was the doctor." As he spoke, his gaze drifted towards the conservatory.

"No, Dad. It's Maggie. You know, from work."

Jackson's father reached across the table and offered Maggie his hand. She didn't know what to do, so she shook it, noticing the distinctive odour of tobacco.

"Thanks for coming. Um... do you want a cup of tea or something?"

Maggie suddenly realised that he thought she'd come to pay her respects. She could feel herself blushing with embarrassment. She was grateful when Jackson intervened.

"I'll make it. Why don't you go and lie down until the doctor gets here?"

He stood up and put the kettle on to boil. His father nodded and turned to leave, but then stopped and looked back at Maggie.

"She was talking about you last night. She really liked you. It would mean a lot to her that you're here." He seemed to be about to say something else, but his eyes clouded over as if he were lost in thought.

"I'm sorry for your loss." The same words she had given Jackson. They seemed so meaningless.

He nodded and then left Maggie and Jackson alone in the kitchen.

She looked towards the conservatory where she'd sat with Manjula only yesterday, remembering the old lady's kind smile and warm hands, wishing they'd met sooner – that she'd had more time with the woman. As it was, all they'd talked about was the Acheri, and Maggie felt that she'd missed the chance to get to know someone special. Another reason to despise Prapti and the evil she'd brought to Thorn Tree.

Jackson abandoned the tea and came and sat back down.

"Why did you come, Maggie?"

She was surprised by his sudden change of direction but plunged in. "I needed to ask Manjula more about the Acheri."

Jackson nodded. "Yesterday when she woke up from her nap, she seemed fine. She didn't really eat anything, but I thought she was just tired. She talked about you. She said she was worried. Worried because she knew you were going to try to stop the Acheri." He looked towards the conservatory before continuing.

"She must have known something was happening to her because she made me promise I'd tell you something." He hesitated, looking down at his hands. Maggie could tell he was trying to compose himself, so she waited.

When he looked up, his eyes were shiny.

"She told me that there might be a way to stop the Acheri. She said the answer came back to her in a dream. She dreamed she was a little girl and she heard her mother talking about it the night they left Naghar. I just wish I'd listened more carefully, but I told her not to wear herself out... I said we could talk about it tomorrow." He ran his hand over his eyes in frustration.

"Jackson, I know this is difficult, but what exactly did she say about the Acheri?" Maggie asked, trying to be gentle with her questions. She could see Jackson was doing his best and badgering him wouldn't help him remember.

"Something about a red... mantle? Yeah, that's it. She said you needed to find a vaidya and use her mantle to destroy the Acheri."

Maggie frowned. She had no idea what he was talking about.

"Do *you* know what any of that means?"

"Sorry." He shook his head. "I was going to ask her to explain it to me today. Sometimes she lapsed back into Hindi when she was tired, so I let it go..." His voice trailed off.

Maggie thought for a moment and then asked him if Manjula mentioned a stranger in her village. A woman that was new to the area, but Jackson shook his head.

"Just the thing about the red mantle. She said you had the heart of a lion and would know what to do." He gave an embarrassed laugh.

Maggie nodded and tried to think.

"Does your father smoke?" she asked.

"Yes." Jackson was clearly surprised by the question.

"Can I have one?"

"Um... yeah. I can get you one. I just didn't think you smoked."

"I don't... I mean, I haven't for about ten years, but right now I need one."

Maggie stared out at the conservatory. Manjula's old leather armchair sat as a painful reminder of its owner's absence. Even if she knew what she was supposed to do, which she didn't, would she have the courage to do it? Was she the right person for all this?

A few minutes later, Jackson returned to the kitchen with a packet of cigarettes and a lighter. Maggie thanked him and asked if it was all right if she went outside through the conservatory to smoke one. Jackson shrugged and nodded, but Maggie could tell the boy disapproved.

"Jackson, would your dad know what a vada is?"

"Vaidya," he corrected. "He doesn't speak Hindi, but maybe. You go smoke, I'll ask him."

When she was outside, Maggie took a cigarette out of the packet and lit it using Mr Palmer's Zippo. She took a long drag. The smoke hit the back of her throat and a rush of dizziness filled her head. Time was ticking away, and the longer she waited, the sicker Harness would get. But with Manjula gone, she didn't know what to do next. *Mantle.* The word could have a number of meanings. Until she knew what vaidya meant, it was impossible to know one way or another.

She'd been running on adrenalin since early morning, pinning all her hopes on Manjula's knowledge. Now all she had was a cryptic message and no time to decipher it. Exhausted and empty, Maggie blew out a cloud of smoke, watching it drift across the backyard.

The news of the old lady's death hit her hard, snatching away any hopes of stopping whatever was killing Harness. Manjula thought she had the heart of a lion, but the old lady was wrong. Maggie was afraid. Afraid to act and afraid to run away. When her marriage ended, she ran. So scared of facing everyone, she'd left Perth and made a big show of starting a new life when really, she was just hiding from her old life.

Face to face with Prapti at the café, she'd been almost too scared to move. How the hell had she convinced herself she was going to take the woman on *and* face a supernatural creature with the powers of a walking plague? Her hands were shaking even thinking about it.

She took another drag of the cigarette, nervously flicking the lighter open and closed in the opposite hand. Her options were little to none. She could do nothing and let Harness die. Annabel would probably be next, followed by God knew who else. There was no way of telling how many people would die before the creature was done with Thorn Tree. Or, Maggie thought as she stubbed out the cigarette, she could drive out to Knoll Road and confront Prapti, probably get herself killed. Whichever way she looked at it, the future was bleak.

The back door creaked open. Maggie turned to see Jackson approaching.

"Have you decided what you're going to do?"

"What do you mean?" Maggie asked, knowing full well what he meant.

"About the Acheri? Whatever it is, I want to help."

Maggie's first instinct was to refuse. The last thing she wanted was for anyone else to get hurt, but could she protect him? Jackson was young, but there was a glint of determination in his eyes that made her wonder if he was tougher than he looked. She knew she couldn't do it alone, and more importantly, she trusted him.

He continued as if sensing her reluctance. "My gran lost her friend to this thing. I'm not going to let that happen to me."

Maggie felt tears sting her eyes. She really had underestimated him. He was a good man *and* a good friend.

"What about your father? You can't leave him alone with... with your gran?"

"It's okay. I just rang Mary again and she said Dr Cole is on his way. She's going to look after his patients until he gets back."

"Did you ask him about vaidya?"

"Yeah. He knew right away. I can't believe I didn't recognise the word. Gran was always going on about it."

He smiled and shook his head at the memory.

Maggie listened with growing excitement. She suddenly saw things very clearly, and a plan started to form in her mind. She looked down at the lighter in her hand and had another idea.

"Jackson." She cut him off mid-sentence. Maggie held up the lighter. "Does your dad have more fluid for this?"

Chapter Thirty-one

Maggie glanced right then left before tearing through the stop sign. She looked over at Jackson, surprised at how unfazed he looked by her driving. They needed to make a few stops before heading out to Knoll Road, and with every new piece of information, time slipped away.

"Jackson, call Mary now and tell her what we need."

Jackson nodded and made the call. Maggie listened as he explained what they wanted. She was impressed by the way he handled himself, explaining their unusual request. While she'd always liked him, she'd also viewed him as shy and eager to please. Maybe he was those things, but she'd realised he was also calm and stoic. Qualities she suspected he'd inherited from his grandmother. If he were ten years older and she didn't have Harness in her life... She left the thought unfinished.

Jackson ended the call. "It took a bit of manoeuvring, but she's going to have it ready for us."

"Wow. You can be very convincing. I'm going to take you with me every time I go demon hunting." In spite of everything they both laughed, lifting the tension.

Maggie pulled up in front of the surgery at 11.30.

"I'll go in," she said. "You know what to get, right?"

"Yes. If the hardware shop's not open, I'll go around the back and knock until Phil lets me in. Won't be long." He trotted off towards the shops, head up, shoulders back. She wondered if he was as unafraid as he appeared.

Maggie left the car and jogged towards the entrance, stopping to read the sign taped to the door: *Flu Centre*.

The sign was written in red pen. It put her in mind of something she'd read about the bubonic plague and how a red X was painted on sufferers' doors. In spite of the heat, the sweat on her neck turned cold. She guessed the sign was designed to keep everyone else away, limit the chances of spreading the sickness. She wondered what people would do if they knew the sickness wasn't spread in the usual ways. Maybe it was better that they didn't know it was a plague that sought out victims with a deliberateness unseen in any normal virus. She could imagine the panic if people knew they couldn't protect themselves from a new type of Black Death.

Maggie pushed open the door to the surgery, surprised to see the waiting room empty.

"They're too scared to come, in case they catch something," Mary said from the reception desk.

"Oh. It's probably the smart thing to do, but–"

"You don't think it matters." Mary finished the thought for her. Her usually easy-going smile was replaced by a drawn, tired expression. Maggie could only imagine what the woman had witnessed.

"Dr Cole told you what I'm doing?"

"Yes. Tony told me."

Maggie braced herself, expecting Mary to call her crazy, maybe give her a tongue-lashing for making up ridiculous stories during a time of emergency.

"I've been a nurse for over thirty years. I've worked in emergency rooms, prisons and even in a mental health facility. I've seen a lot of misery. *And* death. I've learned to keep an open mind." She paused and looked around the empty waiting room. "This isn't a flu outbreak – not like

212

any I've ever seen. It's something... sinister. If you can do anything to stop it, do it soon, before more children die."

Maggie couldn't hide her surprise. She'd expected Mary to scoff at the notion of supernatural forces. A week ago Maggie herself would have done just that. But one thing was clear: the events of the last few days had blurred the line dividing dark and light. It seemed, like Maggie, Mary felt the line wavering.

"Do you have it?" Maggie asked.

"Yes. I haven't even looked at it since the nineties." Mary reached under the desk and lifted the black plastic bag towards Maggie. "I don't know how it will help, but I hope it does."

Maggie took the bag and thanked her. Before she left, she turned back.

"How is he?" She didn't use his name, afraid she'd break down.

"Harness? He's strong. He'll hang on as long as he can." Mary gave her an encouraging smile and stood up. "I'm going over to check on him, I'll walk out with you."

The two women left the surgery. Maggie waited while Mary locked the door, then, just before they parted, Maggie pulled the woman into a hug. It was a quick one-armed embrace that took Mary by surprise. She responded by patting Maggie on the back.

"Thank you for looking after him." Maggie let the woman go and jogged back to the car before Mary could see her tears.

She sat behind the wheel, grateful for a moment to be alone before Jackson returned. He'd been strong and steadfast up until now, but he'd just lost his grandmother. Maggie couldn't afford to let her emotions rub off on him. She grabbed a tissue out of her bag and watched Mary as she began the short walk to Harness's house.

More than anything she wanted to be with Harness, holding his hand so he'd know he wasn't alone. But she'd set a path for herself; if she stopped now, he'd die. Of that she was certain. For the first time since she'd made the decision to stop the Acheri or die trying, she let the truth creep into her mind. She wasn't doing any of this for the children of Thorn Tree. Her reasons weren't noble like Jackson's, they were selfish. *I want to save Harness, that's all that really matters.* And worse, she was willing to risk Jackson's life and anyone else's who could help. She looked at her reflection in the rear-view mirror and wondered if she was really any better than Agnes.

The sound of the boot slamming brought her out of her reverie. Jackson came around the car and hopped in.

"Okay. I got them. Did you see Mary?" He turned to look at Maggie and stopped. "What's wrong? Did something happen with Mary?" he asked, taking in her tear-stained face.

"No... She had it for me. Everything's okay. It's just Harness... You know Sergeant Gibson, he's sick."

Jackson hesitated for a second. "Sorry. I didn't know that you and he were... um... you know..." His voice was tight. He looked away, avoiding her gaze.

Maggie wondered if he was angry because she hadn't told him about Harness sooner. Maybe he realised she wasn't a heroine trying to save the town, just a selfish woman hell-bent on saving the man she loved. They drove in a stilted silence for a few minutes. She thought of trying to explain, but what was there to say? They both had their reasons for risking their lives, what difference did it make?

Jackson was the first to speak. "So, where are we going?"

"If we're going to do this, we'll need help."

* * *

Ten minutes later Maggie pulled into Doug Loggie's driveway and turned the car off. His ute was parked under the carport. As they approached the front door, Maggie noticed the lasagne and note were gone, which she took as a good sign.

"I don't know about this," Jackson said, standing back from the door to let Maggie knock. "Do you think he'll believe us?"

She'd been wondering the same thing. Doug was a good friend; she hoped telling him her crazy story wouldn't ruin that. "We'll soon see."

They heard sounds from inside the house, the echo of footsteps. When Doug finally opened the door, Maggie's heart sank. He was dishevelled, unshaved and bleary-eyed. White hair standing up like fluffy horns as though he'd been sleeping, the odour of tobacco and whiskey clung to him like a second skin.

"Oh. Hello, Maggie, Jackson." He ran his fingers through his hair, trying to make himself more presentable.

"Hi, Doug. How are you doing?" Maggie realised it was a stupid question even as she asked it.

"I've been better. Thanks for the food and the note. Sorry I didn't answer the door, but I was sleeping," he said and looked over her shoulder as if something in the distance had caught his attention.

"I understand."

The bags under his eyes told a different story; it didn't look like he'd been doing much sleeping. Now that she was about to add to his misery, guilt wrapped up in sadness almost overwhelmed her.

"Do you mind if we come in?"

"Oh. Yes. Sure. Sorry, Maggie, I didn't mean to keep you standing on the doorstep." He stepped aside and let them into the house.

The sitting room spoke of his late wife with floral furnishings and bright yellow throw cushions. With the curtains closed and an overflowing ashtray on the coffee table, the usually cheerful room looked like a cave of despair.

Doug must have caught Maggie's expression. Grabbing a half-empty whiskey bottle and the ashtray, he left the room. Maggie glanced at Jackson. His usually tanned skin looked ashen in the gloom. Both men were grieving. Jackson's pain was fresher, but Doug's would probably stay with him like a shadow. An unwelcome twin, shading every day of his life.

When he returned, Doug opened the curtains, letting the early afternoon sunlight fill the room.

"Please, sit down." Doug gestured to the sofa, taking the armchair opposite them. He didn't offer any apologies or explanations for the whiskey bottle or the ashtray, and Maggie admired him for it. He looked from Maggie to Jackson, obviously wondering what the visit was all about.

"I'm so very sorry about Maureen." She wondered how many more times she'd repeat the same platitudes before this plague was done.

"Thank you, Maggie. You're a good girl to come and check on me like this, but I'm fine, really. I just need time to wallow."

Maggie felt a blush creeping up her neck. She *had* been worried about him, but her reasons for being there were far from altruistic.

"That's not really why we're here." Maggie swallowed. "We need your help."

He looked confused, but nodded for her to continue.

"Have you heard about the children?" she asked.

He nodded again and ran his hand through his hair. "Yes, I heard. Yesterday when I went into town to buy whiskey and smokes. The place was deserted and then Gib Pierce, you know from the liquor shop, told me why." He let out a deep sigh, but didn't continue.

"Doug, I think..." She hesitated and glanced at Jackson before continuing. "*We* think that the thing killing those children also killed Maureen."

Doug's brows furrowed, deep lines creasing his forehead.

"No. That can't be, Maggie. She'd just finished chemo, so she hadn't been out or had any contact with anyone but me. You see, her immune system took a battering, so we couldn't risk her catching anything. Whatever bug killed those children couldn't have got to her." He looked down at his hands. "I think maybe her body just couldn't take anymore and that's my fault... She didn't want to go through another round of chemo, but I kept pushing her. I–" His voice was husky, and when he looked up, his eyes were wet with unshed tears.

Maggie's chest tightened. Doug hadn't just been grieving, but suffering under the weight of his guilt.

"Doug, it wasn't the chemo or the cancer that killed Maureen. It was something much worse. Worse because it was deliberate." Maggie struggled to keep her voice from rising. She could see her words were upsetting him, but couldn't stop.

Doug looked away, towards the empty rocking chair that sat near the fireplace. When he spoke, his voice was soft, but firm.

"I think you two should go now. I'm tired."

"Come on, Maggie." Jackson clamped a hand on her elbow, urging her to stand.

"No." She jerked her arm out of Jackson's grasp. "Just listen to what I have to say and then if you still want us to go, we will. Please!"

She was crying now, tears running down her cheeks and dripping onto the red scarf still wrapped around her neck.

Doug looked back at Maggie, then at Jackson. His expression softened and he nodded. "Okay. I'll listen, but not in here. I need a smoke. We can sit out the back."

The three of them moved to the back veranda where they sat at a table with bench seats on either side, Doug on one side and Maggie and Jackson on the other. The four corners of the veranda were dotted with large terracotta pots, overflowing with purple petunias.

"It's nice out here." Maggie nodded at the spotlessly maintained lawn and fruit trees, a pretty and peaceful space that in many ways reflected Doug and Maureen's relationship.

Doug nodded. A smile lifted the corners of his mouth. "Yes. Maureen loved this garden. We both did. We had a lot of happy times out here, we…" He trailed off and took a cigarette out the packet he'd been holding.

Maggie took the packet Jackson had given her earlier from her handbag. For a minute or so no one spoke.

"I didn't know you smoked, Maggie," Doug said around a plume.

"I didn't know you did," Maggie said with a smile.

"I quit about thirty years ago. Maureen read somewhere that it might help us with trying for a baby, so I stopped. Now seems like a good time to take it back up."

Maggie nodded and puffed on her cigarette. She'd have to quit again, go through the torture of nicotine withdrawal all over again, but it seemed like a worry for another day. Her main concern right now was convincing Doug to help them. He was a friend and a good man. Maybe that's what led her to Doug *and* Jackson. If they were going to take on evil, they'd need good people to do it. She wanted to believe that there *was* good at work in Thorn Tree, as well as evil. Maybe with enough good on her side, the scales might tip in her favour.

"All right," Doug said. "I'm listening."

Maggie told Doug about her first meeting with Prapti. Then about Manjula and the run-in with Prapti at the café. She told him about Annabel and the other sightings of the little girl, including what Ollie said about his car accident. Finally, she went through the research she'd done online and, after lighting another cigarette, she got to Harness. She didn't leave anything out, including Harness's description of the demon.

Maggie talked for nearly half an hour. During that time Doug smoked two more cigarettes, but never interrupted. His expression remained the same, bushy brows knitted together in concentration. It was a crazy story. Sitting on the veranda in the early autumn sun, it seemed so far-fetched that she was beginning to feel like she was wasting her time.

Doug took his time before speaking, maybe weighing something up in his mind.

"Jackson, why are you here?" The question wasn't what Maggie had expected, but Jackson seemed unsurprised.

He held Doug's gaze with a directness that didn't waver.

"My grandmother died this morning. She'd been haunted by the Acheri all her life. Her last words to me were about stopping it and that's what I'm going to do."

Doug looked back at Maggie. "So, you're saying this woman... Prapti, brought a demon to our town and it's killing people?" He spread his hands wide. "Why?"

"I think it has a purpose. It wants Annabel, just like it wanted Manjula's friend, Meena. But I also think it kills because that's what it does. It kills." She waited for him to speak, but when he remained silent, she continued, "It sounds unbelievable, but I know it's true. If I had any doubts, they disappeared when Harness got sick."

"Maggie, I've lived a long time. Long enough to know only a fool dismisses things because they sound unbelievable."

"So you believe us?"

"Yes, I believe you. What now?"

* * *

Doug made three cups of strong instant coffee which they drank while Maggie outlined her plan.

"Okay." Doug set his cup down. "It sounds like you have it all worked out. I think we should take my ute, though. If we're going off-road, it'll be safer than using your car."

"All right. I'll move it out of the way and we can load up the ute," Maggie said, getting up and draining the last dregs from her cup.

219

"Give me five minutes, I need to grab a few things out of the shed. I'll lock up and meet you both out the front," Doug said, grinding out his cigarette in a chipped saucer they'd been using as an ashtray.

Jackson and Maggie headed back through the house and out to the car. Just as Maggie opened the car door, Jackson stopped her.

"Do you think he's up to this?"

Maggie thought for a moment before answering. "He'll be okay. What about you? How are you feeling?"

Jackson shrugged. "I don't know. Ask me when it's over." He gave a nervous laugh.

Five minutes later, Doug appeared at the back of the carport. Wearing a red trucker's cap and carrying a shovel in one hand with a pitchfork in the other, he looked like he'd stepped out of a painting by Grant Wood.

"What's the pitchfork for?" Maggie asked.

"What would angry villagers be without one?" Doug said, tossing the garden equipment into the back of the ute. Jackson barked out a laugh, hawking like a kookaburra. The sound was so comical, Maggie found herself laughing along with him, enjoying a moment of lightness.

When everything was loaded, they climbed in with Maggie squeezed in between the two men. The clock on the dashboard read ten after one, still hours before sunset. It would be a mistake to try and confront Prapti and the demon after dark. So far, the demon had only been spotted at night. Maggie hoped it meant the Acheri was weaker in the day. Any advantage, no matter how slim, was worth grabbing.

"All set." Doug reversed out of the driveway, the ute bouncing onto the road.

"Are you sure you know where Knoll Road is?" Maggie asked, gripping the seat.

"I know where it is. I haven't been up that way in years, though. I don't know about an old shearer's cottage, but if it's there, we'll find it."

Chapter Thirty-two

"We'll find it." Annabel blinked, unsure of her surroundings.

"It's all right, love. We're at the motel, remember?" Her mother's voice was soft, comforting. Annabel lay back on the bed and allowed herself to relax. She remembered listening to the voices and sounds buzzing in her head until she couldn't think.

"Where's Daddy?" she asked without opening her eyes.

"He's just popped out to get us something for lunch. He should be back any minute." Her mother's voice was closer now, she could feel her sitting on the bed. "What will we find?"

Annabel thought about the dream she'd been having. A scary lady with long black hair was dancing around in an old shack waving something silvery and sharp in the air. She was waiting for someone, but Annabel couldn't remember who.

She tried to think, but the buzzing started again, blocking her thoughts. "I don't know. I'm trying to…" The buzzing became a humming, and a name clarified amongst the background din – *Maggie*.

Annabel sat up, eyes wide. Her mother was beside her. Golden light from the window spilled into the room, blurring everything but her face.

"What is it? Tell me what's happening." Her mother's voice was still soft, but there was pain in her tone.

Before Annabel could answer, the door opened and her father walked in carrying a plastic bag.

"There wasn't much open, so I just got some orange juice, bananas and cookies." He dumped a plastic bag on the table in front of her mother. "The streets are deserted. I don't think I've ever seen Thorn Tree so quiet." He pulled some coins from his pocket and slapped them on the table.

"Daddy." Annabel was having a hard time hearing her own voice over the confusion in her head. "I think Maggie's in trouble. There's a scary woman waiting for her. She knows Maggie's coming and she's going to hurt her." She had to speak slowly, making sure each word came out.

Her father came over and sat next to her mother on the bed and put his arm around Annabel's shoulders. "It's alright, Bell Pepper. I'll go and see Sergeant Gibson and tell him to check on Maggie. Okay?"

"He's sick, Daddy." For a moment there was silence in her mind. "I'm not sure how sick, but I don't know if he can help her."

Her father's gaze flicked to her mother. Something passed between them. Annabel had seen them exchange a look like that a million times, but this time there was fear mixed in with the *Are you thinking what I'm thinking* look.

He turned his attention back to his daughter. She didn't know how to put her feelings into words, only that Maggie was trying to save her from the monster. If the scary lady from her dream knew Maggie was coming then something terrible would happen and the monster would come back tonight. She could feel the creature as surely as she could feel her dad's arm on her shoulder. The monster wanted to hurt her and tonight, there would be nothing to stop it.

She'll get me just like she got the others. Her dad studied her face for a moment and nodded.

"All right. I'll walk over to the police station and get someone to check on Maggie. You two eat something. I won't be long." He kissed her on the head.

Her mother walked him to the door, they kissed, and then he was gone. Annabel and her mother sat at the small dining table nibbling on the cookies and sipping orange juice that neither of them really wanted. Her mother kept glancing out the window watching the street. Annabel listened to the buzzing. She caught an echo. Maggie's voice seemed far away, but for a second, it sounded like she was laughing. Annabel hoped that meant that she was all right.

Chapter Thirty-three

Doug spotted the turn for Knoll Road. The bitumen was bleached almost white with age, the road cracked and neglected. Jackson and Maggie both agreed they'd never been out to this part of Thorn Tree before.

"We're not in Thorn Tree anymore." Doug jerked his chin at the road ahead. "These old roads are ghost tracks leading up into the hills. There used to be small towns and settlements; most of them were destroyed by bushfires between eighty and a hundred years ago and never rebuilt. That's why the bush grows so thick out here. After a big fire, it comes back stronger than ever."

Maggie glanced at the trees crowding the road like long, dry fingers reaching out to prevent them passing, their shadows casting jagged lines across the bitumen. She could hear the sound of a lone crow squawking in the distance. "Ghost tracks," as Doug called them, was a fitting title. Eager for a distraction, she leaned down and fiddled with the radio.

"Mind if I put some music on?"

"Help yourself," Doug said without taking his eyes off the road.

Maggie ran the dial across the display, but each station crackled with static. She pulled the phone out of her bag and checked for a dial tone. Nothing but crackling and a faint high-pitched screech.

"Jackson, is your phone working?" Maggie asked.

Jackson took out his mobile and put it to his ear. "No. Just static." He put it back in his pocket.

"There's a magnetic field in the ground out here. Probably interfering with the signal." Doug glanced at Maggie. "Nothing works out here."

She nodded, but wasn't convinced that was the only reason they were suddenly cut off from the rest of the world. She wondered if Prapti knew they were coming. The woman had been spying on her over the last few days, but it would be impossible for her to be following them out here without being spotted.

She searched through her bag and found the notes she'd made before leaving home that morning. *A Familiar is a demi-supernatural being with mystic powers which they use to spy on people.* The words looked sinister and foreboding. How could she have been stupid enough to think they could just drive out here and surprise Prapti?

"I think she knows we're coming." Maggie held the paper up.

"How could she?" Jackson asked.

"She knew where I'd been, who I'd spoken to. I thought she was following me – you know, parking near my house and watching me. I think it's more than that. I think she's got some sort of telepathy or... or something with the birds lets her know what people are doing. I know it sounds crazy–"

"No more crazy than anything else you've told me about the woman," Doug said, cutting her off. "She might know we're coming and that loses us the element of surprise, but she's not all-powerful or she would've stopped us before we got this far. I'm betting she doesn't know everything we have planned."

Maggie thought for a minute. It made sense. If Prapti knew what they were planning, then why hadn't she done something to stop them?

"He's right, Maggie," Jackson said. "For all we know, she can read people's minds, but that doesn't mean she knows everything. From what you've told me, her only other power is saying mean things."

Maggie couldn't help smiling. "I hope you're both right. I guess we'll soon find out."

They drove on in silence for a while, each of them lost in thought. Even with the windows down, the air in the cab was heavy with the scent of tobacco and sweat.

The incline in the road increased until it was clear that they were heading up into the hills. But it wasn't until the thick bush gave way to sparser growth that they could really see where they were going.

"Do you think we've passed the turnoff?" Maggie turned, searching the road behind them.

"No. I don't think so, but the bush was so thick back there it would have been easy to miss. We'll keep going for another ten minutes or so and if we don't see anything, we can always backtrack." Doug pulled off his cap and wiped his forearm across his face.

Maggie wished her phone was working so she could call Mary and check on Harness. Her mind drifted back to the night before, the way Harness touched her face as they made love. She'd never felt that connected to anyone before, not even her ex-husband. Last night was different, like she was finally where she was supposed to be. The thought of never feeling that way again was worse than the fear of facing the demon.

A loud *bang* brought her out of her reverie. The car lurched forward and then spun to the right. Jolting forward, Maggie slapped her palms on the dashboard. A shudder travelled up her arms, jarring her shoulders.

Doug struggled with the wheel, trying to bring the ute under control as it veered towards the edge of the road.

The tyres squealed as the steering locked before the vehicle shuddered to a stop. The contents of the back of the ute clanged from one side to the other.

"You okay?" Doug sounded breathless.

Maggie nodded, too shaken to speak. Jackson said he was fine and climbed out of the cab. Before following him, Maggie wiped her damp palms on her jeans and let out a shaky breath.

Doug bent and examined the front right tyre, which was completely shredded. He pulled something out from under the wheel and stood up.

"Barbed wire. Not supernatural powers, just an old-fashioned booby trap." With a disgusted grunt, he flung the mess of tangled wire into the bush.

"I guess that means we're getting close." Maggie couldn't pull her gaze away from the shredded rubber.

"I guess I'll get the spare." Head down, Jackson headed for the rear of the ute.

Maggie grabbed a cigarette out of her bag and lit it. Her heart was doing a weird jittering and blood was whooshing in her ears. They were getting close. She could feel the tension twisting in her gut, making the cigarette taste like sour milk. She tossed it onto the track and ground it out before following Jackson.

He had the back of the tray down and was reaching for the spare.

"You okay?"

"I'm good." He spoke over his shoulder. "I've decided that when this is over, I'm leaving. Leaving Thorn Tree."

Jackson bounced the spare tyre onto the ground and then reached in and grabbed the jack. Maggie watched him, not sure how to respond. Over the last week, she'd come to rely on him, not just in the café, but as a friend. She couldn't imagine life in Thorn Tree without him.

"I'll miss you." It sounded lame, but she meant it.

"Well, you've got the cop now and I need to get out. I can't live with my parents forever."

Maggie was surprised by the hurt in his voice. She'd always thought he might have a crush on her, but because of the age difference had never given it much consideration. She wondered how she could have been so blind and insensitive.

"Jackson, I'm sorry if I've hurt you. I never realised–"

"Forget it." He cut her off. "It's not your fault. I'm just being an idiot. I need to get this tyre changed."

He turned his back, rolling the tyre along the cracked road. Maggie put her hand on his arm and stopped him.

"You're not an idiot. You're kind and brave and I consider you my friend. If you have to go, I understand, but I'll miss you." She let go of his arm, not sure what else to say.

He nodded without looking up and continued rolling the spare towards the front of the ute. Fifteen minutes later, with the shredded tyre in the back of the ute, they were moving.

They'd been driving less than five minutes when Doug spoke.

"There it is." He pointed to the left about ten metres up the road. Maggie registered a gap in the bush, a dirt road, barely visible until they were almost on top of it. She wondered how Doug, who she guessed was about seventy, had spotted it so easily.

"How did you–"

"There are skid marks on the road," he said, answering her question before she could finish. "It looks like someone drives in and out of there in a hurry."

Maggie looked back at the road and saw black marks scarring the bitumen. She was no expert, but the lines looked fresh, as though someone was using the turnoff regularly.

Doug turned onto a side road that was little more than a gravel and red-dirt track with weeds growing up the centre. The path snaked its way uphill as the vegetation became sparser. Nothing but tall gum trees grew amongst small clumps of twisted scrub.

"This area used to be grazing land before the bushfires drove the sheep farmers out. We must be getting near the edge of the National Park, so it can't be much farther."

Maggie was only half-listening; her attention was focused on the hills ahead, which she scanned for some sign of the cottage.

Skin tingling with gooseflesh, her senses felt heightened – ragged. It was an unpleasant feeling, like sitting on the dentist's chair as he leaned over, razor-sharp needle poised to enter the soft flesh of her gums. Only at this moment, the dentist would be a much easier option.

The car jumped slightly as they drove over a hump in the track. As the vehicle rose, Maggie caught a glimpse of something dark and angular on the horizon. A snatch of black only visible for a fraction of a second, long enough to recognise the tip of a roof.

"Stop!" Maggie grabbed Doug's arm. He stomped the brake, grinding the vehicle to a jarring halt.

"I think I spotted it, but I need to get a better look."

"I don't see anything," Jackson said, searching the hills.

"Let me out. I want to get on top of the cab so I can see."

Maggie headed to the back of the vehicle and unbolted the tray. She clambered up on the back of the ute and made her way to the cab, taking care to avoid stepping on any of the gear they'd packed. Jackson followed a step behind while Doug stood next to the vehicle, hands on hips, gazing up at them.

"Here." Jackson crouched so she could use his knee to step up onto the roof.

She braced herself with one hand on his shoulder as she climbed onto the roof. She was about to turn and offer him her hand, but Jackson gave a small jump and lifted himself onto the cab in one easy movement. The increased height gave Maggie a better view, but it was still difficult for her to make out anything but the topmost peak of what appeared to be a black roof.

"It looks like two buildings," Jackson said. "I'd say the smaller one in the front is the cottage and the one behind it with the bigger roof might be a shearing shed."

"Any idea on the distance between the buildings?" Maggie turned to look at him. The afternoon sun was on his left, momentarily blinding her.

"Hard to say, maybe twenty or thirty metres."

Maggie could hear his words, but his face was obscured by a halo of sunlight. For a second, he looked ethereal, like an angel. A cold shiver ran up her spine. She turned away off balance and sat on the roof so she could slide down to the vehicle's back tray.

After they'd both clambered down from the ute, Maggie pulled the old red towel out of the black backpack she'd borrowed from Jackson. She tore it in two long strips and handed one to each man before tossing the bag back into the ute.

"Tie it around your neck. It might help."

Doug took the strip of fabric, but hesitated. "What is it about the colour red?"

"I don't know," Maggie answered honestly. "I didn't read anything about why it would deter the Acheri, just that it would."

"Red is the colour of power, it's supposed to open a pathway for justice. It's also the colour of blood, which is a symbol of life."

Noticing the way both Maggie and Doug were staring at him, Jackson flushed.

"It comes up in lots of mythologies from all over the world." He paused, and when neither Maggie nor Doug spoke, he added, "I looked it up last night after talking to my gran."

"That's good enough for me," Doug said, tying the strip of fabric around his neck.

"Okay." Maggie tossed the pack back in the back of the ute. "We need to separate. I'll take the car and drive up to the house. Once I get to the top of that rise" – she pointed to an area about fifty metres ahead – "she'll be able to see me. Hopefully she'll think I've come alone. I'll keep Prapti occupied while you two approach. I'm guessing the demon is in the outbuilding. That's where you both come in."

"What about the paint?" Doug asked.

"I'll park the ute on an angle so when you approach the house, you can grab it out of the back. If everything goes to plan, Prapti will be too busy with me to look out the window and see you or Jackson."

"What if Prapti gets past you and reaches us before we get to the shearing shed?" Jackson asked.

"You'll have to... subdue her." Maggie looked from Jackson to Doug, noting their grim faces. It was clear the idea of subduing a woman didn't sit well with either man, but now wasn't the time for scruples.

"She's a killer." Maggie waited until both nodded their agreement.

Before she got in the ute and drove away, she kissed Doug on the cheek and wished him good luck. When she approached Jackson, she felt a little awkward, but if they were going to do this, then she was determined to do it properly. She stood in front of him, rolling up onto her tiptoes, and wrapped her arms around his neck. She pulled him into an embrace.

"Be careful." She whispered the words close to his ear, feeling his breath on her face.

After a slight hesitation, his arms came around her, holding her in a tight squeeze before releasing her and gently pushing himself back. An image of him surrounded by sunlight flashed in her mind. Whatever happened next, she'd always hold this moment in a corner of her heart. A memory to take out and examine whenever she thought of him.

The two men watched Maggie climb into the ute and drive towards the rise.

Chapter Thirty-four

"Don't die on me." Rodney took his hand off the wheel and tapped the slumped figure on the shoulder. He waited, heart pumping like a fire hose.

"I'm not going to die." Harness's head rolled to the left. His eyes opened with all the speed of a senior citizen waking from an afternoon nap. "Just keep your eyes on the road."

Rodney let out a breath and nodded. "Just checking."

They'd been driving on Knoll Road for what felt like an eternity. The antiviral injection and fluids had helped, but Harness felt like there was a brass band working on either side of his head, but instead of a tin drum, someone was playing a tune on his skull. The road doubled then came into focus. Staying upright without sliding onto the floor of Rodney's truck took every bit of strength left in his body. He put his hand on the Smith & Wesson Police Special that was sitting on the seat between him and Rodney. The cold metal felt good against his hot skin. He hoped he'd have the strength to use it when the time came. But with each fit of shivering, he wondered if he'd have enough energy to lift it, let alone shoot straight.

"This was a bad idea. I should've come on my own." Rodney gave him another edgy glance.

"Look, Rodney, I don't want you getting mixed up in all this. Just drop me off and then drive back to town."

Harness hated the waver in his voice as he tried to suppress a cough bubbling its way out of his chest. Rodney was clearly regretting driving him out here. It wouldn't take much for him to change his mind and turn the car around.

He leaned his head back against the seat and closed his eyes as the vehicle rattled over the uneven road. Less than an hour ago, Harness had been in his bed struggling to breathe. When he'd questioned Mary on Maggie's whereabouts, she'd been reluctant to talk. It was only when he tried to get out of bed that she'd given in and told him about the shearer's cottage. Within moments, Rodney showed up and, while Mary protested, Harness had convinced him to drive him to the cottage to look for Maggie.

"Why did you come to check on me?" Harness spoke without opening his eyes.

"What?"

"You showed up at my house to check on me. How did you know I was sick?"

Rodney gave a long sigh. "Annabel told me. She was worried about you." He paused. "She's worried about Maggie too. I said I'd check on you."

Harness opened his eyes and watched Rodney drive.

"Tell me what Annabel said about Maggie."

Rodney recounted the incident in the motel room.

"Annabel said the woman knew Maggie was coming." Rodney took his eyes off the road and glanced at Harness. "She told me the woman was going to hurt Maggie."

Harness sucked in a breath that stabbed at his chest like a nail. "Can this thing go any faster?"

Chapter Thirty-five

The ute's bonnet tipped over the rise, giving Maggie her first real look at the single-storey shearer's cottage. Sitting on a flat area directly beneath a steep hill covered in greyish-green shrubs and long yellow grass, the cottage looked ancient. Maggie let the vehicle roll forward, taking in the building's grey walls, which were scarred and blackened, suggesting it had escaped a fire at some point. What remained of the building looked brittle and ready to collapse. Behind it was a larger structure, partially obscured like a hulking giant.

Maggie's heart rate kicked up a notch as she eased the vehicle forward towards the final incline. The porch spanning the front of the house had come away from the main structure, dipping dangerously to the right. Tin sheeting on the high and unusually pointy roof was stained orange with rust, but intact, with a stone chimney rising to a jagged spike at the rear of the structure. The windows were hidden beneath the shadow of the crumbling porch roof. The overall look of the place reminded Maggie of a witch's house, sinister and desolate. Like a crouching monster, it seemed to be waiting for her – trying to make itself less threatening. *It couldn't look more terrifying if there were bats flying out of the chimney.* A dry pant emerged from her lips, as close to a laugh as she could muster.

In front of the house and to the right sat a large black van. The vehicle looked newish, but was covered in dust from numerous journeys on the dirt road that accessed the property. A group of weeping peppermint trees grew around the left-hand side of the house; their fibrous trunks and graceful dome shapes offered a spot of colour to the ramshackle scene.

Maggie accelerated, wincing at the rumble of the ute's engine. Her gaze kept jumping from the cottage to the structure behind it. The shearing shed was bigger than the cottage but half-hidden by its location. It had the same scorched look as the front building. Maggie's plan rested on the Acheri occupying the outer building and Prapti the cottage. She wasn't sure why she had planned it this way, but her gut told her the demon wouldn't be living in a house. A creature like the one Harness described would want something more crude and earthy, making the old shearing shed the perfect setting. So much of her plan rested on gut instinct, she hoped hers was right.

Maggie proceeded up the hill towards the cottage where the dirt road abruptly ended. Whether by luck or planning, Prapti had chosen a location that would make it impossible for anyone to approach without being seen. Recognising the pointlessness of trying to surprise the woman with a silent approach, Maggie floored the accelerator and drove straight at the house. At the last minute she spun the steering wheel and brought the ute around and to a stop next to the van, sending up a cloud of dust and gravel.

She hoped that it looked like an angry move, one that disguised choosing a strategic parking spot. By parking on the far side of the van, Prapti might not see Doug and Jackson unloading the gear. If everything went to plan, the men might be able to get from the ute to the shed without being seen.

That's a big if, Maggie thought as she turned the engine off and grabbed the spanner from under the passenger's seat. She shoved the heavy tool down the back of her jeans and pulled her T-shirt over it. The metal felt icy cold against the skin on her lower back. Cold, but reassuring.

She stepped out of the car, leaving her bag on the seat. If Prapti was watching, she wanted her to see that her hands were empty and believe she was unarmed and vulnerable. Maggie walked around the van and up to the house, noticing a large group of crows in the weeping peppermint trees, their beady eyes watching as she walked. A light breeze ruffled the leaves and started the birds squawking.

A murder of crows, Maggie thought grimly, half-expecting the creatures to swoop down on her and begin pecking her eyes out.

The birds gave no sign of attack, but continued their watchful vigil as she climbed the steps and stood on the sagging porch. The breeze was doing more than unsettling the birds; it carried a strange odour that Maggie couldn't quite identify. The smell reminded her of unwashed potatoes, but mixed with something metallic and unpleasant. Maggie grimaced and tried to breathe through her mouth.

The now visible windows were blackened using either dirt or paint, it was hard to tell, but it looked deliberate. The cottage was incredibly isolated, making the blackened windows unnecessary for privacy. It occurred to her that she'd seen Prapti twice; once at night when she was introduced to her at Agnes's party and the other time in the late afternoon in the unlit café. *Maybe Prapti doesn't like the light?* If she could get Prapti out into the sunlight or get some light into the cottage, it could work in Maggie's favour.

The front door was made of a solid wooden panel, splintered and slightly warped. Maggie tried the knob, it was unlocked. She hesitated. Her hands were shaking again. Once she stepped into the cottage, there'd be no turning back. *I might be making things worse. Worse for Harness and worse for everyone in Thorn Tree.*

Maggie let go of the doorknob and balled her hands into fists, opening and closing them a few times and taking deep breaths. Adrenalin was coursing through her body like wildfire, making it difficult to keep her mind focused. If she didn't act now, Doug and Jackson would come over the rise and the whole plan would be ruined. She reached out and turned the knob.

The door opened a few centimetres with a crunch of grit and dust, then stuck. She put her free hand flat on the wood and pushed. When it didn't budge, Maggie wedged her shoulder against the door and, bending her knees, shoved.

The door popped open and swung inwards, taking Maggie with it. She stumbled into what she guessed was the main room. The smell was stronger inside and now mixed with the thick stench of human waste. Maggie gagged and covered her nose. An old fireplace and wide wooden mantle dominated the room, near it an archway that probably led to the kitchen. Along the left side of the room were two doors both standing half-open, probably leading to the bedrooms.

Maggie stayed in the entrance. Even with the front door standing open and a few rays leaking through the blackened windows, gloom cloaked the area. Amongst the other odours, she detected wood smoke, telling her someone definitely lived in the hellish cottage. A few steps into the room, she noticed a battered saucepan in the remains of a wood fire. On the mantle above, something glinted, capturing a beam of light.

She glanced at the bedroom doorways, the archway to the kitchen, and then back out the front door, listening intently as she crept forward.

The object came into focus and her stomach lurched. The thick stench in the air and the horror before her almost knocked her off balance. She'd prepared herself for a physical attack, not the twisted nature of what was laid out on the wooden mantle.

A little tin whistle, its dark blue paint faded and aged. The instrument could have come from anywhere, but Maggie knew it was Meena's, the little girl Manjula left behind in India. She knew with every cell in her body that it was the same whistle she'd seen in the photograph.

She swallowed back the sour taste filling her mouth and let her eyes scan the trophies littering the shelf. A red and white yo-yo with a bit of frayed string clinging to the centre, a baby's bottle encrusted with grime. There was a gap in the collection, an empty spot waiting to be filled.

A spot for Annabel. Maggie couldn't explain how she knew these things, but the knowing was undeniable. Unable to drag herself away, Maggie looked over the keepsakes. A morbid collection gathered from countless dead children. Children Prapti and the demon had killed for what looked like decades, maybe longer. Some of the things looked very old and fragile. A single lace bootie, yellow and brittle with age, lay next to a tin soldier. Maggie picked up the toy; it had the look of an antique probably dating back to the First World War. She put the little soldier in the palm of her hand, feeling its weight. Most of the green paint had peeled off, the tiny helmet dented almost beyond recognition.

The toy felt cold against her skin. As her fingers traced the soldier's face, she thought she heard an echo – singing. A childish voice grew clearer as if singing in her ear. *I found a trail of the mountain mist, the mountain mist, the mountain mist.* Without realising it, Maggie's lips were moving, whispering the lyrics as they played in her mind. Tears welled in her eyes. Some poor little boy had played with this toy over a hundred years ago and now it sat in this desolate place as a macabre reminder of his life and death. There probably wasn't a living soul left to remember him.

Maggie's eyes drooped. The lullaby pulled at her soul with its tragic sweetness. *It would be so much easier to just surrender to the song and rest, anything else would be pointless.* Her legs unlocked at the knees, as if gravity pulled her downwards. *Would it be so bad if the mist took away all the pain and struggling?*

"Maggie, I didn't hear you knock."

The woman's voice snapped her back to the moment. Maggie's eyes opened and the toy dropped into the hearth. The singing ceased, vanishing like the mist in the lullaby, leaving her off balance and slightly dazed. She turned, stumbling, and knocked a small stool over, sending it rolling across the gritty floor.

Prapti stood in the bedroom doorway, hands at her sides, head cocked slightly, her pose mirroring that of the crows gathered outside the cottage. She remained still, making no move to approach. For a moment neither woman spoke.

"It's all right, Maggie." Her sonorous voice was affable, as if they were old friends. "I've been looking forward to seeing you again. I'm glad you're finally here."

On the drive into the hills, Maggie had played this moment over and over in her mind, trying to decide what she'd say to the woman responsible for so much death and sorrow. She'd thought about the moves she'd make, how the confrontation would end. But now, standing in front of Prapti, her resolve slipped and all the condemnations flew from her mind. All that remained was fear – and hate.

"I know why you're here and what you think you're going to do."

Her oversized mouth drew into a grin, exposing large teeth and turning her expression into something resembling a wolf preparing to pounce.

When Maggie found her voice, it came out as a feeble croak.

"I know you're a killer."

Prapti took a step forward – just one, silent and threatening. Maggie's eyes moved to the woman's feet. They were bare and covered in grime as though she'd been walking through dirt.

"You try to label us, but know nothing of our nature. We are creatures of the darkness, but our purpose is divine. The Devi seeks only to uphold the equilibrium, to... keep the *balance*. There's darkness and light in this world... We cannot allow the light to overtake the darkness, balance must be sustained." As she spoke, her eyes shone with religious fervour.

"So you keep the balance by killing children that are special or gifted?"

Prapti took another step and nodded.

"Your understanding is crude, but correct."

"So what about the other children? What about the elderly and the sick? They can't all be a threat to... to your... *balance*? Why are they dead?"

Maggie's voice rose. She had to keep Prapti talking, but the woman was closing in, cornering her in the shadows of the filthy room.

"Do you think you're the first to challenge us?" The friendly tone was gone now. "There have been many like you. Simple-minded savages desperate to protect their simpering offspring, or worse, their lovers." She huffed out a joyless laugh. "Yes. I can smell him on you. He'll be dead by morning and then they will throw his body in the truck with all the other carcasses."

She closed her mouth, oversized teeth clanging together like scissoring blades. The mocking smile pushed and stabbed at Maggie until anger broke through the fear and slammed everything into focus. Prapti's black pupil-less eyes, her grime-stained neck and dirty black dress all emerged out of the fear. It was then that Maggie realised Prapti held something in her right hand, half-concealed by the folds of her dress.

A meat cleaver, large and blindingly shiny amidst the filth. Maggie's brain was sluggish, slow to comprehend what it saw, as if whatever spell the toy soldier spun still clouded her mind. *It's the cleanest thing in the house.* The thought was fleeting, a moment's distraction before her instincts surfaced. The woman was closing on her, and if Maggie didn't act, she'd die here. Her blood would cover the grimy floor. Any chance at real happiness would be hacked to pieces. Blood rushing in her ears, she reached around to the back of her jeans and touched the spanner.

Prapti swung her hand back and forth, bringing the cleaver in and out of view.

"I did warn you to stay out of this, Maggie, but you didn't listen. I won't lie, I'm glad you ignored my warning. I've been looking forward to this moment. I'm just sorry I won't be able to spend as long with you as I would've liked. You see, we're leaving tonight with one last stop on our way out of Thorn Tree." Her smile widened until the entire lower part of her face seemed only teeth. "There's a very special little girl we're anxious to meet."

Maggie's fingers closed around the spanner.

* * *

"The door's open."

Jackson crouched low as they approached the ute. Doug followed, noting the half-open door. His knees throbbed from the uphill walk over the rise and the muscles in the base of his spine spasmed, sending jolts of pain up his back. They hadn't talked much since Maggie left, but he knew Jackson was worried. Doug saw the way the kid looked at her. He could see Jackson was head over heels for her.

"She's counting on us to do our part," Doug said quietly, and began unloading the paint. If Jackson panicked and ran into the house before they completed their part of the plan, then the Acheri might escape and they'd miss the only chance they were going to get.

As much as Doug wanted to protect Maggie, he was here for one thing: the monster that killed his wife. Since Maggie and Jackson had shown up on his doorstep, all he could think about was destroying the evil creature that took Maureen away from him. *Maureen.*

His vision blurred and his chest constricted. *It shouldn't have been like this, not for Maureen. Not for those little ones.* He hated the creature as much as he hated the cancer that sucked the life out of her, only now he had something tangible, something he *could* fight. He'd stop it if he had to tear it apart with his bare hands.

Doug screwed his eyes shut, forcing down the emotions. He watched the kid unloading paint tins from the back of the truck. If he had to, Doug would put himself between Jackson and the monster. The idea of being with Maureen before the day was out appealed to him a hell of a lot more than returning to their empty house.

They unloaded the rest of the gear as silently as possible, dividing up the two cans of paint, shovel, pitchfork, two screwdrivers and the black backpack. Doug took the lead, heading for the back of the house. His eyes and ears weren't as good as they used to be, but there was nothing wrong with his nose. Something rotten was festering in the shed. The stench wafted on the breeze like a poisonous cloud.

At the rear of the cottage, Doug put everything on the ground and pulled a screwdriver out of his back pocket. He paused and waited while Jackson did the same. In spite of the cool breeze, the kid's hair was plastered to his head with sweat, but he showed no other signs of fear.

"Ready?" Doug asked.

"I'm ready."

When both ten-litre tins were open, Doug stood back. Jackson grabbed the first can and hurried towards the back of the cottage. Without hesitating he pitched the red paint over the back door. Colour exploded with a dull *splat,* running down the charred panels in shocking red streaks. The door looked like the backdrop for a firing squad.

Without pausing to admire his handiwork, Jackson went to the shearing shed, carefully tilting the tin to leave a trail of red between the cottage and the entrance of the outbuilding. Doug grabbed his tin and followed, making a red trail that ran parallel to Jackson's, a stark thick line staining the dead weeds and dirt between the cottage and the shed. When they reached the shed door, Doug looked back and surveyed their work.

They'd created a path from the shed to the house about two metres wide, bordered by red paint. Doug was about to work on the shed when he noticed Jackson had stopped and was gazing at the back of the cottage.

"Did you hear that?" Jackson held the paint in one hand, frowning at the house.

Doug shrugged. He wouldn't admit it, but he knew his hearing wasn't what it used to be. He had no idea what Jackson was talking about.

"It's coming from inside the cottage." Jackson ran his fingers over his chin, leaving a smudge of red on his jawline. "Sounds like plates smashing."

Doug could see the kid was about to abandon the plan and go running for the cottage.

"That's a good sign," Doug said. Jackson looked at him, confused. "She's struggling with the woman, keeping her from coming out here," Doug continued. "Now we need to do our bit to help her."

Jackson stared at Doug for a second, his dark eyes searching the man's face. He could see the kid was torn, wanting to help Maggie but hesitant to let her down.

"She's counting on us."

Doug kept his tone even, ignoring the voice of guilt whispering in his mind. *You'll have to live with this. No matter how much whiskey you pour down your throat, the kid's face will still be there.* Jackson nodded and hefted the can, splashing paint along the walls of the shearing shed. Doug glanced at the cottage. Whatever was happening in there couldn't be helped. If Maggie didn't make it, there would be one more burden to add to his soul.

They moved quickly, each splash thumping the timber walls like a bloody slap. Within minutes the outside of the shearing shed glistened with fresh red paint.

When they came together at the back of the building, the two men splattered the remnants on the rear doors, draining both tins. The only part of the shed not stained were the double doors facing the cottage.

Without speaking, they returned to the front of the structure and collected the pitchfork and the rest of the gear, leaving the half-empty backpack near the cottage. Jackson pulled up clumps of the long, dry grass and piled them at the back of the shed while Doug collected sticks and any other dry debris he could find in the ramble of dead bushes and scrubby grass. The sweet, rotten smell still hung in the air, now mixed with the sharp scent of paint to create a swell of cloying air. When the pile was big enough, Doug squirted lighter fluid over it and the back doors. The breeze grew stronger but blew in their favour, towards the shed.

"I think it would be easier if we just went in and dragged it outside," Jackson said.

"Do you really want to grapple around in the dark with that thing? We still have no idea what it's capable of."

Jackson thought for a moment.

"What if Maggie doesn't come out?"

"Then we do it ourselves."

Doug pulled the lighter out of his pants pocket, picked up a handful of dry grass and lit the pile. The two men watched while the stack caught fire and began to burn. Smoke bellowed up the back of the shed, darkening the clear blue sky.

"You know we could get ten years in prison for starting a fire this time of year." Jackson gave a nervous laugh.

"Let's hope it doesn't get out of control," Doug replied, picking up the pitchfork.

When the two men returned to the front of the shed, Jackson moved to open the double doors that faced the cottage and stopped.

"Is that a car?" This time Doug definitely heard something and nodded.

"I reckon someone's just pulled up out front."

"What should we do?"

"Open the shed." Doug ignored the sounds of a car door slamming. They had a job to finish.

Jackson nodded and flung the double doors wide. The rancid smell of rotten root vegetables mixed with a hint of sulphur hit him square on. The drumming flared in Doug's head, not quite blocking the sound of Jackson gagging and coughing. The rhythmical beating pulsed and constricted as though eating at his thoughts.

He looked at Jackson, who had one hand over his mouth, grimacing. Doug wondered if he was reacting to the smell or the drumming. Doug turned his gaze to the inside of the shed and saw only darkness. As his eyes adjusted, he noticed the smoke filling the building, and then spotted a pile of rags. For one sickening second, he thought the shed was empty and the creature had managed to escape, but then the pile shook and jerked forward.

"Get behind the red line!" Doug shouted over the drumming inside his head.

Jackson stood in the doorway staring into the shed, too fixated to take in Doug's voice. Doug reached out and shoved Jackson in the chest. He stumbled back behind the line.

They stood on either side of the red-lined path, Doug with the pitchfork and Jackson holding the shovel out in front of him.

"If Maggie doesn't come out in time, try and keep it off me while I get to the backpack." He was yelling, trying to make himself heard over the crackling fire and the incessant drumming.

"Will do!" Jackson's voice was high-pitched and edged with panic.

A croaking sound rose from inside the shed, like a groan that grew into a throaty guttural cry, sending chills down Doug's spine. He glanced over at Jackson, and they made eye contact. The kid looked dazed, jittery, but to Doug's relief, he held his ground. The intensity of the wind increased and the drumming grew louder.

Chapter Thirty-six

Prapti leapt, and for a split second seemed airborne. The cleaver rose in a vicious curve. Maggie ducked right, avoiding the weapon. Instead, the impact of Prapti's body forced her back into the old dresser, which split on collision, sending brittle wood and crockery smashing to the floor.

Sharp splinters cut into Maggie's back. She struggled to keep her footing as she slid sideways, feet crunching over shards of china. In the same instant Prapti turned, swinging the cleaver in a deadly arc. Maggie heard the blade whip through the air and dove to the side, lifting her left arm to shield her head. She let out a cry and pain blazed up her forearm, making her knees shudder. If she fell, Prapti would be on her in a second.

Maggie staggered, clutching her injured arm. Agony tore through her flesh. Her knees buckled, this time almost collapsing, but she managed to stay on her feet. For a second they faced each other. Prapti, seeing the blood covering Maggie's arm, gave a triumphant laugh. She raised the cleaver for another attack then stopped and looked towards the back of the house.

"Devi!" The guttural shriek echoed off the dark walls.

With Prapti's attention diverted, Maggie grabbed the spanner from the back of her jeans. Prapti turned back with teeth bared, her eyes glazed with hatred and something else – a shifting, watery look that could have been panic. Maggie swung the spanner at the woman's face with as much force as she could muster. The heavy tool collided with Prapti's jaw, rocking her face with a sickening crunch. Prapti sagged to her right, but didn't drop. She lifted her head, glaring through tangled hair, jaw hanging at a strange angle elongating her face.

Prapti grunted and charged, driving Maggie downwards. Her back slammed into the floor, sending a shaft of pain up her spine, but her fingers remained tightly clamped around the spanner. Prapti's weight came down on top of her and the air burst out of Maggie's lungs in a painful *whoosh*. The woman gripped Maggie's throat with her left hand, still holding the cleaver in her right. Face hovering close enough for Maggie to smell her dank breath, Prapti drew herself up until she crouched over her then brought her knee down on Maggie's injured arm.

Maggie choked out a scream, bucking her body in a desperate attempt to heave the woman off. Prapti held on, increasing the pressure on Maggie's throat, leaning over her until her face was only inches away. She stared into Maggie's eyes as if searching for something, then drew up slightly and spat. Blood and teeth sprayed Maggie's face and eyes, blinding her.

As the pressure on her throat increased, mercifully the pain in her arm subsided. Her vision blurred. Maggie's lungs, desperate for oxygen, burned. Prapti's fingers squeezed her throat until it felt like the bones were crumbling. Maggie bucked, this time with less strength as the fight drained from her body.

Her eyes darkened, vision narrowing to a point where she saw herself holding Eddie. He smiled and grasped her finger in one of his chubby little hands. Maggie smiled back, whispered his name and felt warmth sweep over her.

All this time, I've been frantically trying to save Harness because I couldn't face the same pain as losing Eddie. Now she'd failed them both. She didn't deserve this happiness. This warmth. Not if it meant giving in and letting the demon win.

Her arms were empty. She no longer held Eddie. Instead, her fingers grasped something cold and heavy. A thunderous *crack* brought her back to the dark, filthy cottage.

Maggie's eyes opened, meeting Prapti's bottomless stare. Maggie coughed and gulped air, like someone breaking the surface after being held underwater. For a moment all she was aware of was the oxygen filling her lungs and the swollen burning in her throat. Sound rushed back and with it the scene came into focus.

Prapti was looking down, not at Maggie but at herself. Maggie followed her gaze and saw a wound on the woman's chest. A fleshy hole near her right shoulder ringed with black charred skin. Dark blood bubbled and ran down her torn dress.

Maggie felt the weight of the spanner in her hand and struck. She caught Prapti on the temple. The impact resounded like a bat striking a ripe melon and the woman fell to the side, pinning Maggie's injured arm. She cried out as she shoved the lifeless body aside and pulled herself free.

"Maggie."

She heard her name and turned to the voice. Harness crumpled in the doorway, gun in his lap. Maggie dropped the bloodied spanner and half-walked, half-crawled to him.

"You're hurt," he said, and coughed.

She put her hand on his face, making sure he was real, and felt the fiery heat of his skin. She looked into glassy, feverish eyes and knew he didn't have much time.

"We need to get you out of here." Maggie's voice came out a croaky whisper. She looked past Harness and saw Rodney climbing the porch steps.

"I heard a sho—" He stopped and took in the scene.

"Jesus. What happened? Your arm."

"I don't have time to explain." Maggie used the back of her good hand to wipe some of the blood off her face and then kissed Harness on the lips. She looked up at Rodney.

"I've got to get out the back and help Doug and Jackson." She stood up.

"I'm coming with you." Harness shoved his gun into the waistband of his jeans and struggled to his feet.

Rodney grabbed him around the waist. Harness leaned his arm around the shorter man's shoulders.

"You heard him," said Rodney. "Let's go."

Maggie wanted to argue, but the smell of smoke wafting through the house reminded her there was no more time.

"Okay." She made herself look away from Harness.

She moved to the back of the house, barely glancing at the filthy kitchen. Her left arm hung useless and slick with blood. Before opening the back door, she paused and forced herself to examine the injury. The cleaver had sliced through a section of her forearm, leaving a gash nearly eighteen centimetres long, revealing tissue and something white. The wound was deepest near her elbow, where a flap of flesh hung down like a limp red tongue. A wave of dizziness hit her and bile rose in the back of her bruised throat.

She knew she needed to put pressure on the wound to stem the bleeding or she'd risk passing out. Maggie looked around the kitchen for something to use, but apart from a pile of firewood and some empty boxes, the room had been gutted. She could hear Jackson outside yelling something about red lines. His words were obscured by howling.

"Maggie?" Harness's voice came from behind her.

"I need something to wrap around my arm." She pulled her T-shirt over her head, hurriedly wrapping it around her forearm and tying it in place using her right hand and teeth. The pain lessened to the point where her whole arm felt numb and useless. Maggie guessed it was nerve damage but couldn't afford to worry about that now.

Dressed only in jeans and a thin black singlet, Maggie pushed open the back door and was blinded by sunlight. Before her eyes could adjust, her other senses were bombarded. The air was heavy with the stench of burning wood and grass. Another odour, rot and sulphur, nearly overwhelmed her. Hot wind assaulted her body. Doug and Jackson's voices were yelling over animalistic howling and snarling.

Maggie blinked a few times and the scene cleared. Doug was on the ground. The creature on top of him resembled a small human, but skeletal and draped in rags. Its skin was the colour of wet ashes, with long grey wisps of wiry hair growing from its large bony head. It was unlike anything she'd ever seen or imagined. Its presence in the daylight seemed impossible, the horror of it making her want to turn and run. Instead she stood frozen as the thing tried to rip her friend apart.

Doug had his hands on the Acheri's shoulders, trying to push it away as its sinewy neck craned forward, teeth chattering centimetres from his face.

"Holy God, what is that thing?" Rodney's voice from the doorway sounded hollow and distant.

Maggie opened her mouth to answer but couldn't make her throat work. Jackson appeared out of the smoke, lunging at the creature and trying to grab it by the neck. With ferocious strength, it twisted in the young man's grasp and flung him backwards into the dirt.

In the seconds when the Acheri's focus shifted to Jackson, Doug turned his head to Maggie. "The backpack," he called through gritted teeth.

It was enough to get her moving. She looked around but couldn't find the bag. Glancing behind her, she saw Rodney and Harness coming out of the house. Harness took in the scene and, drawing strength from somewhere, pulled his arm from around Rodney's shoulder and took a step forward. In one fluid move he drew his gun from his waistband.

"Get down, Maggie!" His voice sounded stronger. He fired three shots in quick succession.

Maggie dropped to the ground and watched transfixed as all three shots hit the Acheri. With each bullet it jerked back, absorbing the impact but not falling. The force was strong enough to drive the demon off Doug, but not kill it. The Acheri turned to Rodney, Maggie and Harness, as if noticing them for the first time. Its yellow and black eyes rested on Maggie. Drumming pounded in her head as if the instrument were being played against her skull. Images bombarded her mind, skeletal children moaning in pain.

Maggie closed her eyes and shook her head, desperate to clear the awful scenes. She forced her eyes open and saw the Acheri draw back its thin, black lips, exposing a mouth overcrowded with long, sharp, yellowed teeth. In the centre of its face was a two-holed cavity. As it sniffed the air, the holes moved in and out, making a puffing sound.

The demon juddered forward, closing in on Maggie, who looked back at Harness wondering why he'd stopped shooting. He'd collapsed, his body spasming. Rodney knelt on the ground next to him, a look of utter panic on his face.

"Rodney, get the gun. Shoot it," Maggie screamed.

When she looked back at the demon, it was almost on top of her. Maggie covered her head with her hands and braced herself. Another two shots rang out, the report like thunder in her ears. The creature howled. Maggie uncovered her head and looked around.

Rodney stood over Harness holding the gun. The Acheri staggered back a few steps, but was still standing. Maggie saw Doug struggling to his feet. Jackson, holding a shovel, approached the creature from behind. The shearing shed was ablaze, ancient wood snapping and crackling as the building burned at a frightening speed. A strong wind drove the heat forward, making it difficult for Maggie to catch her breath.

She looked around, frantically searching for the backpack. The smoke thickened. Soon it would be impossible to see anything, and their only chance to stop the Acheri would be gone. If it got away now, they all would get sick and die, it was only a matter of time. First Harness, then the rest of them.

She could see the Acheri shrouded in smoke a couple of metres in front of her. It moved in a jerky side-to-side shudder, but she couldn't tell if it was getting closer or moving farther away. She noticed a dark shape on the ground near the demon. *Please, let that be the backpack.* Maggie got to her feet and moved towards the Acheri.

The drumming in her head neared to deafening. In spite of the blazing fire's heat, she shivered as chills invaded her body. Just walking the few metres towards what she hoped was the backpack, her breath laboured and muscles strained. Maggie forced herself forward, eyes constantly moving between the demon and the dark shape on the ground. Nearing her target, she realised the Acheri was indeed moving away.

Does it feel outnumbered, or has if successfully infected those who posed a threat?

Determined not to let it escape, she crouched down and grabbed at the shape on the ground. The smoke made it difficult to see, but as soon as her fingers closed, she felt the familiar nylon straps. Maggie grabbed the bag and fumbled one-handed for the zip. She looked up to make sure the demon hadn't changed direction and noticed Jackson raising his shovel above the Acheri's bony head. She was about to call out to him when something shifted in the corner of her eye. As Maggie turned to look, a soulful cry of sorrow and outrage split the air.

"Devil!" Prapti bounded towards Jackson with the cleaver raised high.

"Jackson." He half turned to the sound of Maggie's voice. The cleaver came down with a sickening crunch. Jackson's head jerked to the right. Arterial blood spurted into the smoky air.

Maggie screamed, her swollen throat burning as she watched helplessly. Jackson's knees buckled. He hit the ground. Prapti turned to Maggie, her jaw hanging disjointed from the upper part of her mouth, the right side of her face bathed in blood, one eye resting on her cheek. Even through her horribly altered appearance, the look of triumph was easy to read.

Maggie stopped screaming and scrambled to her feet. Prapti stepped towards her, the bloodied cleaver still in her hand. The woman meant to kill her, but Maggie would be damned if she'd die cowering on the floor. She held the backpack in front of her.

"Come on, you crazy bitch. Take your best shot." Maggie spat the words.

The left side of Prapti's face drew up in a half-smile. She charged, but before she could make contact, Maggie felt herself pushed aside. A pitchfork punched Prapti in the stomach, the sharp prongs pierced the woman's abdomen. For a moment, she looked confused, then bucked and jerked in an effort to free herself. Doug pushed the handle forward. There was a meaty squelch as the prongs pushed through flesh and bone. He drove the weapon forward, the force pushing Prapti to the ground. She emitted a low gurgling sound, twitched and then stilled.

Doug wasn't taking any chances. He held the handle of the pitchfork, pinning the woman to the ground. He turned to meet Maggie's shocked gaze.

"Do it now."

His words echoed in her ears, but didn't register. She looked down at the backpack. Her movements felt dull and slow, like trudging through water. She put the bag on the ground. Using her good hand to unzip it, she pulled out the long, red woollen coat Mary had given them.

A vaidya's mantle or medicine woman's cloak, she thought numbly as she dragged it out of the backpack. She hoped to God it would work.

The outline of the Acheri engulfed in smoke moved farther away. The red paint that kept the Acheri trapped between the shed and cottage had been disturbed when Doug had fallen and struggled with the demon. Now the Acheri crossed the line and lurched into a veil of smoke.

Maggie tried to stand. Her whole body wracked by chills, she staggered, nearly losing her footing. Strong arms lifted and supported her from behind.

"Whatever you're planning on doing, we'd better make it quick," Rodney said, glancing back at Harness's still form near the back door.

"I need to get this around the Acheri," Maggie responded through chattering teeth.

She wasn't sure if she felt cold because of blood loss and shock or if the Acheri's poison was already attacking her body. Rodney nodded and locked his arm around her waist. With Doug still pinning Prapti's body to the ground and Harness unconscious, Rodney and Maggie moved as one towards the Acheri.

Chapter Thirty-seven

Heat from the fire, like a blast of hell, threatened to overwhelm Maggie. Her skin burned and yet somehow, she continued to shiver. The smoke was almost worse than the heat; it filled her mouth and nose, stinging her already injured throat. Her eyes burned and watered.

Rodney coughed. In his struggle to breathe, he rattled both their bodies. A jolt of white-hot agony spiralled up her arm. Maggie gasped, pushing back a wave of dizziness. The demon made its way around the side of the outbuilding. Maggie blinked rapidly, trying to clear her eyes to keep the ghostlike figure in view. She wondered why a creature who had lunged forward with so much speed now moved so slowly. *Is the heat from the fire slowing it down or all the red paint?*

Rodney kept his arm firmly around her waist, propelling the two of them with enough momentum to gain on the creature. They rounded the side of the shearing shed and were engulfed by more smoke. Maggie heard Rodney's laboured breathing, but every other sound melted away. It was as if the smoke had swallowed them, shutting out the daylight, leaving only them – and the Acheri. For a second, Maggie lost sight of the creature.

"Wait." She was panting, her voice the only sound in the silent smoke-filled landscape. "Where is it?"

"I can't see. It was just ahead of us."

The two of them stood still for a moment, straining to catch any sign of movement. Suddenly, something broke through and hit Rodney in the chest. Maggie saw a flash of grey and heard hissing just as he took the impact. In an instant Rodney let go of her and disappeared.

"Rodney." She croaked in desperation and clutched the coat to her chest.

Holding her breath, she waited, unsure of what to do or where to go.

"It's here." Rodney's voice came sudden and urgent from behind her. She spun around.

The creature's outline became visible through the haze of smoke. It crouched over something on the ground. Its bony head swayed snakelike as its overly long arms worked with shuddering movements. Maggie took a short breath, heavy with smoke, and ran towards the demon. Rodney lay on the ground beneath the Acheri, his shirt ripped open where deep cuts crossed his chest. His chest rose and fell — still breathing, but otherwise unmoving.

The demon turned, catching Maggie's reflection in its yellow eyes. It let out a rolling croak that turned into a snarl and bared its teeth, clacking them together like castanets. Maggie stopped short as terrible images assaulted her mind.

She saw a primitive village burning. People screamed as flames scorched their skin. A child, a little girl no more than ten, was tossed into the flames by a group of screaming women dressed in rags. The girl's terrified cries pierced the air. Her arms and legs kicked and lashed out helplessly in the flames.

Maggie tried to block the horrific image, but even as she brought the coat up to cover her face, she could still see the girl's flesh melting away from her body. Her face scorched of skin and tissue, the fire stripping her to bare bones.

Even in her horror, Maggie knew she had to block the images and keep moving. She lowered the coat from her face and blindly tucked it up under her right arm. In her head the girl screamed and reached out, imploring, begging someone to help her. Maggie overlaid the image with Eddie, and then Harness's face. With her right hand, she squeezed her injured arm. Searing pain shot through her, overriding the mental horror show.

Maggie pulled the coat from under her arm and threw it over the Acheri. The demon snarled and jerked away with the coat hanging from its back. Maggie darted forward, pulling the coat up and around the creature. She yanked the belt free from the loops and flipped it over the Acheri's head. Maggie tried to tie it in a rough knot behind the demon's back, hoping to secure it long enough for it to work, but the belt slipped awkwardly through her hands.

The demon bucked and shrieked with supernatural strength. If the heat of the fire had weakened it, the touch of the coat had re-energised the creature, sending it into a frenzy. Maggie couldn't tie the belt on the writhing demon with just one hand, so she settled for holding it tight with her good hand. The Acheri spun around in an attempt to shake the coat off and took Maggie with her. For a second Maggie felt herself lifting off the ground and almost lost her grip on the belt. When she landed, her right knee hit the ground, sending pain vibrating up through her hip.

The Acheri lunged, dragging Maggie forward. Still on one knee, she tried to plant her left foot and lean back, but it was hopeless. The demon's unnatural strength was too much for her; she had no choice but to be dragged forward. The creature's body shifted and undulated under the coat as it jerked towards the burning shed.

Maggie could hear the fire cracking and the thunderous sound of timbers snapping. At the entrance to the shearing shed she realised the demon, in its panic, had dragged her back to its den. The doors stood open blazing with red-hot flames. Thick black smoke billowed out – the entire structure was only moments away from collapsing in on itself.

Suddenly the pull on the belt lessened. The creature's strength ebbed. It paused only a second, but long enough for Maggie to get her right leg under her and stand. She twisted the belt into a rough knot and let go. She expected the Acheri to dart away from her, but instead it turned back.

Its face melted and bubbled as though the heat came from inside its skull. The lower part of its jaw fused to its neck and one side of its forehead bulged into a huge blister. All that remained were its eyes – yellow and burning with hate. It looked at Maggie with malevolence that seemed to reach into her soul. It wanted to attack her, to tear her to pieces, but hesitated. Maggie's hand drew up to her throat – the silk of the red scarf still clung to her neck.

Then it struck her; the Acheri had not actually hurt her, Jackson or Doug. It had attacked Rodney, the only one of them not wearing red.

She pulled the scarf from her neck and rushed at the demon. It limped back a step, the look in its eyes changing from hate to fear as Maggie shoved the scarf into its fused-open mouth.

She felt its teeth tear at her hand but she pushed with all her might. Drawing back from the demon, Maggie watched it shudder. Thick yellow fluid spilled out of its mouth, soaking the scarf. Still fighting for freedom, it gave one last jerky spin, lifting the bottom of the coat like a child spinning in a new dress. The edge of the coat whipped through the flames on the door of the shed and caught fire. It burnt with an eerie speed. Within seconds the demon was alight.

Howling with pain and surprise, its cries echoed off the hills. Then it stood unmoving as it was consumed by the fire. Maggie watched as the coat and the creature melted into one, finally crumbling and becoming part of the burning building. Overhead, a cloud of black rustled and swooped. Crows flew in every direction.

For what seemed like an hour, Maggie watched the fire destroy the old outbuilding, but in fact it could have been only minutes before the heat and the smoke forced her back to action. Covering her mouth, she turned away from the inferno.

Someone called her name – she saw Rodney walk out of the smoke to the left of the fire. He rushed towards her and grabbed her arm, pulling her away.

"We need to get out of here or we'll be overcome by the smoke." He pushed her from the scorching flames.

They found Doug sitting next to Jackson's lifeless body. During her battle with the Acheri, Maggie had been focused and resolute in the knowledge that she would give *her* life if necessary. But now, staring down at Jackson's body, she realised that it had not been her life – that sacrifice was her friend's.

He'd come here not just because of his grandmother, although that was part of the reason, but because he was good and kind and had wanted to protect her. He'd loved her even though he knew she didn't love him back.

Maggie sank down next to Doug. She placed her hand on Jackson's chest; it felt still – hollow. His face was turned towards her, eyes open and staring blankly. Everything about him crystallised into perfect focus: his light brown eyes; his dark, messy hair; the washed-out tan of his skin – all were clearly defined in the bright afternoon sunlight. Maggie put her head on his chest and let the tears come.

She wanted to go back to that moment on the road when he'd told her he was leaving Thorn Tree – tell him how much she cared about him and how proud she was to have him as a friend. But she'd hesitated and let the moment pass. Now she'd never be able to tell him he was the bravest person she knew.

"Maggie." She heard Doug's voice near her ear and felt his hands close over her shoulders. She tried to shrug them off, but he held her fast.

"The fire is spreading. We've got to go." Urgency edged his voice.

Maggie closed her eyes and let her forehead rest on Jackson's chest. She knew she had to move, but guilt and sorrow washed over her so powerfully, she didn't think she could stand.

A voice cut through the pain. "Maggie, we need to take Jackson home."

Harness. He was alive!

Standing over her, he offered his hand. As if in a dream, she reached out and let him pull her up. For a second she stared at him, unable to believe what she was seeing. He looked terrible, but he was real.

"Ness." She managed to croak out his name and then his arms were around her.

She'd fought so hard to save him and now she could forget all the horror, if only for a moment. He led her away from the fire to the front of the house. Doug and Rodney carried Jackson's body back to the ute, and then they drove away.

Chapter Thirty-eight

Maggie unlocked the back door and turned on the lights. Everything was as she'd left it almost two months ago. The Hawk's Nest had remained unopened and unused while Maggie and a lot of other people in Thorn Tree took time to heal.

In the weeks that followed the fire, there'd been an investigation into the cause and the deaths of Prapti Gautam and Jackson Palmer. The official story was that Maggie, Doug and Jackson had gone to the cottage at Prapti's request. She'd claimed to have information about the source of the sickness sweeping the town. When they arrived at the cottage, it was on fire and Prapti attacked them with a cleaver, killing Jackson and injuring Maggie. Doug had finally overpowered her with a pitchfork he found in the backyard.

The story made sense and officially the case was closed. While there were many unanswered questions, no charges were laid. Maggie watched the early morning light struggling to push through the windows, amber rays not quite stretching all the way across the kitchen. After the fire, no further deaths had occurred relating to the unidentified virus. They'd stopped the Acheri, that had to mean something.

Agnes suffered a stroke on the way to the hospital and was unable to give the police any information on Prapti. Maggie heard she was staying in a rehabilitation hospital in Perth. If Agnes ever recovered sufficiently to return to her home in Thorn Tree, Maggie wondered what she would do if she came face to face with the woman who had invited evil into their lives. Sometimes the thoughts kept her awake at night.

Since the fire, Maggie had attended so many funerals, she'd developed an aversion to flowers. Each time she watched someone she loved or cared for being lowered into the ground, their casket draped in blossoms, she thought of Agnes. A dark place inside Maggie began to grow, taking root right about the time they buried Eddie. It was a place where hatred lived, and in the early hours of the morning when the faces of the dead filled her mind, Maggie thought of Agnes and hoped the woman suffered every day for the rest of her life.

Soon after Maureen's funeral, Doug put his house up for sale and moved to Margaret River to live with his younger brother and his wife. Maggie rang him a few times, but the conversation seemed difficult and stilted, both of them struggling to find things to talk about. She decided to leave it a while before calling again, but in her heart, she knew she would probably just settle on sending him a Christmas card once a year.

Now Indian summer had turned into autumn and as life has a habit of doing, it moved on. Maggie stood for a moment looking around the empty cook's kitchen and allowed her thoughts to turn to Jackson. She pictured him standing there talking and laughing about something a customer had said. The wave of guilt, now so familiar she almost felt comforted by its presence, washed over her. Of all the horror she'd been through, perhaps the hardest part was losing Jackson — knowing *she* was responsible for his death. A burden she'd have to live with, the price she'd pay for having Harness in her life.

Since the day of the fire, she and Harness had grown closer than she ever thought possible. His recovery from the sickness was swift. It was as though whatever poison the Acheri breathed into him had vanished along with the demon. He didn't remember much of what happened at the shearer's cottage, but enough.

At first, they had talked about that awful day and the events leading up to it. Now, it was something they shared, but felt no need to discuss. They enjoyed an intense and passionate relationship which began under perilous circumstances, leaving Maggie secretly fearful that normal, mundane life would see it fizzle.

She supposed her fears stemmed from guilt and a deep-seated belief that God or fate or whatever force was controlling her destiny would never allow her the long-term happiness she craved. She had threatened Agnes, an old woman, sacrificed the life of one friend and risked the life of another because she refused to lose the man she loved. *Do I deserve happiness?*

Maggie didn't know the answer, but when she thought of Annabel, safe and happy playing with her new red setter pup, she knew she'd do it all over again.

She put her bag down on the kitchen bench and struggled to work the zip. It had taken two painful surgeries to come close to repairing the damage to her left arm. She'd regained some movement, but still faced maybe a year's worth of weekly visits to the physiotherapist, painful events where the exercise was often enough to bring tears to her eyes. The crude scar that ran half the length of her forearm would be a permanent reminder of her encounter with evil. The surgeon who'd repaired the nerve damage had suggested plastic surgery, but Maggie refused. The scar was her link to Jackson and what they'd fought for that day. She wouldn't see that memory erased or minimised in any way.

During her recovery, she relived that day at the shearer's cottage a thousand times, always coming back to the images the Acheri forced into her mind. At the time it felt like the creature was trying to torture and hurt her, but Maggie wondered if it had been trying to tell her something.

Maybe it knew it was about to die and was trying to explain its own terrible beginnings? Had it once been an innocent child put to death because of primitive superstitions? Maggie knew she'd had no choice but to kill it. She despised the evil thing it had become, but could still feel sadness for the child it had once been.

The back door opened. For a second, Maggie expected to hear Jackson's voice, but it was Tess. For a moment, neither spoke.

"Are we really doing this?" Tess looked older, the lines around her eyes were deep and a few greys stood out in her brown hair, but she was functioning again.

Ollie made what the doctors called the best recovery possible. He would always walk with a limp but the headaches might improve over time. Thanks to Rodney, he was able to return to his job at the orchard on light duties.

Now they were going through their daily routine and waiting for a time when life would make sense again. It had been Tess's idea for the two of them to open up the café, insisting that it was time to get back to living a normal life.

"Yes, I'm glad I let you talk me into it." Maggie patted her friend's hand, then, feeling tears stinging her eyes, pulled her into a brief one-armed hug.

"Things have to go forward or they'll start moving backwards... and I couldn't bear that." Tess pressed her lips together.

Maggie could see her friend struggling to keep her emotions in check, so she changed the subject.

"I'm thinking of adding sliders to the menu, what do you think?"

"Sounds very trendy. Do you think Thorn Tree's ready for it?"

Maggie smiled and just for a second it seemed like old times.

THE END

List of Characters

Maggie Hawkbetter – café owner
Harness Gibson – police sergeant
Tess Becks – Maggie's friend
Ollie Becks – Tess's husband
Eddie Becks – Tess & Ollie's baby
Jackson Palmer – works at the café with Maggie
Manjula – Jackson's gran
Cilla – works at the café with Maggie
Robert – Cilla's son
Agnes Wells – Mayor of Thorn Tree
Stan Wells – Agnes's late husband
Sandra Michaels – Tess's mother
Mark Leary – police constable
Jason Attwell – police constable
Annabel Chapel – young girl with psychic senses
Lisa Chapel – Annabel's Mother
Rodney Chapel – Annabel's Father
Marley Dicks – mother of baby who dies
Zoe Dicks – Marley's baby
Dr Cole – town doctor
Mary Cole – Dr Cole's wife
Doug Loggie – Handyman and Maggie's friend
Maureen Loggie – Doug's wife
Barry Tucker – petrol station owner

Mike Tolman – school principal
Richard – Maggie's ex-husband
Franklin Wooten – quarantine officer
Thomas – abused child
Aunt Liv – Thomas's guardian
Tyson – Liv's boyfriend

If you enjoyed this book, please let others know by leaving a quick review on Amazon. Also, if you spot anything untoward in the paperback, get in touch. We strive for the best quality and appreciate reader feedback.

editor@thebookfolks.com

www.thebookfolks.com

Also by Anna Willett

BACKWOODS RIPPER
RETRIBUTION RIDGE
UNWELCOME GUESTS
FORGOTTEN CRIMES
CRUELTY'S DAUGHTER
VENGEANCE BLIND
THE WOMAN BEHIND HER

SMALL TOWN NIGHTMARE
COLD VALLEY NIGHTMARE
SAVAGE BAY NIGHTMARE

ANNA WILLETT

A GRIPPING ACTION SUSPENSE THRILLER

BACKWOODS RIPPER

Paige and her husband Hal are on a babymoon, a romantic holiday before their child is born. When misfortune strikes and Hal is injured, they are left stranded in the wilderness. Paige finds two women who offer to help. But when they turn nasty, how far will she have to go to protect her unborn child?

Available on Kindle and in paperback from Amazon.

Mina's father was a brute and a thug. She got over him.
Now another man wants to fill his shoes. Can Mina
overcome the past and protect herself? 'Cruelty's
Daughter' is about a woman who tackles her demons and
takes it upon herself to turn the tables on a violent man.

Available on Kindle and in paperback from Amazon.

Made in the USA
Monee, IL
02 January 2021

56188223R00163